WOLF HUNT 2

JEFF STRAND

Wolf Hunt 2
© 2014 Jeff Strand

Dark Regions Press, LLC
6635 N. Baltimore Ave., Ste. 241
Portland, OR 97203
United States of America
DarkRegions.com

Library of Congress Cataloging-in-Publication Data available by request from the publisher.

Printed in the United States of America

Edited by: Chris Morey
Cover Art by: Frank Walls
Cover design by Irina Summer
Interior design by Cyrus Wraith Walker

ISBN: 978-1-62641-078-7

CHAPTER ONE

Catching Up With George and Lou

George Orton and Lou Flynn sat in their living room, which was also their kitchen and bedroom, sipping margaritas and watching a terrible but weirdly addictive *telenovela.*

"That kid's not really his," Lou said.

"Y'think?"

"It's Ramon's."

"You're out of your frickin' mind. She doesn't have any feelings for Ramon."

"That's what makes it so tragic! She's carrying his baby and she doesn't even love him. Ignacio suspects, though. You can see it in his eyes."

"No way in hell did she hook up with Ramon," said George. "They're totally wrong for each other."

"You can't tell me there's no way they didn't hook up even once. He's hot, she's hot, they're both recovering alcoholics—I'm telling you, that baby is his. Just watch. You'll see that I'm right."

"Not a chance."

"Want to put some money on it?"

"Nah."

"One peso. Just to make it interesting."

"We're not going to be here long enough to find out how it turns out."

Lou sighed and reached for his drink. He reached with the wrong arm—the one that no longer had a hand—then switched and picked it up in his right hand. He kept one of four different handkerchiefs wrapped around the stump. Today's was dark blue. "I know we said that we were just laying low for a while, but I like it here. Nobody telling us what to do. Catching up on our reading. Learning a new language."

George glared at him. "You understand that we're living in a shithole, right? An inferno shithole. I used to fantasize about beautiful women; now I fantasize about not being drenched with sweat twenty-four hours a day. I whack off to pictures of glaciers. Don't you miss AC?"

"Sure, I wish it wasn't so hot," Lou admitted, "but isn't it kind of nice to lounge around in shorts? We always had to dress up before. I hate ties."

"Don't talk about ties. If you remind me that we own a tie, I'll use one to hang myself."

"I'm not saying that if I could pick anyplace in the entire world to live, this would be it. I'm just saying that being broke and hiding out isn't as bad as I thought it would be."

"Well, thank you Mr. Pollyanna Sunshine Sparklepants. Who needs running water when I've got a great big ray of optimism with me? Your radiant smile just fills me with—"

A bullet came through their wall, shattering George's margarita glass.

Several more gunshots fired as George and Lou dove to the floor. They'd been living in Costa Rica for two months, and about three days ago George had finally gotten out of the paranoid habit of keeping his gun with him at all times.

George scrambled across the floor toward his bed as bullets continued to tear through the very thin walls. There were at least two different shooters.

Lou let out a cry of pain.

George glanced back at him. Lou hadn't been shot; in the chaos of the moment he'd tried to crawl with his stump.

The shots stopped just as George reached under the bed and grabbed his loaded revolver. He could return a few blind shots and hope to get lucky, but lots of little kids lived in this area, and George didn't want to take a chance on shooting one who was trying to see what the excitement was all about.

George grabbed Lou's gun and slid it across the floor to him. Because their crappy floorboards were warped, it came up a couple of feet short.

Another shot. This one cracked the TV screen.

George fired at the new bullet hole in the wall. Somebody on the other side let out a yelp. Disappointingly, it didn't sound like a fatal yelp.

He looked around at the dozen or so bullet holes, trying to keep track of all of them at once, waiting for somebody outside to block the light. His whole body was tense and somehow he'd found new sweat to pump out of his pores.

One of the holes right next to the window darkened.

George fired. A few specks of blood hit the glass.

He got to his feet and rushed for the front door. It was a risk, but hiding under the bed wouldn't keep him alive for very long. He opened the door, quickly peeked to the right, and saw a man clutching at his bloody side. He'd dropped his gun.

George shot him in the leg. He fell to the ground.

Lou followed George outside. "I'll check on the other guy," said Lou, hurrying around the corner of their shack. The injured guy made a grab for his gun, but George stepped on his hand and crouched over him.

It was a young guy, maybe twenty-one or twenty-two. Nobody George recognized.

Some of the neighbor brats were already coming over to see what was going on, so George shooed them away. "Get out of here! You wanna get shot?"

Lou came back around. "Other guy's dying. I don't see any more of them."

George pushed the barrel of his revolver against the young guy's face. "Are there any more pieces of crap like you around here?"

The young guy shook his head. "Dude, call an ambulance."

George glanced at his wounds. "You're not going to bleed to death yet. Did Bateman send you?"

"Bateman? Where've you been? Got his head chopped off weeks ago."

"Oh. Good. So you work for Dewey?"

"Yeah."

"You seem pretty green. Is that the best he can do, send a kid after us?"

"Ummmmm ... how important do you guys think you are? This was a training job for me. I don't even get paid. You killed my mentor!"

"How much cash do you have on you?"

"Why?"

"Because I'm going to steal it, numbnuts. Roll over."

The kid rolled over with a wince. George took his wallet out of his back pocket and flipped through the contents. About sixty bucks in United States currency. George was ashamed to admit that this was a pretty big score.

More children were starting to gather. George waved his gun in the air. "I said, get out of here! What's the matter with you?" The children scattered.

"You gonna kill me?" asked the kid.

"Nah. Lou's going to use his switchblade to carve a message into your back to deliver to your boss. It'll say 'To whom it may concern, please note that Mr. George Orton and Mr. Louis Flynn wish to express their displeasure over the fact that a low-level underling was sent to end their lives. They would like to officially register a complaint about this disrespectful treatment, and formally request that it never happen again. Most sincerely yours, George and Lou.'"

"That a joke?"

"Yes."

"I don't wanna die."

"I already said that we weren't killing you. Stop being so whiny. What proof were you supposed to bring back?"

"Proof?"

"Proof of our demise. Photographs of our corpses? Our heads? What?"

"Nothing."

"Yeah, right."

"Seriously. You think I want severed heads in my car when I'm crossing the border? And I can't go around taking pictures of dead bodies when I've got my phone set to synch with the Cloud." The kid coughed up some blood. "Not to be rude or nothing, but again, you're not as big of outlaws as you think you are."

George shrugged. "Fair enough. So are you willing to go back and tell them that you killed us? It's win/win."

"Sure, sure. I'll do that. No problem."

George glanced over at Lou. "Pack our stuff. We're getting out of here."

Lou, looking sad, walked back inside their shack. He came back out a moment later and tossed George's vibrating cell phone to him. George frowned and touched "Accept Call" on the screen. "Ricky?"

"Thank God you answered! Hey, I know I'm not supposed to know that this phone number exists, but I need to warn you that Dewey sent two men to hunt you down. They could be at your place any minute now. I'm taking a huge risk by telling you this, and I could end up on their list if anybody finds out that I gave you a heads-up, but you and Lou need to get out of there as soon as possible!"

"You're a bit late."

"Oh, no! Did they get Lou?"

"No."

"Oh. Okay, good to hear. You're not going to squeal on me, are you?"

"Nah."

"So how are things going? Is Costa Rica nice? I thought I might check it out someday."

George hung up on him and stuffed the cell phone into his pocket. Lou went back into their shack. George returned his attention to the kid.

"The story is, your mentor put a bullet in Lou's forehead. Then I killed your mentor. He died bravely. I shot you, but you took me out before I could finish you off. Sound okay?"

The kid nodded. "Yeah, yeah, I'm all for that. Can you take me to the hospital?"

"Nope."

"C'mon, Mr. Orton. I've got a shot leg."

"A good Samaritan will help you out." George waved his gun at the children again. "I said, get out of here, you suicidal twerps! Don't you know what bullets are?"

George knew that the kid wasn't really going to stick to their story. Still, they had to abandon this place anyway, so he and Lou might as well buy themselves some time by pretending that they believed that he'd lie on their behalf.

It didn't take long for Lou to fill the trunk of their car with their meager possessions, and they drove off, unsure of the next stop on their journey.

―――――――

"It's frickin' freezing," said George. How did anybody live in this environment? He and Lou were wrapped in blankets, huddled next to their tiny space heater, but it wasn't doing enough to counteract the Northern Ontario climate.

"It's not so—"

"Do not say anything positive about our situation! I mean it, Lou. This is not a time for the glass to be half-full. This is a time for misery and complaining."

"I'm just—"

"I will break a fucking icicle off my chin and stab you with it if you try to be happy."

"Maybe you should grow a beard like mine. They're pretty warm."

George ignored him. They sat there for a while, shivering.

Lou finally spoke again: "Better than being hot, though, right?"

"Yes. And having a toenail yanked out is better than having a fingernail yanked out."

"Is it? I'd think that a toenail would be worse."

"Are you crazy?"

"They're bigger. More surface area to hurt."

"You only have one hand," George said. "How can you possibly say that you'd rather have a fingernail ripped out?"

"I guess I was being more hypothetical about it. And maybe you're right; I bet a finger has more nerves."

George sighed, watching his breath mist in the air in front of him.

Lou smiled. "At least I have one less hand to be cold."

Their front (and only) door burst open. Three men rushed inside, all of them wearing facemasks and holding guns.

"Lose the blankets!" said the man in front.

George and Lou tossed their multiple layers of blankets to the floor, revealing their lack of weaponry.

"At least shut the door behind you," said George. "You're letting out all of the heat."

A fourth man walked into their shack, closing the door behind him. Jonathan Dewey grinned at them. "Hello, George and Lou. How nice to finally meet you in person."

CHAPTER TWO

An Unhappy Crime Lord

George squeezed his eyes shut as the gasoline splashed against his face, but there was nothing he could do to keep it out of his nostrils. He couldn't stop himself from coughing, so some gas got into his mouth as well.

"Don't be stingy with it," said Mr. Dewey, as one of his men, a mean-looking ginger, poured fuel from the plastic container directly onto George's head. "That's right, get him all nice and drenched."

The other two guys had taken Lou outside. While being tied to the wooden desk chair, George had listened closely for the sounds of his partner having the crap beat out of him, but hadn't heard anything. He hoped that didn't mean they'd quietly murdered him.

The ginger shook out the last few drops of gasoline, then let go of the container. It bonked George on the head and fell to the floor.

Mr. Dewey casually slipped a hand into the pocket of his coat. "Tell me, how does it feel to be such a fire hazard?"

"You practice that line on the way over?"

"No, George. I did not." Mr. Dewey took out a lighter. "Do you really think that now is the time to be disrespectful? My last memory of you is not going to be of you saying something clever. It's going to be of you shrieking in *absolute agony* while your body burns. Do you think you can be witty while your hair is on fire?"

George did not think he could be witty under those circumstances.

He had no intention of leaving this world begging for his life. At the same time, there was no good reason to let Mr. Dewey light him up without finding out if a sincere apology might help.

"I'm sorry we messed up," George said. "I'm not trying to offer excuses, but jobs go bad all the time, and this one involved a werewolf. If any job is going to go bad, it's going to be the one with the werewolf, right?"

"Do you have any cloth?" Mr. Dewey asked.

"What?"

"You heard me."

"We've got towels in the bathroom."

Mr. Dewey shook his head. "Too soft. I just want to make sure I don't get gasoline on myself." He walked over to the kitchen sink, unspooled some paper towels, and wrapped them tightly around his fist. Then he punched George in the face, almost knocking the chair over. He unwrapped his fist and tossed the paper towels into the sink.

"The werewolf was in a cage," Mr. Dewey said.

George's newly split lip felt like it had already been lit on fire. "Yeah, yeah, he was. But we weren't given proof that he was a real werewolf."

"You didn't *need* proof! He was in a cage! All you had to do was not open the goddamn cage!"

"I understand how it can seem like we were irresponsible," George admitted. "But we didn't just open up the cage for kicks. Nobody told us 'Hey, don't get too close to the bars, because he can change his human arm into a werewolf arm whenever he wants.' I'm not saying that Lou and I didn't screw up, but the disaster would have been avoided if we'd been given all of the information up-front."

"Are you blaming me?" Mr. Dewey asked.

George shook his head. "I'm blaming Bateman. He's the one who briefed us."

"Throwing a dead man under the bus. Very classy."

"It's the truth," said George. And it was, although George wouldn't have fallen into a deep moral quandary if it weren't.

"Do you know why I wanted you to bring me a werewolf?"

George had a couple of theories, but sharing them would get him punched again. "I heard that you wanted to get bit."

"That's right. I'm dying. Brain cancer. Inoperable."

"Sorry to hear that."

Mr. Dewey smiled. "Yes, I'm sure you're heartbroken."

"So ... you thought that becoming a werewolf could cure you?"

"Complete change in my body chemistry? Worth a shot."

"Fair enough."

"Which means that when Ivan escaped, and you failed to recapture him, you cost me my last opportunity at life." Mr. Dewey flicked on the lighter and waved the flame a couple of feet in front of George.

"Wait!" George said. He could not immediately think of a reason that Mr. Dewey might want to wait, so he said "Wait!" again as he desperately tried to come up with something.

"And why would I do that?"

"Ivan can't have been the only one. There's got to be another werewolf out there, somewhere!"

Mr. Dewey let the flame go out. "Actually, there is."

"For real?"

"Yes. In Minnesota, if you can believe it."

George didn't think that any one place was a more surprising werewolf location than any other place. "Lou and I have dealt with these things," he said. "You need us."

"And your experience is the only reason you're not going to die tonight," said Mr. Dewey, putting the lighter back into his pocket. "You're going to get the wolf for us, and you're going to bring it back. If you do this, we're even. If you screw it up again, I won't grant you the mercy of just burning you to death."

Mr. Dewey gestured, and the ginger cut the ropes. George stood up and resisted the urge to shake the gasoline off his body like a dog after a bath.

"Lou too, right?" he asked.

"Of course."

George's bullshit meter was going off in a big way. Yes, they had experience with Ivan the Werewolf, but that experience had involved frantically chasing after him while he went on a gleeful slaughter spree. Lots of innocent people had died before they were able to force-feed Ivan some silver. There was nothing about that day to indicate that George and Lou might be good candidates for a second werewolf-delivery assignment.

Still, he wasn't going to argue. He didn't care if there was more to the story as long as he wasn't going to be burned alive.

"So what's the next step?" George asked.

"You're going to take a shower at gunpoint. And then we will demonstrate how to properly transport a werewolf."

George and Lou sat in a cage in the back of a van.

It was the exact type of cage Ivan had been in, and though this was more than a little demeaning, George was not inclined to complain about his accommodations right now. At least the van had heat.

Mr. Dewey was in a different vehicle. Two of the men who'd kidnapped them, but not the mean-looking ginger, sat up front, no longer wearing their ski masks, listening to an audio version of a James Bond novel. The driver's name was Sean, or maybe Shaun or Shawn; he hadn't spelled it. The passenger was Brent. They were both ugly gentlemen in their late twenties, although Sean's perfect grooming indicated that he didn't wish to be ugly, while Brent clearly didn't give a shit.

"What did they do to you?" George asked Lou.

"Nothing, really. Took a blood sample."

George sighed. It made sense that they thought Lou could be a werewolf, since one bit off his hand. The first night of the full moon had been a long, sleepless night for them (even though the cycles of the moon had been irrelevant for Ivan, and there was no reason to believe it was relevant for anybody else) but Lou had shown no signs of lycanthropy.

"At least we don't have to hide anymore," said Lou.

George knocked on the cage bars to get the driver's attention. "Hey! How long until we get there?"

"About fifteen hours."

"Are you kidding me?"

"Nope."

"You're not really going to make us stay in this cage for fifteen hours, are you?"

"I sure am."

"Do we at least get stretch breaks?"

Sean looked at them in the rear-view mirror and grinned. "Nope. And were you wondering why there's a bucket in the corner?"

"Aw, that's not cool."

"But please, feel free to try to talk us into letting you go. We could use the entertainment. And who knows? You might touch our hearts."

George adjusted his position, unsuccessfully trying to find a comfortable way to lean against the bars. This was going to be a long drive.

CHAPTER THREE

A Long Drive

Sean hadn't been entirely truthful. They were allowed out of the cage right before they crossed the Canadian border, and George and Lou were instructed to play along if they didn't want something horrible to happen. They didn't want something horrible to happen, so they played along. Then they went back into the cage.

George and Lou slept part of the way, so the trip wasn't as excruciating as it might have been. And a few hours in, Brent took pity on them and tossed a deck of cards into the cage. Sean and Brent did not take pity on them after going through a drive-thru; the two men up front gleefully gobbled down their cheeseburgers without sharing. George couldn't resent them too much for that behavior, since he'd done the same thing to Ivan.

George was very happy to see the "Welcome to Minnesota" sign, and even more happy when they were welcomed to Tropper. After driving down a ridiculously steep and icy road, they pulled into a small warehouse.

Sean shut off the engine, then both men got out of the van. George waited patiently for the back door to open, but after a couple of minutes it became clear that they weren't going to be released quite yet.

"Why do you think they really want us on this job?" Lou asked.

George grinned. "You don't buy the whole 'you've got experience with werewolves' angle?"

"Not really. That would be like hiring the designers of the Hindenburg because they've already made a blimp."

The rear of the van had heavily tinted windows, so they could only see through the front windshield, and nothing was happening out there. After about fifteen minutes they heard a sliding door open and then close again. A few minutes after that, the back doors of the van opened.

"Okay, freedom time," said Sean. "Try anything and you'll be kneecapped. Understood?"

"Understood," said George.

"Understood," Lou agreed.

Sean unlocked the cage and swung open the door. George and Lou crawled out, then climbed out of the van.

Mr. Dewey was there, along with Brent, the mean-looking ginger, and three other white men. Mr. Dewey was apparently not one to hire women or minorities. All of the men had guns. Not small ones. There was also a thin old man, wearing a dark blue suit and keeping his balance with a cane. The guy looked like he had to be in his nineties, and he quivered a bit as he stood there.

Almost in unison, the men pointed their guns at George and Lou. Without being asked, George and Lou put their three hands in the air.

"This is them," Mr. Dewey said to the old man.

The old man nodded and slowly walked over to them. He was so unsteady on his feet that George worried he might fall over, and George wondered why he didn't have anybody assisting him. A pride thing, probably.

The old man walked right up to George and looked at him closely, as if examining a horse. George almost made a smart-ass comment ("Should I open my mouth so you can check out my teeth?") but decided against it.

He turned his attention to Lou and examined him just as closely. Then the old man nodded with satisfaction and took a step back. "Yes, that's them."

"We're not here to con you," said Mr. Dewey.

"Of course not. That doesn't mean I shouldn't inspect them. We'll be off now." The old man turned and began to slowly walk away. Without looking back, he gestured for somebody to follow.

"So ... do we go with him?" George asked.

"You do," said Mr. Dewey. "Lou stays here."

George shook his head. "No way."

"Surely you're not so stupid as to think you have a choice."

"We work as a team," George said. "Case closed."

"Not anymore."

"I'm not going to leave him here so you can experiment on him. We do this together or not at all."

Mr. Dewey laughed. "Experiment on him? This isn't a Nazi death camp, George. But we can turn it into one, if you want to make this difficult for us."

The old man stopped walking. His shoulders slumped, and he turned around. "I'll bring both of them."

"That wasn't the deal," said Mr. Dewey.

"We have a job to do. I'd rather not have it complicated by him being obstinate."

"He'll be a lot less obstinate after we cut his nose off," said Mr. Dewey. "Break a couple of fingers ... a little sandpaper on an eyeball ... I think he'll cooperate just fine."

"You don't know me very well," said George, who hoped that this would not actually come down to lost noses, broken fingers, or sanded eyeballs.

"I'm taking them both," said the old man. "There will be no further discussion."

Mr. Dewey looked very much as if he wanted there to be further discussion, but he said nothing. Who *was* this old bastard?

The old man turned around and resumed walking. George and Lou followed. They walked over to a small, economical, fuel-efficient silver sedan. The old man opened the door and slowly eased himself into the driver's seat.

"I want them back here as soon as it's done," Mr. Dewey said.

The old man gave him a dismissive wave and closed the door. George and Lou looked at each other, shrugged, and then got in the car. George sat up front.

"He's very irritable, isn't he?" said the old man, starting the engine. He put the car into reverse. The car jolted backwards and George decided that it might be a good idea to put on his seat belt.

One of the men opened the sliding door, and they drove out of the warehouse into a sunny but snowy day.

"You got a name?" George asked.

"Do you think I might not?"

"Just asking."

"My name, to you, is Mr. Reith. We are not equals and you are not on a first-name basis with me."

"I can live with that."

"You will find me to be much more pleasant company than Mr. Dewey, but don't confuse friendliness with weakness. Rest assured that I can make awful things happen to you."

George nodded. "Point taken."

"So, gentlemen, we're going on a werewolf hunt. You were responsible for the death of Ivan, correct?"

"Yes, sir."

"Good. He killed my grandson. May the son of a bitch rot in hell."

"Amen."

"I hope he suffered."

"It was pretty quick, but it hurt."

"Excellent." Then Mr. Reith frowned. "Unfortunately for you, Ivan's fate would have been even worse if you'd delivered him to Mr. Dewey like you were supposed to. It would not have been 'pretty quick.' I do not expect you to botch this one."

"We won't," said Lou from the back.

"I'm glad to hear that. The file is in the glove compartment."

George opened the glove compartment and took out a folded manila envelope. It was very thin, and when he opened it, the only thing inside was a wallet-sized photograph.

"Are you kidding me?" George asked.

"No."

"What is she, twelve?"

"Fourteen."

George passed the photo back to Lou. It was a school picture of a girl with long straight brown hair. She looked happy but was apparently too cool to smile for the camera. She was cute; the kind of girl who would be getting boys into serious trouble in a couple of years.

"She's a werewolf?" Lou asked.

"We believe so, yes. There's no evidence that it has manifested itself yet."

"Well, I'm sorry to tell you this," said George, "but we don't kidnap little girls. I'm not saying that Lou and I are top-notch people, but we don't mess with kids."

"Then I'm afraid you'll have to revise your moral code."

Lou passed the picture back up to George. George stuck it back in the envelope, folded it, and put it back into the glove compartment. "Sorry. Not gonna happen."

"Then what's your plan from here?" asked Mr. Reith. "Kill me and steal my car? Go into hiding again?"

"I think we could get your car without killing you."

"They found you in Costa Rica. They found you in Ontario. They'll find you again. I suppose I can understand your loyalty to your partner, but are you really going to risk an excruciatingly painful death for a teenage girl you don't even know?"

"Pretty much, yeah."

The old man let out a derisive snort. "If I had more energy, I'd put that to the test. My guess is that your objections will only last until the knife blade touches your throat. But those days are over for me, so what if I assure you that the girl won't be harmed?"

"Yeah, right," said George. "You want me to believe that we're going to deliver her to a psycho like Dewey and she won't get hurt?"

"All he wants her to do is bite him."

"Uh-huh. You just said that if we'd delivered Ivan, he would have had a worse fate than getting sizzled from the inside."

"Ivan was a reprehensible monster who would never be missed. But an adorable fourteen-year-old in a small town like Tropper? She *will* be missed. She'll be returned safely."

"Seems like it would be kind of easy to pin this crime on us, considering that we'd be the ones actually committing the crime."

"Yes, and then you would lead the police to Mr. Dewey. We're all criminals here, George. Nobody is going to frame anybody. What you have to do is decide if you believe me when I say that you will regret not going along with this. My opinion? You should believe me."

"All right, for argument's sake, let's say that I—"

"No. Not for argument's sake. Either you believe me or you don't. I'm too old to waste time speaking hypothetically."

George looked back at Lou. Lou shrugged. George gave him a look that said *How about you contribute more to the decision-making process than a shrug?* Lou shrugged again, then nodded.

"Fine," said George. "We believe you."

"Perfect. Then your job is to acquire the little girl. As you heard, Mr. Dewey is impatient, so you have two hours."

"Two hours? That's it?"

"If you're good at what you do, it's more than enough."

George opened the glove compartment and took out the folder again. "What's her name?"

"That's your job."

"You don't know?"

"I didn't say that I don't know. I said that it's your job. You're being given an opportunity for redemption in a business that doesn't offer many second chances. I'd encourage you to quit asking unnecessary questions and get to work."

They drove for a few more minutes, and then Mr. Reith pulled into the parking lot of a strip mall. He kept the engine running as he handed George a key and a cell phone. "The blue van is yours. There's one contact number programmed into this phone. Call it when you've got the girl. I would not advise you to call with any message but 'We've got her.'"

"Understood."

"There's a tranquilizer gun and two darts in the glove compartment, just in case."

"Tranquilizers didn't do any good against Ivan."

"Then hopefully you won't have to use them. The dose is intended for a wolf, not a girl, so don't use it unless things get out of control."

"Also understood."

"Perfect. Now get out of my car."

George and Lou got out of his car. As Mr. Reith drove away, they walked over to a dented, dirty blue van with tinted windows. George unlocked the doors, and they got inside without a word. He started the engine and turned on the heat.

"I can see a lot of potential problems with what we're about to do," George said.

"Yeah. Not quite foolproof, is it?"

"We could bolt."

"You want to?"

"I don't know. I didn't enjoy the gasoline shower. I really thought he was going throw that match on me. I'd rather do a long stretch of prison time for attempted kidnapping than burn to death."

"What if they kill the girl?" asked Lou.

"We won't let that happen."

"What if we don't have a choice? I mean, let's face it, we're not actually going to have a choice, right?"

George let out a long sigh. "Probably not. But, ultimately, you and I are shitty human beings, and we do shitty things to people for a living, and I'm more inclined to go for it and hope that this works out happily for everyone than to get set on fire for a teenage girl I don't even know."

"Before we went to Costa Rica, you kept saying that you wanted to become a better person."

"I do! But not at the cost of all my skin! It's hard for me to quantify just how much I don't want to get set on fire. So, yeah, I'm putting self-preservation at the top of my list."

Lou was silent for a moment.

George held his hand next to the vent to get more hot air. "Hey, if you don't want to do this, I'll look the other way and you can run. I'll make something up; tell them that some guys in ski masks threw you into the trunk of their car. I can handle this one solo."

Lou shook his head. "That's not how we work. I'm with you."

"Thanks. We won't mess this up."

"Of course we won't."

Lou glanced in the back. "Then again, he didn't even give us a cage."

CHAPTER FOUR

Creepy Stalkers

George and Lou sat in their van, parked across the street from Tropper High. They didn't think that the "big scary guys questioning strangers about a picture of a cute teenage girl" tactic should be their first course of action, and since it was mid-afternoon and school would be letting out soon, they decided to just scope out the place and hope to see their target.

"This is so inappropriate," said Lou.

"I know."

"What if we have to talk to her? What do you say to a fourteen-year-old girl? They scare the crap out of me. I don't know what they're into."

"Music."

"But not *real* music. Not anymore. They listen to that stuff ... I forget what it's called ... that stuff where people are singing but it's not really their voices...?"

"Robots?"

"Not robots. It's got that weird sound so that it's kind of like a computer is helping them sing. It's for when they can't really sing but they've already got the record contract so they need the computer to mess with it."

"I have no idea what you're talking about," said George.

"Auto-tune. That's it."

"That tells me nothing."

"Bob Dylan didn't need auto-tune."

"You hear that?"

"What?"

"Listen."

"What?"

"It's the sound of kids on your lawn. Better go shake your fist at them. Want me to get you some Geritol from the local apothecary?"

Lou ignored him. "What if she wants to talk about Beyoncé?"

"Why the hell would she want to talk about Beyoncé?"

"That's who kids listen to these days!"

"We're kidnapping her! She's not going to start a conversation about shitty music."

"I hope she doesn't have a tramp-stamp. I hate those things."

"Can you please stop talking like an old person?"

"Actually, kids may have moved past Beyoncé. I think she's one generation before where we are now. We're fossils, George."

"We're in our mid-forties!"

"These days, that's ancient."

George shook his head. "Incorrect. Being forty-four is *younger* now than it used to be. People are living longer and being less mature. We can be forty-four and walk into a toy store to buy a *Star Wars* action figure without embarrassment."

"I'm only forty-two."

"I know how old you are. I'm just saying that if my dad had bought a *Star Wars* figure when he was that age, he'd have been filled with shame to be doing it. He'd have pretended it was for me. We're not ancient. I know what Facebook is. I know how to tweet."

"You tweet?" Lou asked.

"No, but I know how."

"How?"

"Don't derail this conversation. There's absolutely no reason that we can't find common ground with a fourteen-year-old girl. Maybe we'll change her musical tastes for the better."

"How do you tweet?"

"Shut up." George slapped the air vent a couple of times. "C'mon, is that all the heat you've got?"

"If we get a chance to talk to her, without just grabbing her and throwing her in the back of the van, which one of us should do it?"

"You're more like a big teddy bear than I am."

Lou nodded. "True. But I'm bigger."

"So?"

"So that makes me more intimidating."

"You're huggable. I'm way scarier."

"I don't think so."

"You just don't want to do it," said George.

"Well, yeah, but I'm thinking of the mission."

"Let's say that a local orphanage needed somebody to play Santa Claus. Who would they pick?"

Lou shrugged.

"It would be you, right?"

Lou shrugged again.

"I've got a harder edge. You're fluffier. If I were a fourteen year-old girl and I saw me in a dark alley, I'd freak."

"You're a better conversationalist."

"This isn't *My Dinner With Andre*. We don't need to ... actually, you know what, if you're this nervous about it you might accidentally say something scary. I'll talk to her."

The front doors to the school opened, and students began to pour out. George and Lou both sat up straight, watching closely. There wasn't much of a chance that they'd be so lucky as to see her in the crowd, but you never—

"There she is!" said Lou, pointing.

It *was* her. She was wearing a simple white dress that didn't seem anywhere near warm enough for this weather. Did her parents really let her go out like that?

The target was talking to another girl as they walked. George couldn't yet tell if they were headed toward one of the buses. If they were, great—a bus would be extremely easy to follow until it dropped her off.

What would really be helpful was a frickin' name and a frickin' address. If the timeline really was this tight, it made absolutely no sense that Mr. Reith would make their job more difficult than it needed to be. Why was George and Lou's "redemption" more important than actually getting the task accomplished?

"She doesn't look like a werewolf," said Lou.

"What would she look like if she was a werewolf? Fuzzier?"

"I mean that she doesn't carry herself like a werewolf. Ivan was all filled with attitude and stuff. She just looks like a normal kid."

The target, who was now laughing with her friend, did indeed look like a normal kid. Not a cheerleader, not a super athlete, not a brooding loner, not a cutter ... just a normal kid.

"Yeah," said George, "but we've only ever met one other werewolf. If we use Ivan as the baseline, all werewolves are smug assholes."

The target and her friend disappeared from sight behind the buses. George watched closely to see if they would emerge on the other end. This really wasn't George and Lou's area of expertise. They were outstanding at the art of intimidation (well, except when George was tied to a chair being doused with gasoline) but they weren't private investigators. Tracking people wasn't their thing.

"You know, my worst childhood memories are from being on the school bus," said Lou.

"Really?"

Lou nodded. "I was the fat kid, at a time before every other kid was the fat kid. I got picked on non-stop. It was awful."

The girls emerged on the other side of the busses. They weren't headed toward the parking lot, so it looked like they were walking home. George started the engine.

"Ready?" he asked.

"They called me The Blob," said Lou.

"Lou? Focus."

"Sorry."

There was a lot of traffic from parents picking their kids up from school, but as long as the girls didn't turn for the first couple of blocks, George was sure he could keep them in sight.

A block away from school, both girls stopped, laughed about something, and then went their separate ways. Though there were still far too many witnesses around to just nab her, this could be a lucky break.

They weren't going to be able to follow her directly with this many cars around, so George pulled into the parking lot of a small library that was next to the school. They watched as the girl walked alone for a few blocks, and then George drove back onto the street.

"We're following an underage girl in a van," said Lou.

"I'm aware of that."

"Not the direction I thought my life would ever take."

"Nope."

"There's just no upside to this situation. There will be no point in my life where I think 'Ahhh, good times.' There's nothing to look back on fondly in my old age."

"What do you look back on fondly? All of the thumbs we broke?"

Lou ignored him and sighed. "I vote we just bail. Floor the gas on this van and get the hell out of here. Screw Reith and Dewey and those other pricks. We can hide. We'll be more careful this time."

"They found us twice and we weren't even in the United States."

"So we hide in a completely different continent. We could live in Australia. Or New Zealand. C'mon, George. This is awful. Let's not do this."

"How are we gonna get to New Zealand?"

"We'll find a way. We're resourceful."

"Can't do it," said George. "Look how quickly we found her. You think somebody else can't find her just as easily? Somebody who doesn't see anything wrong with killing little girls? It looks like we're doing something horrible—and we are, I'm not trying to deny it—but we're also probably the only line of defense between her and Psycho Dewey. If we're the ones who kidnap her, we can at least do everything in our power to keep her safe."

"She got a crap deal on guardian angels."

"Tell me about it."

"You're right, you're right," said Lou. "We'll stick to the plan. But if we do this and she dies, that's it for my mental health. Just put me in a strait jacket and hide me away. I'm done."

"Fair enough."

The girl turned right. They followed her, pulling into a nice suburban neighborhood.

She was alone. There didn't really seem to be anybody lingering outside of their homes, shoveling snow or anything. If they were going to just grab her and speed off, this was probably their best opportunity.

"I'm gonna loop around the block and get out at the corner," said George. "Don't open the back door until I've got her—we don't want anybody to see the van with an open back door and get suspicious."

"Got it."

"But open it as soon as I've got her. We can't be struggling outside the van waiting for you to open the door."

"Got it."

"If she changes into a werewolf, shoot her with the tranquilizer dart. Don't shoot her with it unless she changes. She'll probably be scratching and biting either way, but that's okay, I can handle it."

"Got it."

"This is the dumbest thing we've ever done, isn't it?"

"Top three."

"Wish me luck."

George parked the van on the side of the street and got out. He didn't want to freak the girl out by running at her, but he wanted to make sure he intercepted her in time, so he settled for a brisk walk.

They reached the corner at the same time.

George tried to give her his least predatory smile. "Hello there."

CHAPTER FIVE

Grab and Go

The girl gave him a wary look. "Hi." It sounded like a question.

"You're Britney's friend, right?"

"I don't know anybody named Britney."

"Oh," said George. Crap. He'd assumed that all fourteen-year-old girls had at least one friend named Britney. He should've gone with Bella. Too late now. "I was supposed to meet her at school for her audition."

"School's that way," said the girl, pointing.

"Okay, yeah, that's what I thought. Just got turned around." George raised an eyebrow. "You look like you can sing."

"How does somebody look like they can sing?"

"I mean that you look like you've got stage presence. That's a rare thing. I'm George."

"Hi, George."

"And you are ...?"

Her eyes narrowed, as if trying to decide if she should run away screaming.

"You don't have to tell me," he said. "I understand. You don't know me from Simon Cowell. I just got turned around, and I was supposed to meet Britney for her audition for this new reality show I'm producing."

"What's it called?" she asked, clearly testing him.

"We're still doing market research on the title. You're part of our core demographic, so maybe you could help. Would you watch a show called *Singers Incorporated*?"

"Who are the judges?"

"Nobody has been hired yet. We're still in the early stages of development."

"Then why are you already auditioning singers?"

How the hell was this little girl outmaneuvering him in this conversation? George was a good talker. He'd been head of the debate team in high school. He could've been a lawyer if he hadn't discovered alcohol during his first and only year in college. Ninety percent of his job involved talking to people and making conversations go the way he wanted. This was insane.

"I like your spirit," said George. "Most kids your age would be saying 'Ooh! Ooh! Put me on your show, pretty please!' but you're actually smart. Let me guess. Straight As, right?"

"Mostly."

"The truth of the matter is that I conned my way into this job, and I don't have a clue what I'm doing. I'm completely out of my element. Do you think you could take a few minutes and answer some questions ... what did you say your name was again?"

"I didn't."

"Well, again, I'm George."

The girl took a step back, but then seemed to decide that, if he lunged at her, there was enough distance between them for her to get away. "I'm Ally."

"Nice to meet you, Ally."

Where was Lou? This would definitely look like a suspicious encounter if anybody happened to glance through their window. For all George knew, he was standing right outside of Ally's home, with her mother dialing 911 at this very moment.

"What questions did you have?" asked Ally, scratching the back of her head. She looked like somebody who was born with straight brown hair but would prefer a purple Mohawk.

George could hear the van approaching.

"For starters, who's your favorite singer?"

"Gigi Kealan."

"Oh, yeah? Great choice. She's definitely somebody we should contact."

"She's my aunt. She doesn't sing at all."

George forced a chuckle. "Now, see, you think you tricked me, but I already admitted that I don't know what I'm doing here. I'm utterly clueless. You are looking at the biggest idiot in the music business. I should be fired. Seriously. My boss should call me up and say, 'Hey, you are literally the least qualified person we could have ever hired for this job,' and fire me. That's why I need you, Ally."

The van came into view. Ally didn't glance back at it. As soon as she did, George would rush her. They were ten feet apart, but George could move pretty damn fast for such a big guy, and he was confident that he could have his hand over her mouth before she got a chance to scream.

"How do I know you're not some pervert?" she asked.

"Do I look like a pervert?"

"Kind of."

"I don't have the energy to be a pervert," George assured her. "I'm old and tired and incompetent. I'm so bad at life that I'm standing here asking a teenager for career advice. Believe me, you've got nothing to fear from me. If I *did* attack you, the encounter would end with me rolling around on the sidewalk clutching my balls."

She giggled at this.

Lou stopped the van.

Ally seemed to notice that the vehicle had stopped behind her, but didn't want to look away from George. If she would maintain eye contact for a just a few more seconds, to give Lou the chance to climb into the back of the van, this would be perfect.

"So who's your real favorite singer?" George asked. "If you could pick your top three dream judges for our show, who would they be?"

What was taking Lou so long to open the door? They'd really lucked out on the privacy issue so far, but eventually somebody was going to drive by or take their dog out for a walk.

Lou slid open the van's side door.

Ally glanced over her shoulder.

George charged.

He lost his footing for a split second and had a horrifying mental image of slipping on the ice and landing on his ass. If that happened, he'd probably just lie there and let Mr. Dewey set him on fire.

But he didn't slip, and managed to lunge forward as intended. If he could get her in time ...

She looked back at him just as he slammed his palm over her mouth. Her scream was completely muffled—nobody would hear it. Without hesitation, he tossed her into the back of the van, quickly climbed in after her, and slammed the door closed.

Done. Only a few seconds' worth of criminal activity for anybody to have witnessed. Unless somebody with too much free time had been peeking through their windows all this time, George felt pretty good about how this had gone.

Inside the van, Lou scrambled up into the front seat as George held Ally against the floor and put his hand over her mouth.

"We're not gonna hurt you," George told her. "I promise."

"He's telling the truth," said Lou, getting behind the steering wheel and driving away from the scene of the crime.

Ally's frantic struggling seemed to indicate that she did not believe them. Fortunately, George outweighed her by at least a hundred pounds, so keeping her under control was not an overwhelming challenge.

"I need you to calm down for us," said George. "Can you do that?"

Ally continued to struggle and scream beneath George's hand, offering no evidence that she intended to, at this particular moment, calm down for them.

Normally in this kind of situation George would give the victim a good thump on the head or briefly remove their access to oxygen, but their victims were almost always sleazeballs. A sweating little weasel who was stealing drug money from his boss *deserved* a very large hand on his throat.

Though they still had over an hour left before Mr. Reith's deadline, they had to assume that once Ally was reported missing, somebody would come forward and say that they'd seen an unfamiliar van before the abduction. So it was in their best interest to resolve this as quickly as possible.

"Ally? Hey, Ally? I need you to listen to me."

She wasn't listening to him. George decided to give her five minutes of freak-out time to get it out of her system.

After five minutes, she was no more calm, so he decided to make it ten.

These icy roads sucked, and Lou's one-handed driving always made George nervous, yet there was no sign that anybody was pursuing them. Yeah, this whole thing could still come to a horrible, horrible end, but for a rushed, half-assed kidnapping that he and Lou wanted no part of, it had gone far better than George could have hoped.

After about eleven minutes of being held down by George, Ally stopped screaming.

"So I'm not producing a music show," George informed her. "We're taking you to meet somebody, but we're not going to let him hurt you. Do you hear what I'm saying?"

George removed his hand from Ally's mouth. She spent a few seconds gasping for breath, then said, "My mom will pay you. Anything you want."

"This isn't about ransom."

"Are you going to kill me?"

"No. I said, we're not going to hurt you. You'll be back home before you know it."

"Are you going to...?" She burst into tears.

"Absolutely not. I swear to you, Ally, nothing bad is going to happen to you."

"I want my mom."

"You'll see her. You may be back before she even knows you're gone. We're going to take you to see this guy, and I won't deny it, he's a piece of crap. But we'll be there with you, I promise." Since they'd just kidnapped her, this probably wasn't the most soothing thought that George could offer.

"We won't let him hurt you," Lou said, looking at them in the rear-view mirror.

"Then why are you taking me to him?"

"He wants you to bite him," George said.

28

"What?"

"He wants you to bite him. That's all."

Ally's confusion seemed to outweigh her terror. "He wants to, like, make a video?"

"No, no, no, it's not a fetish," said George, immediately wishing he hadn't said "fetish" in front of a fourteen-year-old girl. "He thinks you're a werewolf."

"What?"

There was no reason not to spill the whole story. "He wants you to bite him so that he can become a werewolf too."

"Is this a fucking joke?"

"So you're not a werewolf?"

"No, I'm not a werewolf! Are you retarded?"

"I'd like to think not."

"Oh my God! Oh my God!" Ally began to sob, presumably devastated that her life could end at the hands of a couple of superstitious idiots.

"Has anybody ever accused you of being a werewolf before?" George asked.

"No!"

"Have werewolves played any role in your life thus far?"

"No! I don't even like werewolf movies! What the fuck is the matter with you?"

"Okay, I'm not going to give you our whole life story, but we were in a situation where we were extremely skeptical about werewolfism—"

"Lycanthropy," Lou corrected.

"Shut up. *Lycanthropy*, and our skepticism worked out badly for us. I'm not saying you're a werewolf. You're probably not. But the guy who's making us do this does believe, so the easiest way to put this behind us is to deliver you, let you bite him, and take you back home."

"You want me to bite a crazy person?"

"It would help us all, yeah."

Ally sniffled.

"I'm really sorry about this," said George. "You seem like a great kid and you don't deserve this."

"If I was a werewolf, I'd change right now and kill both of you," said Ally.

George nodded. "And I wouldn't blame you one bit."

"I'd rip you to pieces and eat your guts."

"Of course. Why would you not?"

"You should've put me in a cage."

"I know, I know. They even had one. Lou and I rode in it all the way from Ontario. It doesn't make any sense."

It really *didn't* make any sense. There was clearly some animosity between Mr. Dewey and Mr. Reith, but considering that the last werewolf-related job had gone so terribly wrong when the wolf was *in* a cage, it was mind-boggling that they only had a couple of tranquilizer darts this time, fourteen-year-old girl or not.

Shit, it was as if Mr. Reith wanted them to fail.

George considered that.

Shit, Mr. Reith wanted them to fail!

George could not immediately come up with a good motivation for this. And he *had* given them the darts, at least. So maybe Mr. Reith didn't want them to fail. Still, something was very wrong here.

"I hope you die!" Ally shouted. "I hope both of you die!"

"I need you to calm down, Ally."

"Just take me home!"

"We will, I promise, as soon as we—"

"Take me home *now*!"

Had her voice deepened? It sounded like it might have deepened. That didn't necessarily signify that anything bad was about to happen, but it was a bit unnerving.

"Take me home! Take me home! Take me home!"

Ally growled.

Then she snarled.

Then she growled again.

Then her face began to change.

And then George suddenly saw the merit in Lou's previous suggestion that they just drive away from this whole mess.

CHAPTER SIX

Those Who Do Not Learn From The Past . . .

Since he was driving on an icy road in the snow, Lou was not able to devote his full attention to the transformation that was happening behind him. But he caught glimpses of tan fur, claws, and teeth in the rear view mirror, and George was helpfully providing exposition as he screamed.

"Jesus Christ! She's a werewolf! She's a werewolf!"

There was a lot of traffic on this four-lane street and Lou was in the left lane, so he couldn't just slam the brakes and scramble into the back to help his partner. He started to swerve into the right lane, got honked at by a jeep he almost hit, and returned to the left.

"Do something, Lou!" George shouted. "She's gonna bite my face off!"

Lou held the steering wheel in place with his handless arm while he reached over and popped open the glove compartment with his right hand. He took out the tranquilizer gun, but it wasn't loaded, so he tossed it onto the passenger seat and grabbed one of the darts, while simultaneously trying to keep his eye on the road and monitor the struggle in the back.

"The tranquilizer gun! Get the tranquilizer gun!" George shouted. He could be forgiven for not noticing what Lou was doing up front, given the circumstances.

Lou couldn't load the gun while driving the van. He tried once again to swerve into the right lane and again got honked at. He'd always envisioned Minnesota as this desolate wasteland with a car every twenty miles, but apparently that wasn't the case. He wasn't going to be able to multi-task right now, so he'd just have to focus on being a safe driver.

"Shit!" said George, offering no additional context.

Lou flipped on his turn signal, waited for the lane to clear, and then finally moved into the right lane. Then he slammed on the brakes, since the cars directly in front of him were all stopped at a red light.

The tires screeched and the van slid forward, finally stopping a few inches away from the rear bumper of the car ahead.

The car behind them struck the van. Not hard. Probably just a minor fender bender. Still, this wasn't a particularly convenient time to have somebody walking up to exchange insurance information.

Lou spun around. Ally was a full werewolf.

She wasn't a huge werewolf. George was still bigger than her, as far as Lou could tell with both of them thrashing and rolling around. Like Ivan, she hadn't changed into an actual wolf. She retained her human limbs, though they were now covered with fur and had scary-looking claws. She didn't have the long snout of a wolf, but she certainly had the teeth of one.

George punched Ally in the face.

Her head flew back and a thick rope of spittle hit the side of the van. She snarled and opened her mouth wide. George punched her in the throat before she could sink her teeth into his face.

Lou loaded the dart.

Ally clutched at her throat and made wolfish choking noises. George shoved her off of him. She struck the side of the van, right where the spit had landed, but recovered immediately and grabbed George's foot by the ankle.

Lou took careful aim as Ally dragged George toward her. If he'd wanted to shoot George, well, he'd have an excellent shot, but since he wanted to shoot Ally, his available shot was total crap. He moved the tranquilizer gun to the left just as George was dragged in the same direction.

"Get out of the way!" said Lou.

"I'm trying!"

"I need a clear shot!"

Ally slashed at George with her claws, ripping open the front of his jacket but not, as far as Lou could tell, George's chest.

"Shoot her, for God's sake!" George shouted.

Lou had a decent shot at her arm. Not good enough to risk wasting the dart. He'd always been a knife guy, not a gun guy, so even at a close distance like this he wasn't comfortable with a moving target.

Somebody knocked on the passenger-side window.

It was a tall beefy guy. Probably the guy who'd hit the van. He looked pretty upset. As far as Lou could tell, his vantage point didn't allow him to see that Lou was pointing a tranquilizer gun into the back of the van, although the shaking and snarling and shouting was probably arousing suspicion.

Lou waved him away.

The guy knocked on the window, more insistently.

"Go away," Lou told him, politely.

That seemed to piss the guy off. He pounded on the window a couple more times, and then—wait, was he really going to open the door?

Yep, he threw open the door.

"What the hell is the matter with...?"

Lou wasn't sure if the man reacted to the werewolf snarls that were no longer muffled by the van door, or the fact that he now had a tranquilizer dart pointed at him, but his mouth dropped open much wider than necessary to complete his question about what the hell the matter with Lou. He stood there for a half-second, raised his hands as if being arrested, then hurried away.

Lou pointed the gun back into the rear of the van. He still didn't have a good shot. Ally tore out another piece of George's jacket, and this time Lou thought he might have seen some blood.

George bellowed. Yep, there was blood on his chest, though no intestines.

Lou considered climbing into the back to get a better angle, but rejected that idea as suicidal.

"Get her in front of you!" said Lou.

George responded. He'd probably said, "I'm trying! I'm trying!" but his words weren't very coherent.

"Dammit, George! Push her!"

Lou got maybe half of what George said next. Enough to figure out that he was saying, "Just throw it to me, you twit!" The "twit" part was definite, anyway. Not a usual part of George's vocabulary.

He tossed the gun to George, who caught it.

Lou immediately turned back around in his seat. It wouldn't do any good to have a knocked-out werewolf if the cops showed up before he could drive away. Well, it would do some good from the perspective of George possibly not getting torn apart, but still, it would've been a lot of moral anguish for nothing if they ended up in prison.

The light had turned green, probably a few moments ago since there were no longer any cars in front of them, so Lou floored the gas pedal. The tires spun for a second, then the van shot forward. He raced across the intersection. There were plenty of places he could've pulled off if he hadn't just been involved in the fender-bender, but now they had to flee the scene.

Hopefully George could get the situation under control by himself.

George screamed. It didn't sound much like the situation was under control.

"Just throw it to me, you twit!" George shouted. "Twit" was not the word he'd meant to use or even a word he'd ever said before, as far as he could remember, but when a werewolf was raking its claws across your skin and drawing blood, it was hard to vocalize more than the screams of pain.

For somebody whose lycanthropy supposedly hadn't manifested itself yet,

Ally had transformed pretty goddamned efficiently. Had she been lying? Did she go out on werewolf romps every weekend?

At the moment, it didn't matter. The slashes across George's chest stung like hell and might require stitches but weren't anything that would cause him to bleed to death. If she got in another good swipe, or got him across the neck, it might be a different story.

Lou was no marksman and it made sense that he'd wait for the perfect opportunity, but still, George felt like his partner should've been able to squeeze off at least one decent shot by now. Didn't matter anymore. Lou tossed the tranquilizer gun to him and George caught it.

Then Ally knocked it out of his hand. George's wrist went numb, but there was no jutting bone or spurting blood. The tranquilizer gun fell to the floor as the van rocketed forward, putting Ally off balance. George took advantage of that moment and punched her in the stomach with his non-numb hand, as hard as he could, doubling her over.

Though he'd assumed that she'd gone totally feral, knocking a gun out of his hand wasn't an animal thing to do. Could he reason with her? Ivan had retained his human personality in his wolf-form, so maybe they could just talk this out.

"Ally!" he shouted. "Ally! Listen to me! We're trying to help you!"

She leapt on him and took a vicious swipe at his face. An inch closer and he'd be missing a nose.

"You can fight this!" George insisted. "Just try!"

Granted, there probably wasn't a lot of motivation for Ally to fight the change at this particular moment. Tearing George to shreds would be in her best interest. But if she *was* a peace-loving teenage girl at heart who didn't want to hurt anybody, and there *was* part of her resisting the murderous urge ...

Ally put back her head and let out a howl. It was not the kind of howl that George could translate as, *Hi, George, I'm doing everything I can to control my inner beast, so just be patient for a little while longer.* It was more like a howl of victory right before devouring her prey.

George punched her again. He wasn't sure if he'd feel guilty about this later. She rolled off of him. Now she was in the perfect position for Lou to shoot her with the tranquilizer dart, if he'd still had it.

Lou took a sharp turn to the left, eliciting a couple of honks. The tranquilizer gun slid back within George's grasp, and he snatched it up. He pointed it at Ally and pulled the trigger.

The van suddenly tilted as it headed down a steep hill, messing up George's aim. The dart flew past Ally's neck, missing by so little that George swore he saw her fur sway.

Then it struck Lou in the shoulder.

Aw, shit.

How fast did these darts work?

Lou plucked the dart out of his shoulder and looked back at them. His eyes rolled to the top of his head and he flopped over in his seat.

Ally pounced upon George. This should have distracted him from the fact that he was now in the back of a driverless van that was rolling down a steep icy hill, but it didn't, not entirely.

There was another dart up front. Other useful items up front included the steering wheel and the brake pedal, none of which were likely to be accessible before the van smashed into another vehicle or struck the curb and flipped onto its side, taking out a few innocent pedestrians. It was probably best for his mental health that George couldn't actually see where the van was headed.

Ally made another close but unsuccessful attempt to bite off his nose. He tried to jab his thumb into her eye. He didn't want to cause her any permanent injury, but he also didn't want to die a gruesome death, and right now his survival instinct trumped his concerns about disfiguring her. It didn't matter, since his thumb missed, and then narrowly missed getting bitten off.

He punched her once more. These blows were undoubtedly hurting his fist more than the were-girl. Still, each one seemed to stun her long enough to keep her from tearing him apart in the next moment.

The van was picking up speed.

Lots of speed.

At any second George expected to hear the *crunch* of something human underneath the tires.

"Ally! We have to stop the van or we're both going to die!"

Ally gave no indication that she understood him, or at least that she cared about his urgent message.

"Ally, please! I don't want to die like this! Neither do you! We need to work together!"

Ally gnashed her teeth.

George was surprised that they hadn't crashed into something yet. It was going to really, really hurt when they did.

Lou opened his eyes.

Where was he?

Oh, yeah, in the van.

What was happening in the van?

Oh, yeah, George was fighting a werewolf in the back.

Lou sat up. His vision was blurry. As far as he could tell, nobody was driving the van. Was that his job? He was pretty sure it was.

Why was the van still moving if nobody was driving?

It was going too fast for safety.

Lou was sleepy.

So sleepy.

He knew that he should be doing something important, something related to the van, especially since there was a very large truck up ahead that George might not know about, but the darkness overtook him again and he toppled back over and went to sleep.

George doubted he had time to overpower Ally and then climb into the front of the van so that he could steer them away from what he assumed was certain death, so he continued his attempts to reason with her.

"Ally! Ally! Can you hear me?"

She tried to chomp off his ear.

"Ally, I need you to—!"

George was not entirely certain what happened next, although it definitely involved the van colliding with something very large. It wasn't a head-on collision, because the van began to spin—until it struck something else. All of the windows shattered, filling the back of the van with light as George and Ally tumbled backwards and slammed into the rear door. Ally struck her head; George struck the door with the entire left side of his body.

With a groan, George sat up. At least the van wasn't...no, actually, it was still rolling down the hill.

Through the broken rear window, he could see that their second collision had been with a grey sedan that now had a crumpled front hood. As they rolled further, he saw that the van had originally hit a U-Haul truck. If they'd hit it straight on, he, Lou, and Ally would probably all be dead now, instead of dead a few moments from now.

George prayed that Lou was still alive. He couldn't see any blood up front, but nor could he hear Lou snoring.

Though Ally seemed stunned, she remained conscious. George kicked her in the head to try to change that. She tried to bite his foot. He kicked her again.

He glanced up front to make sure the van wasn't seconds away from crashing into another vehicle. They'd rolled into the opposite lane, and the snowplow coming toward them did not give him a warm happy feeling.

CHAPTER SEVEN

Crash

Ally's eyes were still open but she wasn't actively trying to kill George anymore, so he decided that his best move was to focus on stopping the van.

He started to crawl toward the front seats, which is when he discovered just how much his body hurt. Though no bones were broken, as far as he could tell, he knew he'd be covered with grotesque bruises, and the agony from merely crawling the length of a van was almost unbearable. In the morning he'd barely be able to move—if there was a morning for him.

He was also pretty sure he was leaving a trail of blood along the floor, though he didn't look back to verify. He hadn't felt this bad since the last time he'd dealt with a werewolf.

George made it to the front seats and reached over Lou for the steering wheel. Nope. His arms weren't long enough. He climbed between the seats, noting that the snowplow was trying to change lanes to avoid the van but was not doing so quickly because, after all, it was a snowplow.

Sure, it was pushing a large pile of snow in front of it, but that wouldn't make this a well-cushioned, fluffy impact.

George grabbed the steering wheel and spun it to the right. The tires screeched and the van went off the road and into a driveway, narrowly missing a tree, two snowmen, and a parked car.

The van did hit the other parked car, though.

George felt as if his body were ripped in two at the waist. Fortunately, the seats kept him from hurtling straight into the dashboard and splattering the contents of his skull. Lou rolled off the front seat.

At least the van had stopped now.

George put his hand on Lou's neck. There was still a pulse. Thank God.

And now Ally's snarling had resumed. She was crawling toward him, teeth bared, claws extended.

Tranquilizer gun. He needed the tranquilizer gun.

No, wait, he'd dropped that in the back. He couldn't remember if it was while he was fighting Ally or during one of the crashes, but either way, the gun was inaccessible.

The snowplow continued on its merry way past the house. Really? The guy wasn't going to stop to see if everything was okay? What a dick.

George looked around for something he could throw at Ally. Nothing was available except maybe a handful of safety glass.

Screw it. George scooped up a handful of glass and threw it into Ally's face. It was a damned good throw. He wasn't sure if he actually got her in the eyes, but she turned her head and stopped moving toward him.

That wouldn't keep her away for long.

Should he continue trying to reason with her, or did that just make him look stupid? Could he look any stupider at this point?

Ally suddenly seemed to realize that the windows were broken. She scurried over to one and poked her head outside.

Crap. If she tried to squeeze through, she could probably make it. Then he'd have a crazed werewolf on the loose, possibly one that might go on a killing spree. Again.

"Hey!" he shouted. She ignored him and continued to push through the window, apparently not bothered by the glass on the edges of the frame. George's first instinct was to lunge forward and try to grab her leg...but was that the best idea, looking at the big picture? How many innocent lives would he save by getting mauled to death before she escaped?

Better plan: get the dart, get the gun, shoot the wolf.

In his current state of agony, George would have preferred moving at a leisurely pace, like that of a ninety-seven-year-old invalid, but the situation didn't permit that, so he climbed halfway into the passenger seat and grabbed the dart out of the glove compartment as fast as he could. Oh, yeah, he'd definitely be paying for that in the morning.

Ally was halfway out of the window. It would've been convenient and hilarious if she got stuck, but she was making fairly rapid progress.

And then she was through.

Shit, shit, shit, and shit.

George scrambled into the back and picked up the gun. He frantically loaded the second dart.

Please don't start slaughtering people. Please don't start slaughtering people. Please don't start slaughtering people.

Two cars being in the driveway didn't bode well for nobody being home. And the snowman was even scarier.

He slid open the van door and got out. Two cars had parked on the side of the road, and one the drivers was already out of his vehicle. Ally wasn't running toward him. Nor was she running toward the open front door, where a woman and a young boy stood. She'd dropped to all fours and was running toward the woods behind the house.

If she made it past the trees, he'd never catch her. Not a chance in hell.

"Animal control!" he shouted, waving the gun in the air. "Everybody stay back!"

The woman ushered the boy back inside and closed the door.

George extended his arm and took careful aim. He'd never fired a tranquilizer dart before the one that hit Lou, and he doubted it was anywhere near as accurate as a bullet. On the plus side, Ally didn't seem acclimated to her new form and her gait was kind of awkward.

Behind him, a woman screamed. George didn't let that distract him. *Focus... focus...*

He squeezed the trigger.

Ally let out a soft yelp.

Holy crap! He'd done it!

She kept running, but her pace slowed. Then she disappeared into the woods.

George turned around. "I need you to clear the area!" he said, trying to sound like somebody in a position of authority. There were two people walking toward him and a couple more cars had parked. "It's too dangerous to be here. Please return to your vehicles."

"What the hell was that thing?" a woman asked.

"It's rabid," said George, not really answering her question. "I need you to vacate the premises. Seriously. It's for your own safety."

A man had taken out his cell phone. Surprisingly, he seemed to be making an actual call instead of taking a picture.

"Sir? There's no need to contact anybody. I have this under control."

"Under control? That thing ran into the woods!"

"I understand that. But there's a serious financial risk if the media ..." *Fuck it.* George didn't have time to try to bargain with these people. He ignored the witnesses and his own agony and hurried off into the woods.

Ally had only made it about twenty feet in before collapsing. She was still in her wolf form, thank God. That would make her a lot more difficult to drag back to the van, but onlookers would be less likely to try to prevent him from taking away a wolf-creature than a teenage girl, although they'd probably wonder why the wolf was wearing a dress.

This would be a hell of a lot easier with Lou helping him, but he couldn't really blame his partner for being unconscious, given the circumstances.

He grabbed Ally underneath the arms and dragged her through the snow. He wondered how efficient the Tropper police department was in responding to emergency calls. Hopefully they sucked.

This wasn't so bad. He'd dragged unconscious bodies before. Getting her back into the van would be more of a challenge, but he had this, no problem.

He dragged her out of the woods and into the yard.

Several people were watching George as he dragged Ally toward the van. He didn't mind gawkers as long as they didn't try to interfere. Hopefully nobody was thinking to take down the license plate number, though George planned to ditch the van as soon as he could. He kept his head down, trying to be as non-photogenic as possible.

"What's going on?" the woman demanded. "What is that?"

"I already told you, it's a ... rabid. It's still alive, as far as I can tell, so any smart person would get back in their car."

"Where are you taking it?"

George started to say "The Center for Disease Control," then decided that starting a citywide panic was not in his best interest. "Just a lab," he said.

"What kind of lab?"

"If you're going to just stand there talking, do you think maybe you could help me with this thing? Take the feet."

The woman did not take the feet.

George dragged Ally to the van. He hoped it was still drivable after three collisions. He'd drawn enough unwelcome attention already—forcing somebody to give him their car would be a last resort.

He left Ally on the ground next to the side of the van and opened the driver's side door. Lou was still flopped over, snoring. Moving his big ass out of the way was going to be much more challenging than dragging a werewolf through the snow.

"You're bleeding," the woman said.

George nodded. "Yep. She got me good."

"Do you need a first-aid kit?"

"That would be lovely."

The woman walked back toward her car. George gestured to his bloody chest. "How come she was the first one to offer? You've all just been standing there watching me bleed. I thought Minnesotans were supposed to be polite?"

Okay, no time to scold. George took a deep breath, then began the unpleasant task of moving his very large partner out of the front seat. George's muscles and bruised-up skin did not respond well to this, and it felt like his arms were being twisted around like a leg coming off a roasted chicken, but he worked as fast as he could and got Lou out of the way without too much wasted time or humiliation.

He turned the key in the ignition. The engine started. Mr. Reith knew how to pick a good van.

Still no sound of sirens, but there was a zero percent chance that nobody had called the cops, so he really needed to get moving.

The woman returned with the first aid kit. "Thanks," said George. "Can I keep this? I think I'll need the whole thing."

"Uh, sure."

"Thank you. If you've got a business card I'll mail you a replacement."

"No, no, that's fine."

"Okay. Back away now."

The woman backed away. George had kept in shape during his months of hiding out (more so than Lou, who'd gone more than a bit soft) so, with some effort and lots of whispered cursing, he was able to get Ally into the back of the van. He slid the door shut.

Inside the house, he could see the woman and boy peeking at him through the window. The woman looked conflicted, as if trying to reconcile her desire to have the wrecked car issue addressed with her desire to not be outside with a thug dragging around a wolf-girl.

"I'll be in touch," George told everybody. He got into the driver's seat of the van, slammed the door shut, and waved through the broken windows. He backed out of the driveway while at least three of the witnesses took his picture. Nothing he could do about that. He had neither the means nor the desire to kill everybody who'd seen him. Mr. Dewey would crap his pants with fury when he found out how badly this had gone, but, in the end, George *had* captured the werewolf, as instructed.

As long as the cops didn't stop him.

George drove away from the scene of the crime, quickly but not too quickly.

CHAPTER EIGHT

Hard Bargain

George did hear sirens shortly after he drove off, but they weren't close enough to create a "floor the gas pedal and scream 'You'll never take me alive, coppers!'" sense of urgency. He was more worried about Ally recovering and leaping out the window again. Until he got something to better secure her, he was going to operate under the potentially fatal assumption that Lou would wake up first, giving him some warning.

Though he wasn't skilled at pursuing somebody, George was quite experienced in the art of the getaway. A few sudden turns and he was confident that nobody who'd witnessed the werewolf action was following him. A few more turns and he was in a nice secluded area, a single-lane path surrounded by woods.

He stopped the van and shut off the engine.

He poked at Lou's side. "Lou? Hey, Lou? Wanna wake up for me, buddy?"

Lou did not stir. This was for the best, since the deeper he was under, the less chance that Ally would wake up at an inopportune moment.

The dashboard was covered with snow and more was falling in through the broken windshield, but George had more pressing issues than being cold and miserable. He took the cell phone out of the glove compartment and called the one number that was programmed into it.

There was an answer after the first ring. "Yes?"

"Good afternoon, Mr. Reith."

"George. I've been watching TV. Not a subtle kidnapper, are you?"

"Nope. You know what would be nice? Accurate information. If somebody tells me that a werewolf I'm carting around isn't going to transform, I'd like for that to actually be the case. That would be a refreshing change of pace."

"I'll note that for the future. Where are you?"

"We're safe."

Mr. Reith was silent for a very long moment. "George," he finally said, "I sincerely hope that you're not planning to add any difficulty to my life."

"Nah. I just have a few questions."

"Now is not the time."

"Yeah, well, you can answer my questions or you can blow me. Why did you send Lou and me on this job?"

"Redemption."

"I'm not buying that. You didn't tell us her name, you didn't give us any time to scope out the situation, you didn't give us the cage or even a frickin' net. We were set up to fail."

"Did you fail?"

"Almost!"

"You were given the opportunity to prove yourself," said Mr. Reith. "I'm honestly astonished that you don't understand or appreciate that."

"Because you're full of shit. No way is The Redemption of George Orton and Lou Flynn more important than delivering the werewolf to Mr. Dewey. So you're going to tell me what's going on, or we'll sell her to the highest bidder."

"Do you have any idea what you're—?"

"Start talking or I'm shattering this phone against a wall."

"Do what you feel is necessary."

"Okay. Blow me." George disconnected the call then powered down the phone so that Mr. Reith couldn't trace it. Or at least to decrease the likelihood that Mr. Reith could trace it. George didn't understand the technology of phone-tracing very well.

If everything had gone smoothly, George might have stuck to the plan, but now he and Lou had become a much more problematic loose end. Mr. Dewey would execute them for sure, unless George could negotiate his way out of this, or maybe figure out the deal with Mr. Reith.

He'd give the old man a few minutes to stew in his own juices, then call him back.

Even if Mr. Reith couldn't trace the location of his cell phone, he might have put a tracking device in the vehicle. If that was the case, hanging out in the van was a terrible idea. Unfortunately, George had an unconscious partner and a werewolf to deal with, and a van that needed to stay off the road as much as possible. He couldn't just leave Lou and Ally here. If Ally escaped, he'd lose all of his bargaining power.

George was a man of action, but his best course of action right now was to sit in this freezing van and wait. And to use the first aid kit to bandage up the gashes on his chest.

Exactly five minutes after he'd hung up, George powered up the phone again and called Mr. Reith back.

"Have you decided to listen to reason?" Mr. Reith asked.

"Nah."

"All right, then. I guess I have no choice." Mr. Reith cleared his throat. "I despise Mr. Dewey. I have hated that son of a bitch for twenty-six years, and yes, I wanted to make him sweat. I was not inclined to let this job go without its share of complications."

"So you're admitting that you set us up to fail?"

"Not to fail. To succeed in a messier fashion."

"Sorry, I'm afraid I have to call bullshit again, sir. As bad as things went, they could've gone a lot worse. You wouldn't risk the whole thing just to stress him out. Either you wanted it done or you didn't. Give me a better answer the next time I call."

George hung up on him and shut off the phone. He usually tried to be respectful toward those who could have him slowly tortured to death, but he needed Mr. Reith to know that he was calling the shots. At least for now.

He poked Lou again. No response. He had no idea how long he'd be out from this tranquilizer dart, but it couldn't be all *that* long, could it?

Why was George even trying to guess? It wasn't as if he was a zookeeper or a big game hunter. They could be out for three weeks, for all he knew.

He sighed. Costa Rica hadn't been so bad.

If only he had something with which to secure Ally.

The seatbelt?

In her animal form, she wouldn't know to press the button to free herself, would she? She might be able to snap it, but, still, it was better than nothing.

Well, yeah, if he wanted a savage homicidal werewolf sitting right next to him, shredding him while he tried to drive.

Not his brightest idea. At least he hadn't said it out loud to anybody.

If he didn't work things out with Mr. Reith on the next call, he was going to have to take the risk and return to the road. He'd much rather wait until nightfall, when there was less chance of being spotted, but he didn't know how much time he had. They'd gone all the way to Ontario to collect George and Lou for this job, so Mr. Reith and Mr. Dewey would at least pretend that they were going to try to talk things out with him.

He wiped some snow off the dashboard.

There had to be a way out of this mess. None came to mind, but he wasn't yet willing to accept that he was screwed. If no plan worked out, he supposed he could always just wait for Ally to change back, drop her off on the side of the road, and then speed out of Tropper and go back into hiding.

Maybe that should be Plan A.

It really sucked not being able to bounce bad ideas off of Lou.

He powered up the phone again and called Mr. Reith. While waiting for him to answer, George had thought that he might start off the conversation by calling him "sweetheart," but by the time Mr. Reith actually answered George had decided that it would be going too far.

"You ready to talk?" George asked.

"I've said as much as you need to hear."

"See, now, I disagree with that, obviously."

"I'm not interested in whether you agree or disagree. I won't be playing your little game, George. Feel free to go to hell. Goodbye."

Mr. Reith hung up.

George glanced at the display to make sure Mr. Reith had really disconnected the call. Yep. He had. Hmmm. That wasn't how he'd hoped this conversation would go.

As long as he had Ally, he still had the upper hand.

Right?

If George called him back, that gave Mr. Reith all of the power. So he definitely wasn't going to call him back. At the same time, no way was Mr. Reith sitting there saying, "Oh well, I guess I'll just let those crazy fellows go. Sometimes these things don't work out the way you hoped."

The van had to be traceable. They needed a new mode of transportation, as soon as possible.

George started the engine and turned the van around. He'd steal the first car he could find. Maybe he could figure out a way to get Mr. Dewey to place all of the blame on Mr. Reith. Yeah, Mr. Dewey had let Mr. Reith take Lou against his wishes, but that didn't necessarily mean Mr. Dewey couldn't put a hit on the old bastard. If Mr. Reith took all the heat for this disaster and got a bullet through the skull, maybe George and Lou could return to their original plan of delivering Ally for a quick bite and then taking her back home.

Now that Ally was no longer trying to kill him, George felt terrible for all of the punching and kicking. It couldn't be helped, but still, it wasn't cool.

He glanced back at her. Her legs had changed into human legs again, though the top half of her remained a wolf-girl. Her dress had been torn during the transformation but it thankfully still covered enough that he didn't know what color underwear she was wearing. He'd try to steal some new clothes for her, just in case. Her shoes were history.

He watched her for another moment, but nothing else seemed to be changing, so he began to drive. He kept the phone in his pocket, not sure if he wanted it to ring or not.

After less than a minute, a truck came into view, driving on the same path, moving toward him.

There was room on the path for two vehicles, if each of them moved to the side.

The truck did not move to the side.

George applied the brakes.

The truck stopped in front of him. There were three men inside. George could already tell that these weren't friendly Minnesota guys out for a drive. Even through their dirty windshield, all three of them had the look of killers.

Or maybe they were just hunters who really liked to watch animals die.

The driver didn't honk the horn to tell George to get the hell out of the way, which wasn't a good sign. People who weren't there to kill him would be annoyed that he was blocking the path.

George popped open his door without swinging it outward. He tried to look calm, like everything in life was simply delightful.

The driver and the man closest to the passenger-side door got out of the truck. George couldn't see any guns, but they were wearing jackets, so they could be carrying anything.

They wouldn't immediately try to kill him. They'd find out if he had Ally first. So he at least had a few seconds before things turned violent.

The two men outside the truck split up, the driver walking over to Lou's window and the passenger walking up to George's. George had still held on to the point zero zero zero three percent chance that these guys had nothing to do with Mr. Reith or Mr. Dewey, but this wiped that out.

"Hello there," said the man outside of George's window. He wore a black knit hat, and had a thick brown mustache and goatee. He smiled, revealing a missing front tooth. His tongue protruded through the gap.

"Hi," said George.

"Looks like you've had some trouble." The man tapped the edge of the shattered windshield with a gloved finger.

"What's up with your buddy here?" asked the other man, reaching in and poking Lou. "Sleeping off a bender?" This man also wore a knit hat, though his was red. He was startlingly handsome. Was he paying the bills with crime while waiting for his modeling career to take off?

"Seriously, guys?" George asked. "Are you really going to pretend that we're meeting by accident?"

Black Hat chuckled. "I guess that *was* kind of silly."

"We're all adults here. Let's not insult each other's intelligence."

"I can respect that. Where's the girl?"

"In the back. Your fuckhead partner can go check, if you want. Not like I can stop him from looking in. The windows are all broken."

"That wouldn't be a trap, now would it?"

"Yes, it's a trap. She's waiting back there with an Uzi."

"Funny guy. I kind of like you."

"This mean you won't kill me?"

Black Hat shrugged. "I'll consider it. Is your buddy dead?"

"Nah. Just sleeping."

"Odd time to sleep."

"I accidentally shot him with a tranquilizer dart."

"You being funny again?"

"Nah."

"Because he could be faking it. Seems like the smart thing for me to do would be to put a couple of rounds into his head, just to be sure."

"You know we're unarmed. That would be a dick move."

"I don't know you're unarmed."

"I would've already shot you. Why isn't your fuckhead partner looking in the back yet?"

Red Hat frowned, as if he thought Ally might really be waiting back there with an Uzi. Black Hat nodded at him, and he walked toward the rear of the van.

The third man, who wore no hat, remained in the truck, watching them carefully.

"Were you told to kill us?" George asked.

Black Hat smiled again. He seemed very proud of that missing tooth. "I've got some say in the matter."

"She's back here," Red Hat called out from behind the van. "Beat up pretty bad."

Had Ally changed completely back to human? George wanted to check but didn't dare to look away from Black Hat.

"That your M.O.?" Black Hat asked. He poked his tongue through the tooth. "Beat up little girls?"

"She's pretty spunky. She'd probably kick your ass for calling her a little girl."

"Is that right?"

"I have no idea. I just needed something to say. She did slash up my chest pretty bad. Got some nails on her."

"Well, George, you're in luck. I don't think I'm going to kill you."

Black Hat's words would have been more reassuring if he wasn't reaching inside his jacket while he was saying them. If George was going to take action to not get shot in the face, now was the time.

George flung open the door.

CHAPTER NINE

Bloodshed

The van door bashed into Black Hat's chest. He cried out in pain. He was a tough-looking guy who didn't seem like the type to make such a sound in response to getting hit by a door, but he'd probably been reaching for a gun, and thus his hand probably got whacked between the door and his gun, which was a pretty good motivation to make such a sound.

George ducked down beneath the broken windows, in case the guy with no hat decided to take a shot at him. He yanked the door closed and then smashed it into Black Hat again, knocking him several steps backwards. George scrambled out of the van as quickly as he could, trying to tackle Black Hat before he could take out his weapon.

If Black Hat had been taking out a pen instead, well, George would figure out a way to cope with his guilt.

Black Hat removed his hand from inside of his jacket, revealing a revolver clutched in fingers that weren't all bending the right way. George was actually glad to see the gun, since it meant he wouldn't waste precious seconds digging through the jacket himself.

Neither George nor Lou had any formal martial arts training, and of the two of them, Lou was much better at delivering karate chops. If he put all of his strength into it, Lou could break somebody's arm. George's karate chop skills were not of the bone-breaking variety, but he did knock the gun out of Black Hat's hand.

To be fair, Black Hat might have dropped it anyway, since he had at least two crushed fingers, but George couldn't stand around to wait for that to happen. They both reached for the ground at the same time, narrowly avoiding cracking their skulls into each other.

George grabbed the gun first.

Though Black Hat was the closer danger, the other two men almost certainly had guns of their own and were thus a more immediate threat. George quickly fired two rounds into the windshield of the truck, missing the guy with no hat, who ducked beneath the dashboard.

He spun around, gun arm extended, but saw no sign of Red Hat.

He spun back around, accidentally bashing Black Hat in the nose with the revolver. Blood squirted from his nostrils.

Though George had already wasted two rounds, now was not the time to conserve the rest of them. He squeezed the trigger, firing point-blank into Black Hat's face, directly under his right eye.

The thug dropped to the ground, instantly creating a pool of red snow. His hat was ruined.

George was surprised that he hadn't already been shot at, so he wasted no time in pressing himself against the side of the van. He still couldn't see Red Hat, so he must've been crouched down beneath the windows.

A shot rang out and a bullet zipped past George's foot.

He cursed and hurriedly put a tire between himself and Red Hat. He glanced back at the truck. No sign of the occupant. Hopefully that meant he was a complete chickenshit, although guys like Mr. Dewey and Mr. Reith typically didn't employ people who were complete chickenshits.

Honestly, this would be a pretty good time for Ally to wake up and transform into a werewolf again. George could use a distraction.

Movement. George caught a flash of Red Hat's jacket around the corner.

He fired.

Missed.

It had only been Red Hat's jacket that was exposed, not the man himself. Dammit. He'd made George waste another round with an obvious trick. He might as well have just waved a red cape and let George charge at him.

The worst part was that his back was starting to hurt from all of this ducking to stay under the van windows. He really was getting old.

He thought he heard the truck door open.

"Any chance you guys want to cut a deal?" George asked. "I've got a buyer for the werewolf. Two hundred grand. Three-way split."

Neither of the men responded.

"I'm serious!" George insisted. "Nobody will know. You'll get chewed out by your boss, but you'll walk away sixty-six grand richer!"

"You believe in werewolves?" asked Red Hat, who had returned to the opposite side of the van. "What the hell's the matter with you?"

"Well, no, I don't," said George. "But you work for somebody who does, right?"

"No."

"Oh. Who do you work for?"

"We work for Desmond Reith."

"Okay, see, he believes in werewolves."

"No, he doesn't."

"Fine. Maybe he doesn't. The point is that I know somebody who does believe, and he's willing to pay us a lot of money to deliver what he thinks is a werewolf girl to him, however stupid and deranged that might be, and you're throwing away your share if you kill me."

"No deal. Sorry."

Red Hat's voice sounded like he was crouched down beneath window level, but not all the way to the ground. George risked a peek under the van. No visible feet. Red Hat was using the same "stay behind a tire" trick.

No, wait, now he saw feet. Not Red Hat's feet, though. Running feet.

The hatless man leaned around the front corner of the van. George noticed a lot of things about him at once (he was pudgier than his partners, was underdressed for the weather, and put too much product in his hair, which probably explained his reluctance to wear a hat) but the most noteworthy element was that he was carrying a submachine gun.

It looked like a Tommy Gun, the kind used by Prohibition-era gangsters. George got the hell out of there as the hatless man opened fire.

Over the noise of the gun George could hear the bullets clanging against the side of the van, and the hiss of a tire deflating. George fled around the back of the vehicle, unable to believe that this psycho would be shooting off dozens of rounds so close to the werewolf.

George rounded the corner to see Red Hat only about three feet away, pointing his own gun at him. The hatless man stopped firing, perhaps to avoid accidentally mowing down his own partner.

George held up his hands in surrender.

"She needs meds," he said.

"Drop your gun," said Red Hat. George heard the hatless man step around the corner of the vehicle behind him.

"I hid the meds. You want 'em? Let's talk."

Red Hat shook his head. "Let's not talk."

"Fine." George made as if to lower his gun, then pointed it through the broken window at Ally. "Put down your guns or I'll kill the girl."

Red Hat didn't even raise an eyebrow. George couldn't see how the hatless man reacted to this, but fully expected a barrage of bullets to tear through his back at any moment.

"I'll do it," George insisted. "I'll waste her. Your boss doesn't give a shit about me, but you get *her* killed and you'll be at the bottom of a lake within the hour."

Red Hat shrugged and lowered his gun. "The kind of guy who'd beat up a girl like that would probably murder her, too, huh?"

George kind of wanted to clarify that the beating had occurred when she was savagely attacking him as a wolf-girl, but this was not the time to worry about what these gentlemen thought of his moral standards.

The hatless man jabbed George in the small of his back with the barrel of the submachine gun. "Go ahead. Shoot her. Give me an excuse to shred you."

"You do that, you'll shoot right through me and hit your co-worker."

Red Hat stepped out of the way.

"So much for that plan," said the hatless man with a chuckle.

"That wasn't an actual plan. I wasn't really hoping that you'd shoot through me to hit him."

"Whatever."

"You're just really anxious to use that machine gun, aren't you?"

"Submachine."

"That an actual Thompson?"

"Replica."

"Still pretty sweet."

"Yep."

"Mind getting it out of my back before I shoot the girl?"

"I don't care if you shoot her."

"You're just saying that because you don't think I'll shoot her."

"I want you to shoot her. Nothing would make me happier. If you shoot her, I'll get to see what this thing can really do."

"You haven't killed anybody with it yet?"

"Not yet."

"How long have you had it?"

"Couple months."

"I guess that's reasonable, then."

"Have you figured out an escape plan yet? I've been talking long enough."

"My plan was to point the gun at the girl. That plan's still in effect."

"It's a shit plan."

"But you haven't killed me yet."

"Then I stand corrected. It's the best plan ever."

A trickle of sweat ran down the side of George's face, which was a pretty impressive feat of anxiety in this cold weather. He had not yet come up with a second part to his plan, and though the hatless man seemed perfectly content to chat with him right now, George had no reason to doubt that he would soon follow through on his own plan to pump dozens of rounds into George's back. He hadn't known the hatless man very long, but George also pegged him for the kind of guy who would continue firing rounds into George's twitching corpse until there were no rounds left to fire.

"So are you going to shoot her or what?" asked the hatless man, grinding the barrel of the submachine gun more tightly into George's back. "Show us how tough you are." The hatless man now began jabbing the barrel into his spine, hard enough that it went past annoying into genuinely painful. "Come on, you say you're amazing enough to shoot a teenage girl; let's see you shoot one. She's right there. Blow her head off."

This would be a fine time for the earth to crack open directly underneath the hatless man's feet, plummeting him into the depths of hell.

However, that did not happen.

I don't wanna die like this, George thought, although after a split-second of consideration he realized that this was indeed a perfectly appropriate way for a guy like him to die. Getting gunned down by men hired to kill him wouldn't be humiliating or, considering the volume of bullets that would be fired into his body, a drawn-out demise. It was how he *should* go, if he was honest with himself.

He didn't want to die now, though.

Ally twitched, and then rolled onto her side.

And then George saw...well, not salvation, exactly, but at least something for them to continue to talk about.

"She's a real werewolf," he said. "She changed when we kidnapped her, and then she changed most of the way back, but not all of the way back. Look at her ear."

"Nice try," said the hatless man.

"That wasn't a nice try," said Red Hat. "Don't give him credit he doesn't deserve."

"Shift your eyeballs for a tenth of a second," said George. "Look at the girl's ear."

Red Hat didn't move. George couldn't tell if the hatless man was looking, but he did stop jabbing him with the barrel of his gun.

"Not gonna lie," said the hatless man. "That's one messed-up ear."

Red Hat's expression was that of a man who knew that he was probably being tricked, and whose best course of action was to stay right where he was, but who also wanted to see a messed-up ear. He kept his gun pointed at George while he carefully stepped close enough to see Ally's head.

Her ear was long, pointy, and hairy.

"Hmmmm," said Red Hat.

"Doesn't prove a thing," said the hatless man.

"It's not scientific evidence of lycanthropy, no," George agreed. "But it's weird, right? Why does her ear look like a werewolf ear? Did I put a prosthetic ear on her? Why would I do that? Was that my ultimate plan, to slap a fake ear on this chick so she'd roll over and you'd see it?"

"Could be a birth defect," said Red Hat. "She was born with a messed-up ear and it got her tagged as a werewolf."

George nodded. "That's a valid theory. An ear that messed up could cause people to say all kinds of things about you. But look at my jacket. Look at all the blood I've got on me. Don't you think this is excessive for a scuffle with a teenager?"

"Teenage girls are the most insane creatures on the earth," said Red Hat, "So, no."

"Good one. All joking aside, though, she's waking up, and we don't have anything to secure her with. If the three of us consider ourselves intelligent guys, shouldn't we at least entertain the possibility that this situation could turn really bad if we don't take a small step to manage it?"

Everybody was silent for a moment.

George had already been sore, and now his arm was getting tired and his fingers were numb from the cold. This would be a terrible time for the gun to slip out of his grasp, but if they didn't resolve this soon ...

"You know what?" said the hatless man to Red Hat. "You probably can't see it as well from over there, but she really does have a seriously messed-up ear. I'm not saying she's a werewolf, not at all; I'm just saying that ears aren't ever supposed to look like that. I think we should restrain her before she wakes up."

Ally's eyes popped open.

George quickly lowered his gun, so she wouldn't get the wrong idea. And then cursed as it fell out of his hand.

The hatless man removed the barrel of his gun from George's back and lifted it toward the window.

Ally hissed.

The hatless man flinched.

The passenger door of the van burst open, bashing into Red Hat.

As the hatless man glanced over at the commotion, George grabbed him by his thick, luxurious hair and smashed his face into the side of the van. The hatless man squeezed the trigger of his submachine gun, firing into the ground right next to their feet.

George bashed him into the van again, trying unsuccessfully to get him to drop the weapon. Bits of snow were flying everywhere.

Lou leapt out of the van. Actually, it was less of a leap than a clumsy stagger, but he did grab Red Hat while he was still off-balance from being struck by the door.

The hatless man screamed in pain, having just fired several bullets into his own foot. This was not enough to make him drop the gun or take his finger off the trigger.

Lou and Red Hat struggled with Red Hat's gun.

There was still some glass along the bottom edge of the van window frame. They were chunks instead of shards, but that didn't seem to matter to the hatless man as George dragged his face across it.

He kept his hold on his gun, continuing to fire into the ground until it ran out of ammo. George dragged his face across the window in the opposite direction, slamming it hard on the edge of the frame.

Though he still didn't drop the gun, he didn't put up much of a struggle when George took it away from him.

George released his grip on the man's hair. His fingers stuck to it for a moment then pulled free. The man touched his mangled face, looked down at his mangled foot, and then spat some blood on George's shirt.

George cracked him on the skull with the barrel of the Tommy gun.

A gun fired.

Red Hat turned around and staggered away, clutching at a gruesome stomach wound. Lou shot him in the back of the head.

George hit the hatless man once more with the gun. His eyeball bulged from its socket just a bit, and then he dropped onto the bloody snow.

"You okay?" George asked Lou.

Lou looked confused for a moment, then nodded. "I think so. I'm not ... I mean, I'm ... things are kind of ..."

George ignored him and peered at Ally, who was frantically scooting toward the other side of the van. "What about you? You okay?"

"I hissed to help you!" she insisted.

"I know."

She slid open the side door.

"C'mon, Ally, please don't make me chase you," said George.

She jumped out of the van. George reached down, with some effort, and picked up Black Hat's gun.

"Lou and I both have guns," he announced. "Don't make us shoot you. We can work this out together."

She ran.

"I hate my life," George muttered as he went after her.

CHAPTER TEN

Meanwhile, Eighty Miles Away ...

Shane Goldwyn looked up at the clock on the wall. 4:15. The same time that was displayed on his computer monitor and on his wristwatch. Forty-five more minutes to go. This day was never going to end.

"Any big plans for the weekend?" asked Patrick, his cubicle-mate.

"It's Tuesday," Shane informed him.

Patrick laughed. "Hey, I start thinking about my weekend plans on Monday morning. Sometimes Sunday night."

"I'll probably just work out," said Shane.

Patrick laughed again. His laugh was unbelievably grating, and he laughed all the time, whether or not anything amusing had been said or done.

"I hear that. Got to keep in shape, my man."

Another annoying habit of Patrick's: he'd say things in such a manner that Shane couldn't tell if he was being sarcastic or not. Was he suggesting that Shane needed to work out more often? Shane was in perfectly good shape. Yeah, it sucked that at thirty-four he had the hairline of a fifty-year-old, but he was tall, lean, and far more physically desirable than a jackass like Patrick.

Okay, that wasn't fair. Patrick wasn't a jackass. Shane was just frustrated with the cubicle situation. A recent acquisition had brought in twelve new full-time employees, but there weren't enough desks for all of them. So Shane's supervisor had announced a new work-from-home program, where Shane would only have to come into the office on Mondays, Wednesdays, and Fridays of even-numbered weeks and Tuesdays and Thursdays of odd-numbered weeks. He had a half-hour drive to work, so the saved commute time would really add up, not to mention that he could be a much more productive employee without the constant interruptions.

Then, management changed its mind, and they went with a "two to a cubicle" system.

He'd wanted to rip down the cubicle walls, and then tear open his supervisor's throat with his teeth. *She* sure wasn't sharing a desk with anybody.

Instead, he'd settled for a one-on-one meeting where he shared his grievance, and she said that she completely understood his disappointment, but that it turned out to not be a feasible arrangement, and perhaps they'd revisit the issue in a few months.

He'd clutched his fists so tightly that the nails dug into his palm, and then thanked her for taking the time to discuss it with him.

At least he had a job. Not everybody could say that, in this economy.

"Maybe I'll do a barbecue," said Patrick.

"In this weather?"

"Yeah, sure. I've got some brats in the fridge that'll go bad pretty soon, and no room for them in the freezer, so I might as well grill 'em all up and share 'em with the neighbors. I've got plenty if you want to come over. Bring your girlfriend."

"I'll ask her," Shane lied.

His cell phone began to vibrate. He slid it out of his pocket and checked the display. Robyn.

"Speak of the devil?" asked Patrick.

"Excuse me?"

"Is it your girlfriend?"

"Yeah." Employees weren't supposed to use their cell phones except when they were on break, and Robyn knew that, so she wouldn't be calling him unless it was important. The rule wasn't strictly enforced, but Shane stood up without answering the call and walked away from his cubicle, just to be on the safe side. He'd call her right back as soon as he got outside.

By the time he'd left the building, she'd sent him two text messages: *U there?* and *Call me.*

"What's going on?" he asked, when Robyn answered.

"Have you heard?"

"If I'd heard, I'd know why you called. Don't be cryptic."

"Ally didn't come home from school."

Shane immediately felt sick to his stomach. He closed his eyes and took a deep breath before speaking. "Okay...but it's only a quarter after four. So she's, what, an hour late?"

"Uh-huh."

"Is today band practice? Couldn't that have run long?"

"It's orchestra, not band. And she's not in it this year."

That was news to Shane, since he'd insisted that his daughter devote at least one more year to that violin he'd bought for her. "How do you know she didn't come home? Did Peggy call you?"

"No, I called her."

"Why the hell would you call her?"

"Are you alone?"

"I'm outside. Why?"

"Is anybody around?"

"There are some people smoking. Tell me what's going on, Robyn."

"You're going to be really upset. I think you should make sure you're somewhere that nobody can see you."

"I'm going to be really upset if you don't start giving me some fucking answers."

"Please don't curse at me."

Shane wanted to crush the phone in his fist, or at least fling it against the building. He didn't.

"I apologize. Now tell me what you know about the situation."

"Peggy still won't let Ally have a cell phone, so it's possible that she just went out with friends after school, lost track of time. But..."

"But...?"

"But the police are investigating a hit-and-run—"

"*What?*"

"No, no, not Ally. Just a car crash. A van smashed into a couple of other cars, and then it smashed into another car parked in somebody's driveway. And, basically, a few witnesses say that a wolf jumped out of the van and ran into the woods, but it wasn't really moving like a wolf, it was running like a human, sort of, and then the driver of the car ran into the woods, and he dragged the wolf back into the van and drove away."

"Okay. All right." Shane's hand was trembling. "All we have to go on is that Ally is late coming home from school, and some people claim they saw an unusual wolf, right?"

"There are pictures online. None of them are any good, but to me it looks a lot like George Orton. And one person said that there was also a big unconscious guy with a black beard in the van."

Shane closed his eyes and said nothing.

"Honey?" Robyn sounded desperate. "Please tell me that you're not where anybody can see you."

"I can control myself."

"But honey—!"

"Stop acting like I'm incompetent! I said I can control it!" A couple of the nicotine addicts glanced over at him and Shane lowered his voice. "I'll be fine. Nothing's going to happen here."

George Orton. Louis Flynn. The thugs who'd murdered Ivan Spinner.

Ivan was no great loss. Shane had never even met him. Still, their kind had to stick together, if only from the perspective of hating those who would take a werewolf's life.

"Has Peggy made any connection?" he asked.

"Between Ally and the wolf? No. Of course not."

"I have to ask, because you said you fucking called her right after hearing that George and Lou were dragging around a wolf."

"Stop cursing at me, Shane. I mean it. Why would Peggy ever think that?"

"Was the wolf wearing any clothes? Because if it's wearing the same clothes that my daughter was wearing to school, that might be a little strange, don't you think?"

"Okay, yeah, I understand."

Lost in the horrific news of Ally's disappearance was the fantastic news that she had indeed—potentially, if this wasn't all one big misunderstanding—inherited his lycanthropy. Now *that* would help repair the father/daughter bond.

"We're going to Tropper. Call Crabs. He's going with us."

"No, honey, not Crabs."

"Don't argue with me."

"Not him, please."

"Who the ... who else are we going to call? Is there a local werewolf emergency response team that nobody has told me about? Call Crabs and tell him we're leaving in twenty minutes. Have a couple of changes of clothes packed for me when I get home."

"We can do this ourselves, Shane. I can't be around him. You know he creeps me out."

"Lou and George have my daughter. They weren't even trying to hide it—I mean, for God's sake, you said there are pictures online. That's a slap in the face. That's a declaration of war. Do you understand that?"

"Yes."

"Call him. Tell him to be ready. I'm leaving now."

Shane hung up. It was going to take over an hour to get to Tropper. An unbearably infuriating hour. Lots of terrible things could happen to Ally in an hour.

If he wanted to keep his job, he knew he should go back in and explain that he had to leave early due to a family emergency. He also knew that if he did so, he'd end up slamming his claws deep into his supervisor's neck and then twisting her head off.

Not a good idea.

He'd save his rage for the thugs. If George and Lou were looking to start a war, he was happy to escalate it.

Copious Frustration

George had only cried twice in his adult life. Once when his beloved Aunt Lori told him that she had cancer, and once more when she told him that she was cancer-free. Apart from that, no tears, ever. But he did almost want to cry when Ally took off running.

"Ally!" he shouted, quickly giving up the pursuit as hopeless. "Get back here! Don't make me shoot you in the leg!"

Ally continued running, apparently not impressed by what she'd seen of George's shooting abilities.

"Can you chase her?" George asked Lou.

Lou blinked as if he didn't quite understand the question, then nodded and hurried after her at about a quarter her speed.

"If you get lost in the woods you'll freeze to death!" George shouted. "You saw that they sent three killers after you! They'll send more! You need us, Ally!"

The idea that she needed the guys who'd kidnapped her and then savagely murdered three human beings right in front of her was going to be a tough sell. Then again, she *had* hissed to help freak out the other guys, so ...

"Lou, that's enough," said George. "You'll never catch her. Let's just clear out."

Lou stopped running. He turned back around too quickly and nearly lost his balance.

"We'll get in the truck and get out of here. New Zealand sounds good."

George walked over to the truck and opened the driver's side door. No keys in the ignition, of course. Black Hat had been driving, so the keys were probably in his pocket. George went over to his corpse, crouched down in the slushy red snow, and patted his pants pockets.

Not there. Not in his outside jacket pockets, either, so George opened his jacket and checked the inside ones. Nothing but some tissue. Black Hat had been the driver, hadn't he? George was sure of that. Ninety-nine percent sure. The hatless, and now mostly faceless, man had definitely been sitting in the middle.

George stopped searching as he heard another vehicle approach.

It could be somebody there to help them.

Most likely it wasn't.

What should they do? Have an exciting shootout, or flee into the woods?

George wasn't up for fleeing into the woods.

On the other hand, if anybody in the approaching vehicle was another Bonnie and Clyde wanna-be, they'd have a hell of a lot more firepower than George and Lou.

# CHAPTER ELEVEN

Suddenly there was a yelp from the woods. Ally.

"You hear that?" asked Lou. "That sounded like she fell. We should go after her."

"All right." Good. Let Lou make one of the frickin' decisions, finally.

George and Lou jogged into the woods, both of them already panting. If he weren't focused on gasping for breath, George would have asked Lou exactly how long he'd been conscious in the van before he threw open the door. That question could wait.

At least the snow made it easy to follow Ally's tracks. After about a minute they found a large indentation where apparently she'd fallen, and just ahead of that the tracks split and veered into two different directions.

George and Lou paused at the intersection.

"She's messing with us," said Lou.

"Gee, y'think?"

Each set of tracks extended for about twenty feet and ended at a tree. She'd done a good job retracing her steps; it was impossible to tell which set of tracks she'd doubled back on.

"Come on out, Ally," said George. "Don't make us shoot you."

She didn't come out.

"You want left or right?" George asked.

"Right."

George walked to the left, not following Ally's tracks but rather staying far enough from the tree that if she was hiding behind it, he could see her before she—

Ally, whose ear was back to normal, charged at him, holding a large branch over her head with both hands.

He pointed his gun at her, though George had no intention of using it. It didn't stop her. She let out a not-quite-werewolfish cry and swung the branch.

George had expected the "pointing a gun at her" trick to work, so he didn't otherwise defend himself to the best of his ability, and the branch got him.

Fortunately for George, he was significantly larger than Ally, and the branch struck him in the shoulder instead of the head. It didn't feel *good*, but despite her spunk and lycanthropy, no fourteen-year-old girl was going to take out George with a moderately sized tree branch.

He yanked it out of her hands and tossed the branch aside.

Ally turned to run, but he grabbed her by the elbow and pulled her back toward him. As Lou came over to help out, George twisted Ally's arm behind her back, using about a tenth of the force he'd use if he were pulling this move on a scumbag.

She cried out.

"I'm going to try once again to reason with you," said George. "My partner and I are awful people, we've already established that pretty well by now, but some of these other people are much worse. They may be here already. Lou and I are doing everything we can to control the situation, but we can't work this out if you keep trying to escape. Can you do me a favor and please just trust me? Can you do that for me? Just relax."

"Would you relax if you found out that *you* were a monster?" Ally asked. She was suddenly sobbing. The fact that it had taken this long to get to the sobbing part was very impressive.

"No," said George. "I'd completely lose my shit."

"Me too," said Lou.

"But we'll get you help," George assured her. "We can sort this out. We just need you to trust us, okay?"

"Okay," said Ally, obviously lying her ass off.

Fine. He didn't need her to trust him, as long as she didn't transform again. He simply wouldn't let go of her arm.

"Thanks. Let's get moving."

"Let me call my mom. I know she's worried sick."

George shook his head. "Can't do that now. Don't have a secure phone."

"No phone is secure. Let me call her and I'll cooperate with whatever you want, I swear."

"You'll cooperate anyway, because I'm saving you from experiments. Do you know what dissection means?"

"Yes. I go to school. Did you?"

George grinned. If she were his daughter, he'd be proud of her. "Well, I don't want to see you get dissected. So let's work together and stop that from happening. Do you know this area?"

"You mean these woods?"

"Yeah. If we keep going, will we get somewhere or will it become a *Blair Witch Project* kind of thing?"

"I think we'd be okay. I don't know. I don't go outside much if I don't have to.

You're breaking my arm."

"No, I'm not."

"It feels like it's going to snap."

"I'm barely doing anything to it. Seriously, Ally, we're all going to die if you keep trying to escape."

"I'm not trying to escape."

"*George Orton!*" shouted a deep male voice from where they'd left the vehicles and the corpses. "*Louis Flynn!* We know where you are. Surrender yourself!"

At this point, George would've actually been relieved if this voice had come from a megaphone and been accompanied by the phrase, *this is the police.* He noted that the speaker had not bothered to say that they'd be unharmed.

"Let's just run," said George.

"Should we split up?" asked Ally.

"No."

George removed Ally's arm from behind her back but didn't let go of her. He kept a tight grip on her elbow as they hurried through the woods.

"You're slowing me down," she said.

"I know."

"They'll see our tracks."

"I know."

"If you let me go, I can get help."

"No."

"You run like my grandpa. We'll never get away."

"I'm not trying to outrun them," George said. If he weren't out of breath, he would have explained that his intention was just to get the three of them deep enough into the woods that the pursuers might be separated from some of their firepower. They wouldn't *all* run into the woods after them. The further he could separate them, the better the chances of taking them out individually.

It wasn't the kind of scheme that would make you rub your hands together and cackle at the genius of it all, but still, it was a halfway decent strategy to use in their goal of not immediately getting gunned down.

"Surrender yourself or we're coming in after you!" shouted the man, as if they weren't already coming after them.

"Let me at least make some fake tracks," said Ally.

"We saw how well that worked out for you before."

"You're being retarded!"

"Don't use the word 'retarded,'" said Lou. "It's offensive."

"Are you kidding me?"

"It is!"

"But it's not offensive to rip up somebody's face on a window?"

"Enough!" said George. "No more talking!"

"You guys are idiots."

"Yes, we are. Deal with it."

Ally muttered something, probably unkind.

"Okay, now it's time to separate. Lou, you wait here, and kill whoever comes by. Ally and I will keep going forward."

"Got it."

Lou was still feeling groggy from the dart, but he didn't say anything. Ally seemed fine, and even though she was a werewolf he didn't want to admit that she had a shorter recovery time than him.

If it were up to him, they'd just let the girl go. If she ran ahead, and he and George stayed back to deal with the reinforcements, she'd probably be able to get away.

George wouldn't like that idea, though, and he'd get pissed at Lou for suggesting it. Better to stay quiet until he caught up on everything he'd missed after getting tranquilized. He felt like he'd slept through some pretty substantial developments.

He snapped out the clip of the pistol and counted the rounds. Four. Not too bad. Better than having to strangle people with his bare hands.

Maybe he should try Ally's footprint trick. Lou trudged off to the side, toward the biggest tree on his left. Since George and Ally had continued walking straight, their pursuers would have three different paths to choose from. If it caused them just a moment of confusion, that might be enough.

Lou walked to the tree, then turned around and walked in his own footprints back to the original path.

"You have ten seconds!" the man shouted.

Lou walked to the right. None of the trees were big enough to hide him very well, but he'd work with what he had.

About a minute later, two men in facemasks and white snowsuits came down the path, each holding a rifle.

Snowsuits? What babies.

They stopped when they saw the path split into three branches.

"Is this a joke?" one of them asked.

Lou stepped out from behind the tree and fired, hitting the closer of the two men directly in the middle of the chest. He dropped to the ground. He squeezed off another shot just as the second man returned fire. The man's shot hit the tree. Lou's shot got him in the stomach. The second man also fell.

White snowsuits would show off spurting blood really well, and disappointingly, there was none. Bulletproof vests. He would've aimed at their heads, but it would've increased the chance that he'd miss altogether.

Oh well. He still had two bullets to finish them off.

Before he could rush over there to deliver point-blank headshots, the two men had already sat up. Damn. Those were some top-notch bulletproof vests. Lou squeezed himself behind the tree again as they opened fire. A chunk of bark flew off and hit him near the eye.

The shots ceased.

Were they reloading?

"Are you George or Louis?" one of the men asked.

"Lou."

"You're more valuable to us alive than dead, Lou."

"I'm honored."

"We'll sleep fine tonight if we have to kill you, but we'd rather not. Your call."

Lou could hear that they were separating. Shit.

He wasn't going to surrender. Better to go out with guns blazing than to suffer whatever fate awaited him back with Mr. Dewey.

The instant he caught a glimpse of the first guy, Lou fired at his head. The guy grunted and slapped his hand over the red streak on his neck, but he'd only been grazed. Not even close to a fatal shot.

Lou felt a sharp pain in his back.

He hadn't heard a gunshot.

He reached around and there was another goddamn dart lodged there.

"You've got to be ..." he began, before everything went dark.

"If we die it's all your fault," said Ally, tugging her arm to make George move faster.

"You know what? Fuck you, kid. I'm still your elder."

"Elder doesn't mean wiser."

"We were forced to do all of this. Lou and I didn't wake up and decide to kidnap you. We don't mess with children. It's one of our rules."

"Flexible rule, though, huh?"

"You're not helping anything. Didn't you ever watch any TV shows that taught you about cooperation?"

"I guess I missed the episode where Grover was a kidnapper."

"You're a precocious little shit. We'd be in much better shape if you'd drop the attitude and work with me."

"Yeah, I'll get right on that."

"I'll make you a deal. You transform back into a wolf, and you can do whatever you want. You can scamper off through the wilderness with all of your animal friends."

"Screw you."

George decided to let her have the last word. If she'd cheerfully gone along with him, he'd be wondering what the hell was wrong with her, so he had to respect her disdain for him.

"Hey, George!" somebody shouted from behind them. It wasn't the guy who'd been shouting before.

George didn't shout anything back. Not all of his recent decisions had been top-notch, but he wasn't about to start foolishly giving away his location.

"I know you can hear me. We've got Lou. Turn yourselves in and we'll let the three of you live. Otherwise, your friend gets shot in the head."

Damn it. It could be a trick, but the shouting did sound like it was coming from where they'd left Lou. And Lou hadn't helpfully announced that no, he was perfectly fine, it was all just a clever ruse, no need for concern.

"We're not going back, are we?" asked Ally.

"We might."

"I'm not."

"If I don't hear anything in ten seconds, he's dead!" the man shouted.

George chewed on his lower lip for eight of those ten seconds. "Okay!" he finally called back. "We're on our way!"

"Are you insane?" Ally asked.

"By now, yes."

"I'm not going with you."

"Yes, you are. I've got a plan. You like guns?"

CHAPTER TWELVE

Plan F

In instances where George was forced to come up with a desperate plan, they usually involved an element that would hopefully cause the person being planned against to say, "What the hell?"

That was the key component of this one. If he could get a moment of "What the hell?" out of the guy or guys who had Lou, he might be able to use that second of surprise to shoot him or them in the face or faces. Plans like this were usually better when you knew how many people you were up against, but George didn't have this luxury.

The part of the plan that sucked was that it required him to trust that Ally, when given a revolver, would not immediately use it against him. Handing his gun over to Ally could be construed as extremely dumb, since she hadn't expressed any real desire to *not* jump at the opportunity to escape from him, but hopefully he could convince her that this plan was a better one than shooting him and running away.

George popped open the cylinder and spun it. "You see that the gun is loaded, right? I'm not trying to fool you."

"Okay."

Actually, he was trying to fool her, a little. He'd rotated the cylinder so that her first couple of shots would be on an empty chamber. That way, if she did try to blow his head off, he'd have the opportunity to try to wrestle the gun away from her.

This also meant that he'd have to squeeze the trigger a couple of extra times before he could take out Lou's captors, but there was no way around that unless Ally suddenly developed a convenient case of Stockholm Syndrome.

"I really need you to trust me on this," said George. "If you run, they *will* find you, and it *will* be horrible. Work with me on this, and Lou and I will drop you off somewhere safe, I promise." George decided that, for now, he was telling the truth.

Then he handed her the gun.

The plan, in its entirety, was that they would walk back and pretend that Ally was holding George at gunpoint. This sight would both surprise and amuse the other criminals, and during their moment of "What the hell?" Ally would quickly return the gun to George, who would then start shooting.

That was it.

Given time, he could probably come up with something better that did not involve a fourteen-year-old werewolf pointing a gun at his head, but right now, this was the best he could do.

"Act like you hate me," said George, as they walked down the path back toward the van, truck, dead bodies, reinforcements, and Lou.

Ally didn't say anything, even though he'd given her an excellent opportunity to make a smart-ass comment like, "No problem."

It didn't take long to reach the spot where they'd left Lou behind. He was sitting on the ground, leaning against a tree, unconscious. *Hopefully* unconscious. George didn't see any blood.

Two men were there in facemasks and white snowsuits that each had what appeared to be bullet holes on the torso. Thanks to the facemasks, George couldn't read their expressions, which was going to make it more difficult to capitalize on any "What the hell?" moments.

Of course, they both had guns pointed at him.

"Don't shoot," said George.

The man who had a hole in his chest instead of his stomach tilted his head a bit. "What's the deal?"

"What does it look like?" asked George. This was worse than that stupid plan to just snatch Ally outside of her home.

"You let her get your gun?"

"Stop talking, everyone!" said Ally. "Don't make me kill him!"

One of the many, many flaws in this plan was the complete lack of motivation for Ally to have brought George back at gunpoint. The plan wasn't supposed to last long enough for the men to question it, but George had anticipated something with a more natural moment to get the gun back from Ally, not something where two men just stared at him with their guns drawn.

"This is some sort of plan, isn't it?" asked the man with the bullet hole in his stomach.

George and Ally neither confirmed nor denied this.

"Drop the gun. Seriously."

"All right," said George, even though he was not the one holding the gun.

He braced himself for the *click, click* of Ally unsuccessfully trying to shoot him in the back of the skull, but didn't hear it. Ally lowered the gun.

"That was a lousy plan," said the man with the bullet hole in his chest.

"I know," George admitted.

"I won't tell anyone about it."

"Thank you."

"Little girl? Drop the gun."

Ally dropped the gun.

"Kick it away."

"Who?" George asked. "Me or her?"

"Doesn't matter. You."

George kicked the gun away. It wasn't easy to do in the snow but he managed.

"Get on your knees and put your hands on your head."

George and Ally both did so.

"Is there another part to your plan that I don't know about? Because if you try anything, I will not hesitate to shoot you."

"There's nothing else."

"Really? That's all you had?"

"Yep."

"That's sad."

"I'm very much aware of that. Can you just take us away now?"

CHAPTER THIRTEEN

Back in a Van

Ally thought she was doing an incredible job of not acting like she was terrified out of her mind. She'd only succumbed to tears once during this nightmare, even though she wanted to cry and scream and beg them not to hurt her. She didn't care if any of these assholes saw her cry, but she needed to stay in control of herself.

Werewolf...

She'd had dreams about being a shape-shifter. But she'd also had dreams about flying, aliens, standing in front of the entire school in her underwear, and a talking fish, and none of those were going to come true.

Werewolf...

She remembered everything that happened. She couldn't control any of it, yet there was no dreamlike haze to it: she remembered the pain of the change, excruciating but over quickly. She remembered the delicious smell of George's blood and how much she wanted to taste it, let it pour over her tongue. She remembered wanting to kill him.

Kill Lou.

Kill anybody else who was nearby.

That last part was what scared her the most. Of course she wanted to kill her kidnappers, but when she'd leapt out of the van, she'd really wanted to go after one of the onlookers. Rip them apart.

Only a sense of self-preservation, which she was aware of even though she couldn't control it, made her run into the woods instead of toward a juicy victim.

She would have murdered somebody.

Gleefully.

Ripped a thick, meaty strip right off their arm and gobbled it down. Loving the sound of their screams as she did it. Loving the smell of their fear almost as much as the taste of their bloody flesh.

She fought with her mother at least once a week, and she despised her gym teacher, but Ally had never in her life wanted to actually kill somebody.

Werewolf...

Or drugs. Maybe they'd given her drugs. Ally had absolutely no interest in drugs or alcohol, even when Lisa and Maddie had made fun of her for refusing to take a bite of a pot brownie. She liked boys but wasn't going to take the chance of one getting her pregnant. Nothing like that was going to ruin *her* life.

Except, apparently, for something she couldn't control.

Was Mom a werewolf?

Was Dad?

Were they both?

She knew for a fact that a wolf hadn't bitten her, so it had to be inherited, right? Was that why her parents got divorced? Supposedly it was because Dad was cheating on Mom, but what if that wasn't really the reason? What if she'd divorced a werewolf?

No. Mom would've told her.

Honey, there's something I've got to tell you. You know that one character in Twilight who changes into a wolf? Edward?

No, Mom. Edward's the vampire.

Jason?

Jacob.

Jacob. That's right. Well, you're just like him. Sorry.

Maybe Mom was waiting for just the right time, and she'd gotten the right time wrong.

Uh-uh. No. Mom started talking about menstruation long before Ally wanted to hear anything about it, so she wouldn't have kept this a secret. Especially if it was a change that made Ally want to kill people.

So Dad.

Dad didn't talk to her much. Called her once a week. Brought her to Minneapolis for the weekend once a month, usually. He'd moved there two years ago, after the divorce, to be with his skank girlfriend Robyn. To be fair to Dad, he was still with the skank, even though Mom had told him, Ally, and everybody who would listen that it wouldn't last.

Dad got angry a lot, but that didn't make him a werewolf.

If anything, it meant that he probably wasn't one. Ally had been furious when she changed.

Well, she'd also been scared. Maybe it was the fear that did it, not the anger.

Or maybe Dad had learned to control himself better.

Oh well. It didn't matter. She was just trying to think about things besides how much danger she was in.

"Ally?"

She looked up at George. "What?"

"You okay?"

"Do you think I'm okay?"

"Sorry. You looked like you were drifting off for a bit."

She and George were seated in the back of a black van. This one did not have windows on the sides. Their hands and feet were bound together by those plastic straps that police used now instead of metal handcuffs. Their hands were behind their back, and Ally's arms were almost completely numb. Lou was also bound up, though he was flopped over on his side, sleeping. They couldn't use the plastic straps on his hands, since he only had one, so his wrist was cuffed to the rear door handle with regular handcuffs. They'd taken George's phone away.

Ally doubted that the plastic straps would hold her if she changed. Unfortunately, she'd been trying to change back pretty much ever since she'd woken up from the drugged dart, and it wasn't working.

The men who captured them knew that, of course. When they tossed her into the back of the van, one of them had made a point of showing her the tranquilizer dart gun he was holding, and he'd also told her that his regular gun had silver bullets.

"Then let me drift," Ally said to George.

George nodded. "Fair enough."

"What are they going to do to us?"

George looked sort of like Dad did when she'd demanded to know why he cheated on Mom. He didn't look away like Dad, but he seemed to be trying to think up a convincing answer on the spot. Finally he just said, "I don't know."

"Are they going to kill us?"

"Want the truth?"

"Yes."

"Gun to my head, if I had to say what I thought would happen, I'd say that Lou and I are toast. But they'll let you go. Even these psychos don't want the heat that would come from killing you."

"Sorry to eavesdrop," said the man in the passenger seat (George couldn't see if he was the one who'd been shot in the chest or the stomach), turning around to face them, "but do you mind if I put in my two cents?"

"Please do."

"They're not letting her go. Not a chance."

"Mind cutting my hands free? I'd like to give you the finger."

The man chuckled and turned back around.

"He's just trying to scare you," George told Ally.

"He did."

"Don't let him. These guys are a bunch of sadists."

"And you're not?"

"No. I'm not. I don't want anything bad to happen to you."

Ally let out an incredulous laugh. Had he really just said that?

"What?" George asked.

"You're a piece of shit, George. You're a child-abducting piece of shit. Don't act like you're some kind of ... I don't know, holy warrior or something."

"I never said that I was a holy warrior or something. Listen, you're not going to say anything about me that's worse than what I say about myself—"

"Your nose is ugly."

"—so why not stop the verbal abuse, okay?"

"What, the big bad gangster can't handle some insults from a tiny little girl? Did I hurt your feelings?"

"My feelings are fine. I just think that there are more productive ways we could be spending our time."

"Our time trapped in the back of a van."

"Yes. That time. We could be using this opportunity to repair our relationship. Right now we need to stick together. Why be a bitchy teenager?"

Ally had a million sarcastic responses to that ... but he was right. She hadn't believed him when he said that he'd let her go, and she knew that he was putting his own survival ahead of hers, yet still, she *did* believe that he'd been forced into this whole thing. He wasn't doing it for money or some disgusting pleasure. If nothing else, he was more on her side than the people she'd be meeting soon.

Time to stop being antagonistic.

Oh, she still planned to see him and Lou dead or in prison, but for now, she'd play nice.

"Fine," she said.

"Yeah?"

"Yeah."

"Thanks."

"So you've seen a werewolf before?"

George nodded. "Yeah. It was a job down in Florida. Lots of dead bodies before we took him out. Lou and I went into hiding, so I don't know for sure how the media covered it, but we don't seem to be in a brand new world that believes in the existence of werewolves, so I assume there was a cover-up."

"I saw stuff about it on Facebook. It wasn't all covered up, at least. People just didn't believe the whole story."

"What did they think happened?"

Ally shrugged. "I don't remember everything. Insane guy in a wolf mask, I think."

George would have buried his face in his hands if they weren't locked behind his back. "Insane guy in a wolf mask. Jesus Christ."

"Makes more sense than the real story."

"Still ..."

"I bet if you checked there are probably like eight billion conspiracy theory sites about it. I think his body disappeared from a Chuck E. Cheese or something before the police got there."

"It was a bowling alley."

"Oh."

"His body disappeared?"

"Yeah."

Weird. "So, any idea how this happened to you? Are you any relation to Ivan Spinner?"

"No."

"Uncle? Cousin?"

"I know my uncles and cousins."

"I meant second uncles or second cousins. I don't know the full names of all *my* relatives. There could be some connection."

"I have no idea how it happened," said Ally. "Maybe I got bit but I didn't notice because I was too busy texting."

George smiled. "Could be. You kids today."

Ally sighed. "Mom won't even let me have a cell phone. I'm going to die without my own cell phone."

The van stopped. George peeked up front, and for a split second he looked extremely worried. Then, as if noticing that Ally was watching him, he smiled again.

"What?" Ally asked.

"Nothing."

"No, what?"

"This is where they gave Lou and me the assignment in the first place."

"Is that bad?"

"All of the scenarios are bad, unless the driver is a double agent and is secretly on our side." George raised his voice, addressing the driver. "Hey, are you a double agent who's secretly on our side?"

"Nope."

"Didn't think so." He looked back at Ally. "This warehouse is where I talked to both Mr. Dewey and Mr. Reith. I was kind of hoping we'd only have to mess with one of them."

"Oh."

"It's okay, though. Stay calm. We'll be fine."

Ally tried to stay calm. The van pulled forward, then turned and stopped. The driver turned off the engine. Both of the men got out.

"Is there anything else I should know?" asked Ally. Her whole body, and her voice, was quivering.

"Just be polite."

The rear door of the van opened.

"They're all yours," said the driver, stepping out of the way.

A very old man, the oldest man Ally had ever seen in real life, was standing there. He looked as if he were going to topple over, despite his cane.

"Hello, Mr. Reith," said George.

"Hello, George," said the old man. There was no trace of amusement in his voice. Not only was he the oldest person Ally had ever seen, but she'd never seen anybody who was so filled with rage. He looked like his withered skin might split apart, releasing streams of lava.

"I know we ended on bad terms."

"Do not speak, George," said Mr. Reith. "Do not say a single word. If you do, I will have you immediately killed. Not one word."

George apparently believed him. He kept his mouth closed and just gave a small nod.

Another man stepped into view. He was significantly younger than Mr. Reith, though still older than Ally's dad. He looked more relieved than angry to see them.

"Good to see you again, George. Don't greet me—I wouldn't want you to die just to be polite." The man looked directly at Ally and broke into a huge, scary grin. "And you're Ally."

"Yes, sir."

"We're going to be very good friends, Ally. I'm Mr. Dewey." He winked at her. "Like the decimal system."

Ally had no idea what he was talking about, but she didn't say anything.

Mr. Dewey gestured to the two men in snowsuits. "Chain her up. We're going to start right away. Drag Lou in there too, in case we need to feed her something."

"Got it," said the driver. "And George...?"

"We'll let George see his future. Put him in the room with Eugene."

CHAPTER FOURTEEN

Slaughter

This was a bad idea. A bad, bad, bad idea.

Robyn was angry about the kidnapping, too. Furious. Ally was a great kid, if understandably hostile toward Robyn herself, and Shane would die for her. But rushing off to Tropper like this, completely unprepared, was not the way to handle it.

Not that Shane would ever listen to her.

He'd offered to drive. Yeah, right. Like she'd let that happen. No better way to spend your evening than speeding down the highway and suddenly having your car driven by a wolfman, right?

At least she didn't have to sit next to Crabs.

He was in the back seat, doing what he did best: staring ahead creepily. He was thirty-five or thirty-six but looked sixty. The pale freak didn't look like a single ray of sunshine had ever touched his skin; did he think he was a vampire instead? He liked to have a few days' worth of stubble, even though his facial hair grew in weird patches. He never stopped sweating. When she was introduced to him, Robyn had desperately hoped that Crabs' nickname had come from some sort of family business on a seaport, but, no, it was from a college experience with a prostitute.

She didn't even know his real name. He called *himself* Crabs, as if he was proud to let the world know that a hooker had accepted his money instead of recoiling in disgust. It was probably on his W-2.

Robyn didn't know of any other werewolves anywhere close to them, but even so, she would never hang out with him if she had any choice in the matter. His presence in her life was almost a deal breaker in her relationship with Shane ... but the werewolf sex was *sooooo* good, and she couldn't get that anyplace else.

Crabs had once made a comment (not a joke—Crabs didn't make jokes) about sharing her with Shane, and she'd calmly but firmly informed him that if he ever put that image in her mind again, she would rip his balls off. She wouldn't transform first; she'd just do it with her human fingernails.

He'd offered to just watch instead.

She hated Crabs.

"What are you doing?" she asked Shane.

"I'm not doing anything."

"You're tearing the seat. Put your hand back to normal."

"It's not 'normal,' it's—"

"It's human. I get it. Stop ruining our car."

"Possessions or sanity," said Crabs from the back seat. "Only one can be pristine."

Shane ran his taloned index finger across the seat, just an inch or so, as if to send the message that he'd tear the car seat whenever he felt like it, then changed his hand back to human.

"I need to stop."

"Why?" Robyn asked.

Shane just looked at her.

"Honey, no."

"I need to blow off some steam or I'm going to lose it."

"We've only been driving for half an hour."

"The amount of time that we have been driving is not relevant," said Shane, emphasizing every syllable, the way he spoke to Robyn's mother in the nursing home. "I need to get this out of my system, and unless you want to be the prey, you'll stop being difficult."

"Don't threaten me."

"I wasn't threatening you."

"That was a threat."

"I apologize, then," said Shane. "But I'm headed for a complete meltdown, and I need ten minutes to unleash this, or I'm going to go batshit crazy right here in this car."

"Intercourse is relaxing," said Crabs.

"What about Ally?" asked Robyn.

"Ten minutes," said Shane. "The next exit—no, the one right after that. There's a homeless shelter."

"You've used that shelter before."

"Not in six months."

"Four months."

"What difference does it make? Do you think they have high-tech surveillance equipment at a homeless shelter? One of the bums there can have an extra serving of soup tonight, thanks to us."

"Bum meat is flavorful," said Crabs.

"All right, all right," said Robyn. "But you have to promise me that it'll be quick. And Crabs doesn't get to help."

"Why not?"

"Because he takes too long and makes too much of a mess."

"Crabs, can you make it quick?"

"Unknown."

"Guess it's me alone then," said Shane. He reached over and caressed Robyn's knee. "Thank you. I really appreciate this."

———————

Six or seven homeless people were standing outside of the shelter, smoking, when Robyn drove up to the building.

"Look at that," said Shane. "If they can afford cigarettes, they should be able to afford food. Someone who doesn't care about their lungs doesn't deserve to breathe through them, right?"

"Just pick one," said Robyn.

Shane reviewed his selection. "The guy on the left. He looks the horniest."

"He looks mentally ill."

"So?"

"So he might be unpredictable."

"Whatever makes you comfortable. How about the one in the orange jacket?"

"Too healthy. He'd put up a fight."

"You choose, then."

"The meth head."

"Which one?"

Robyn pointed. "Brown jacket and mismatched gloves."

"Ah. Good choice. Let's go."

Robyn turned back to face Crabs. "Stay in the car."

"I will. It has your scent."

Acknowledging his sick comments was never a good idea, so Robyn ignored him and got out of the car. She and Shane walked over to the huddle of vagrants. She tapped the one in the brown jacket on the shoulder.

"Wanna job?" she asked.

"Doing what?" He had more teeth than she'd expected, though the front ones all looked as if they'd been outlined with a thin black magic marker.

"Over here. It's private."

Without waiting for him to respond, she and Shane walked about twenty feet away. The vagrant followed, looking uncertain.

"I don't have time to do a long pitch, so here's the deal: we run a porn site where guys like you get to have sex with girls like me. We'll pay you a hundred bucks, blur your face, and give you a packet of the good stuff for your trouble. Sound okay?"

"I ... I ... I'm not sure I can ..."

"We'll let you pop a Viagra on the way."

"I really get to fuck you?"

"Please don't use the f-word, but yes." Robyn opened her purse, reached inside, and took out a pair of twenties. "Forty now. The rest after you get off. Are we cool?"

The vagrant vigorously nodded. "Yes, ma'am."

She and Shane began to walk toward their car. "Come on, then. Get in the backseat. Don't talk to the man back there."

Crabs scooted over obligingly as Shane opened the back door.

"Who's he?" the vagrant asked.

"Sound guy."

"I don't know ..."

"Get in or not. Doesn't matter to us. We can go right back and pick someone else."

The vagrant got into the car.

"Thank you for this," said Shane to Robyn before they got back inside.

Typically they did this at least three or four highway exits from where they picked up the prey, but this one reeked even more than usual and Robyn needed him out of the car before she threw up.

There were a few good desolated spots where they could lead somebody off to the slaughter. Robyn picked the park. Even in the middle of summer, this park was usually abandoned, thanks to the rusty slide and the swings that looked like they might snap off if an even moderately overweight child sat on them. In the winter, Robyn and Shane could be pretty much guaranteed that nobody would see them even walk past the teeter-totter, much less what was going to happen in the wooded area beyond the park.

Sometimes their prey didn't figure out the real deal until right before things started to go badly for them. This particular vagrant was slightly smarter, and he hesitated as soon as they parked the car.

"We're doing it here?" he asked, warily.

"No," said Robyn. "Past the trees."

"Kinda cold."

"Yes. And?"

"I didn't think it was going to be outside."

"Well, now you know."

"Nah, nah, this isn't ... I don't wanna do this. I want to go back."

"Afraid of being cold? Don't you live outside most of the time? What's the problem?"

"I don't want to do this."

"Why not?"

"I just don't."

"Do you think we're going to harm you?"

The vagrant said nothing.

"Do you think we're going to kill you?" Robyn asked.

"I don't know."

"You know."

"Please don't hurt me."

Robyn looked over at Shane. "So are you going to gag him or what?"

"In a minute. Let him sweat a little longer."

"What about your daughter?"

For a split second Shane looked as if he wanted to tear Robyn apart instead of the vagrant, but then he nodded. "You're right, you're right."

Shane got out of the car and then opened the door to the back seat. There was a struggle, though not much of one, before he got the gag on the vagrant and dragged him outside.

"You stay in the car," Robyn told Crabs. "I mean it."

"I take orders."

Robyn got out of the car. Shane and the vagrant had only gone about ten feet before he stopped. "What about Crabs?"

"I told him to stay in the car."

"No, let him watch." Shane raised his voice. "Come on out, Crabs. You don't want to miss the show."

Robyn sighed. It wasn't even worth arguing, despite the sheer stupidity of this whole venture. She completely understood these primal needs, but if you were going to drop everything (including, possibly, your gainful employment) to rescue your daughter, shouldn't she be the priority?

The vagrant was sobbing, and he kept stumbling, though at least Shane didn't have to literally drag him by his feet, which sometimes happened.

Once they were out of sight of anybody who might drive by the park, Shane punched the vagrant in the stomach, really hard, doubling him over.

Then he changed.

And *that* was why Robyn stuck with him despite all of his many flaws. He was a fine-looking man as a human, but as a wolf ... dear lord. Thick black fur.

Muscles everywhere. Golden eyes that almost seemed to glow.

Yeah, she fantasized about doing Johnny Depp or Michael Fassbender, but neither of them could compare to the scorching-hot male specimen standing right in front of her.

Shane usually gave the prey a few moments to think about the situation they had suddenly found themselves in, but this time, Shane just bit off his thumb.

The vagrant shrieked as loudly as one can shriek when their mouth is covered by a thick ball gag.

Shane bit off the remaining fingers of his left hand, one at a time. Of course, he could've chomped off the entire hand in one bite, but he never did. Part of the reason was that it was simply more fun to bite off individual fingers instead of an entire hand, but also, there'd been a time that Shane bit off somebody's hand and almost swallowed it before Robyn screamed her warning that the victim had been wearing a silver wedding band. Silver dissolved their kind from the inside. He'd been understandably paranoid since then.

Shane bit off all of the fingers on the vagrant's right hand, laughing a wolfish laugh as ten gouts of blood sprayed everywhere.

Crabs watched, breathing heavily. As always, he looked like he wanted to start playing with himself. The pervert probably *would*, if he didn't know that Robyn would freak out.

Shane slid one of his talons across the vagrant's neck, slowly, deep enough to trace a thin red line but not enough for blood to spurt.

Then, the time for subtlety apparently over, he slashed his claws across the vagrant's upper thigh, taking out a huge chunk. The vagrant clutched at his wound as he tumbled to the ground.

Shane couldn't talk as a wolf, so he switched back to human to say, "You like that? How'd that feel, huh? How'd that feel?"

He actually didn't need to do a full transformation to speak, but having a human head on a wolf-man body looked ridiculous.

He kicked the vagrant in the stomach. When the vagrant moved his hand to grab his stomach, Shane kicked his leg wound. "Feels good, huh? Feels nice? Having a good time? Way better than a porno shoot, huh?"

Shane transformed back, and then went absolutely berserk on the vagrant's leg, slashing it apart, strip by strip, until there was more bone visible than flesh.

The vagrant remained conscious. Robyn was impressed.

"You like that?" asked Shane, human again. "Like that, faggot? Like seeing the inside of your leg?" Shane waved over at Crabs. "C'mon, Crabs, get over here! It's not fair for me to have all the fun!"

Crabs glanced at Robyn, as if asking permission. Robyn shook her head.

Crabs ignored her and hurried over to the fallen vagrant.

"Let's wishbone him!" Shane said. "C'mon, he's still got a good leg! Let's wishbone him!"

Crabs transformed. He looked even worse as a werewolf than he did as a human, with his greasy fur, bony arms, and a hairless tail that made him look more like a giant rat than a wolf.

Shane took one of the vagrant's arms, while Crabs took his good leg. They lifted the thrashing vagrant off the ground, then tugged.

Last time, they'd been disappointed when the victim came apart at the waist. This vagrant played by the rules, and his arm ripped off. Shane let him drop, then tossed the arm victoriously into the air. After it landed, he picked it up again, bit off the rest of the hand at the wrist, swallowed, then tossed it to Crabs, who took a generous bite for himself.

Shane changed to human yet again. He wiped the blood off his mouth and clapped his hands together. "Let's burn him! C'mon, let's set him on fire!"

"Shane, we have to get going!" said Robyn.

"Let's burn him! Let's watch his skin turn black! C'mon, Crabs, you've got a lighter, right?"

Crabs, still a werewolf, shook his head.

"Robyn...?"

"Why would I have a lighter?"

"There's got to be a lighter somewhere. Let's go get one. C'mon, let's burn him! We'll siphon some gas from the car! We'll light him up real good!"

"*Shane!*"

"Blisters everywhere!"

"For God's sake, Shane! This is why you hardly get to see your daughter!"

Shane's gleeful expression vanished. He looked at Robyn with pure hatred in his eyes as he walked through the snow toward her.

"Oh, Jesus, Shane, I'm sorry ... I wasn't ..."

He walked right up to her, their faces inches apart. "If you ever say anything like that again, I'll beat you into a coma."

"I know, I know, I wasn't thinking."

"Think next time."

"I'm sorry. That was an awful thing to say. I'm just stressed out right now."

Shane raised his fist. Robyn recoiled.

He held his fist there for a long, excruciating moment, then lowered it. "You're lucky that I don't want to have to explain the bruise."

"I'm sorry," said Robyn. "It'll never happen again. I wasn't thinking."

Shane gestured to the carnage. "You ruined it. I could've been relaxed for the rest of the trip, but you fucked it up for me. Completely fucked it up. Nice going. Great job."

"He's still alive."

"The moment's over. He can just bleed out for all I care."

"But—!"

"Don't try to repair this." He turned to Crabs. "Let's throw some snow on him. We'll clean this up on the way home."

"Shane—!"

"Stop talking," Shane told Robyn. "Just stop talking before I go out of my fucking mind. Get me a towel and some new clothes from the trunk."

CHAPTER FIFTEEN

Eugene

George didn't fight or protest as two of Mr. Dewey's men placed a black cloth sack over his head and yanked him to his feet. He couldn't walk very well with his feet cuffed together, so he let the men drag him across cement for about thirty seconds.

One of the men let go of him just long enough to open a door, then they dragged George through the doorway and threw him to the floor. The men left, locking him inside the room.

George was pretty goddamn angry right now, but a temper tantrum wouldn't do him any good since he didn't have the convenience of being able to transform into a werewolf and snap the restraints, so he just lay there quietly.

Somebody sniffled.

"Hello?" George asked. "Eugene?"

"What do you want?" The voice sounded human enough, although raspy, like he had severe asthma.

"I don't want anything," said George. "It's not like I came in here of my own free will."

Some chains rattled. More sniffling.

"You okay?" George asked.

"Why would I be okay?"

"Can you see me, or do you have a bag over your head, too?"

"I can see you."

"Can you move around? Can you get this bag off me?"

"I don't want you to see me."

"All right. Fair enough. Is there a chair or something, or should I just stay on the floor?"

"There aren't any chairs."

"Floor it is."

The chains rattled again. George wondered if Eugene could reach him even if he wanted to. Probably not.

At least I know I'm not stuck in here with a homicidal monster, George thought. *Reith and Dewey wouldn't let me die without watching the fun.*

Then it occurred to George that Mr. Dewey and Mr. Reith could easily be watching the fun through a video feed, and he stopped being soothed.

"I'm George," he said.

"I have a cousin named George."

"Oh, yeah?"

"Yeah."

"You like him?"

"Does it matter?" Eugene sniffled. "You're not him. It's just a name."

"So, Eugene, I'm told that you're my future. Is this something that will upset me?"

Eugene let out a pained half-laugh, half-cry. "I'd say so."

"Well, my imagination is pretty vivid, so if you could help narrow it down, I'd appreciate it."

"George, do you believe in werewolves?"

"Yes, I do. I really, really do."

Eugene let out another half-laugh, half-cry, though this one was heavier on the cry. "Everyone around me is delusional."

"I take it you're not a believer?"

"No. I don't believe in werewolves, vampires, mummies, fairies, dragons, the tooth fairy, or any of those other things that sane people outgrow by the time they start first grade," said Eugene, his voice cracking.

"In my own defense, I only believe in werewolves, not the other things. Well, mummies, too. Those exist, but I only mean wrapped-up dead Egyptians, not the shambling, living kind."

"Unbelievable. My eight-year-old was smarter than you."

"Was?"

"Yeah, was. My son is dead, okay? Want to hear about my daughter? She's dead, too. She got to die with pieces of her brother's brain stuck to her dress. She bought that dress with her own money. She really wanted this light blue dress, but we'd already bought her back-to-school clothes, and we told her that we'd match whatever money she saved toward the dress. When the ice cream man came around, her brother bought a great big ice cream sandwich, but not her, no, she wanted that dress. My wife—she's dead, too, in case you were wondering—tried to convince me to get it for her early, but, no, this was the chance to teacher our daughter a valuable lesson. She saves up for a dress as a kid, she becomes a better adult, right? She saw it through. Bought the dress. Wore it once. Now she's dead. My son's dead. My wife's dead. Bang, bang, bang. All dead."

"Jesus. I'm sorry."

Eugene gasped for breath as if he were choking, then managed to say, "Thank you. I appreciate that."

"How long has it been?"

"I don't know. There are no windows in here. No regular meals. They put me to sleep a lot. Weeks. I don't know. I've only been here a day or two. Before that I was somewhere else. I don't know."

"I'd really like to see who I'm talking to."

"I bet you would."

"If I can see where I am, it'll be a huge help in figuring out how to get out of here."

"We're not escaping, George. This is where we die. Here or on the surgery table."

"How about this? You take this sack off my head, and I promise I won't look at you. I just want to see the rest of the room. Get my bearings."

Sniffle. "Okay."

The chains, which may have only been one long chain, rattled as Eugene walked over to where George lay.

"Close your eyes."

"They're closed."

Eugene yanked the sack off of George's head and returned to where he'd been standing. George sat up, turned his head away from Eugene, and opened his eyes.

Bare cement walls. Steel door. Fluorescent light bulb on a ceiling too high to reach. Dried streaks of blood on the floor that looked like they'd been cleaned up but not well enough. The whole room was about the size of his bathroom at home, and his bathroom was not luxuriously sized.

"Thanks," he said.

"Was it Dewey who killed your family?"

"I don't know who Dewey is. I don't know who anybody here is. They never say their names. I never ask. Don't care to know them on a personal level."

"Was it a middle-aged guy or a really old guy?"

"They wore facemasks. They sounded young. They knocked on the front door while we were eating dinner, forced us all into the living room at gunpoint, down on our knees, then just went down the line. Brian, gone. Jenny, gone. Rhonda, gone. All gone. Just me." Eugene wailed and made a sound that might have been him tearing at his hair. "Just me."

"And they brought you here?"

"They handed me a body bag and told me that I had to clean up the mess first. Then they said they were just kidding. Ha ha. Funniest joke ever. I'm still laughing. Still laughing."

"You don't have to talk about this if you don't want to."

"I'm already talking about it. Why stop now? They put a bag over my head, maybe the same one they put on you, took me out to their van, and threw me in a cage. A cage! Who the hell gets thrown in a cage? Told me I could take a pill or get an injection. I took the pill. Woke up on a table. I've been on that table ten, eleven, twelve times, each time it just gets worse."

"Okay, Eugene, let me ask you a question. Have you ever heard of Vito 'Beak Man' Trunson?"

"No."

"You wouldn't have. He's not well known. Morbidly obese guy—sloppy fat, not the kind where you have an eating disorder, but the kind where you just don't give a shit. Body odor so horrific that you can almost *see* it. But those don't matter. Even if he were thin and fit and smelled like spearmint, he would be the ugliest human being you have ever laid eyes on. I'm not exaggerating. He is one ugly, *ugly* gentleman. Truly repellent. Ironically, his nose is the most attractive part of his face. I've been forced to have long conversations with him, conversations where I am physically ill just from the sight of him. What I'm saying, Eugene, is that I've seen Vito 'Beak Man' Trunson, so your appearance is not going to faze me."

"You're wrong."

"I'm going to have to turn around at some point. It's not fair to restrict me to looking at half of the room."

"Not yet."

"All right. So why did you ask me if I believe in werewolves?"

"Because whoever is keeping me prisoner does."

"Does he think you're one?"

"No."

"Then why is it relevant?"

"He's trying to turn me into one."

George took a moment to process that tidbit of information. "I beg your pardon?"

"You heard me."

"Say it again to verify."

"He's trying to turn me into a werewolf."

"That's messed up."

"Yes. It is."

"So we have our common ground." George really, really, really wanted to turn around now, but he didn't want to lose Eugene's trust. "Any special reason why he selected you?"

"No idea."

"Nothing?"

"Not a clue."

"No wolf research in your family history? Weird uncles? Anything? Think hard."

"George, you seem like an okay guy, but do you really believe that this conversation with you would be the first time I've tried to figure out why I was picked?"

"Point taken. I apologize."

"There may be something. I'm sure there is. But I've been locked in this room for a hell of a long time without much to do except think about my dead family and why I'm here, and I can't come up with a thing."

He let out a sudden sharp cry that made George flinch, and then there was a *thunk* sound that could have been bone against concrete.

"Eugene …?"

Thunk.

"I'd like you to stop whatever you're doing."

"I don't want to stop. I want to die."

"You've been here all this time without going suicidal," George said. "It'll hurt my feelings if being around me is what pushes you over the brink."

The thumping stopped.

"I'm turning around now," said George.

"I can't stop you."

George turned around.

"Not so bad," he said, forcing his face to remain casual and not give away the fact that "not so bad" was one of the least sincere things he'd said in a lifetime filled with saying insincere things.

"Is that so?"

"Yeah. I thought it would be way worse."

"You're looking pale, George."

"I'm fine."

"Do you want to sit down?"

George shook his head, even though he did.

Eugene was emaciated to the point where you could clearly see which ribs were broken. No regular meals? They were practically starving him to death!

He was naked except for a pair of boxer shorts, which may have fit properly at one time but were now barely staying in place.

But George's first clear thought was, *Oh my God. They're frankensteining him into a werewolf.*

Because that's what it looked like: human parts combined with wolf parts. But whereas Frankenstein's monster, though slipshod, was the work of somebody who was at least *trying* to make something halfway decent, Eugene was either the work of children or the mentally ill.

He had large patches of thick hair on his body, in three different colors: black, auburn, and gray. Each patch appeared to have been attached in a different manner: sewn, stapled, or even burned on around the edges. One of them on his upper leg had clearly just been glued, because a thick trail of dried glue ran all the way down his leg. Where there weren't patches of hair, there was red, raw skin. Cuts. Gashes. Burns. A three-inch circle on his chest had been made with what George wished he didn't know from personal experience was acid.

Parts of him seemed to have been replaced with those of an actual wolf. His left hand, for example, was a wolf paw, attached to the stump with thick white stitches. His right hand was human except that his fingernails were talons. The talons had not been simply stuck to his existing nails; the talon of his ring finger dangled, revealing the scabby skin underneath.

A pentagram had been carved on his palm.

One ear was a wolf ear. It flopped uselessly.

His nose was a snout. Off-center.

His mouth seemed fine. So did his eyes.

The word "WOLF" was carved onto his forehead. Also on his chest, his right arm, and both legs.

Large wolfish teeth were stuck all over his chin and shoulders.

Eugene had a lot to cry over. Hell, George almost wanted to cry himself.

"I don't get...I mean, I don't understand this."

"I'm glad," said Eugene. "I'd be worried about you if you understood it."

"Are they trying to make you *into* a werewolf? Is that it? But that doesn't make sense. It's like they, I don't know, it's like the Mr. Potato Head version of a werewolf."

Eugene turned to face the wall.

"Hey, buddy, no reason to get shy now," said George. "Let's try to get used to each other."

"I'm showing you my back."

The word "WOLF" was carved on there six or seven times. More teeth. A couple of incompetently inked wolf tattoos. A long dried-out tongue was sewn to his lower back, where a tramp-stamp would go.

Honestly, George couldn't say for sure that, in Eugene's place, he wouldn't have bashed out his brains against the concrete wall long ago.

What was the point of doing this?

Mr. Dewey wanted to catch a werewolf and force it to bite him. That made sense, in sort of a fucked-up way.

Making his own werewolf was even more fucked up, but still, at least you could follow the weaving path of logic.

This? Eugene wasn't an attempt to create a werewolf that hadn't worked out. This wasn't somebody trying and failing to make a lycanthrope. This was a psychologically unsound kid playing with his toys.

So here was the path of logic: Mr. Dewey buys Ivan the Werewolf, thinking that turning into a werewolf himself could be a miracle cure for brain cancer. Loses him in transit. Doesn't have any other werewolf options available at the moment. Becomes werewolf-obsessed. Goes from being just regular criminally insane to whack-nut batshit crazy. Takes it out on Eugene.

"Let me tell you something," said George, "I have never in my life met anybody who needs revenge more than you. Work with me, and we're going to get out of this place, and we're going to *destroy* the people who killed your family and did this to you. I promise."

"You can't promise that."

"Yeah, I can. They've got an innocent girl here, fourteen years old, and I'm getting her and my partner out of this place. Help me out and I'm taking you with me."

"Because you feel sorry for me or because you're opportunistic?"

"Both. Mostly the latter, but that's irrelevant. We can do this."

Eugene wiped a tear from his eye. "And if not ... I'm your future, right?"

"No offense, but screw that. We're getting out of here."

CHAPTER SIXTEEN

Pressure to Change

Ally blinked against the bright light as the man in the snowsuit pulled the hood off her head. He was no longer wearing his facemask, so she could see that he was a few years older than her, about the age of a college student but probably not actually in college. It was perfectly warm inside, so he didn't need to wear his snowsuit. Ally assumed that he just wanted people to see the bullet hole in the chest.

She was seated in a room that was about the size of one of her classrooms at school. It had cement floors, walls, and ceiling, and there wasn't much in there except for a few shelves containing boxes and what looked like various construction tools. She was bound to a metal chair with thick leather straps—three across her chest, one over each wrist, and one over each ankle. Even if she transformed she didn't think she could snap these.

Lou was seated next to her, in the same kind of chair with the same leather straps. He was still unconscious, his head lolling off to the side as he slept.

There were two chairs across from them. In one sat the old man with the cane. In the other was the man who'd introduced himself as Mr. Dewey.

Neither of them smiled.

The college-aged guy (Ally supposed you'd call him a "henchman") picked up a hypodermic needle from one of the shelves. Ally immediately tensed up, but then he injected Lou with the needle instead. The henchman stepped out of the way, folding his arms over his chest as he leaned against the wall.

Lou's eyes popped open. He looked around, completely disoriented, as he struggled against the straps.

The two older men let him thrash around for a few moments, then Mr. Dewey spoke. "That's enough."

"Where's George?"

"He's still alive."

"Let me see him."

"Or what? You'll struggle helplessly some more? Can't you two be in different rooms for fifteen seconds without mooning over each other?"

"I'm serious, if you hurt him I'll—"

"You'll do something bad to me. I get it. He's with Eugene."

"Who's Eugene?"

"Eugene is my stress relief. Now shut up or I'll cut off your other hand."

The look that Lou gave Mr. Dewey was so filled with pure hatred that Ally actually recoiled, even though Lou was sort-of on her side. Mr. Dewey didn't appear concerned in any way. And despite the anger in his eyes, Lou did indeed remain silent.

Mr. Dewey turned his attention to Ally. "This can be very easy for you, young lady," he said. "Easier than a trip to the dentist with no cavities."

Though Ally wasn't scared of the dentist, Mr. Dewey's reassurance didn't comfort her in any way.

"I know the setup here looks very sinister," Mr. Dewey admitted, "but there won't be much more to this than me asking you some questions. If you answer them honestly, this will be over quickly and we'll send you on your way."

"I want to call my mom first."

"No."

"I've been gone for a while," said Ally. "She's scared out of her mind. You don't know her. She has panic attacks. She could end up in the hospital."

"Then I guess you'll be motivated to get this over with as quickly as possible. Cooperate with me now, and when you tell your mom you're safe, it'll actually be true."

Ally nodded.

"Question one: can you control when you change into a wolf?"

"No."

"Did you know you could do it before today?"

"No."

"What were you feeling before you changed?"

Ally hesitated. "I was feeling at peace."

Mr. Dewey sighed and leaned forward in his chair. "That is an incorrect answer. Since you'd just been kidnapped, your emotional state was not 'at peace.' You're already lying to me, Ally. That's not good."

"What I meant was that right as I changed, I felt at peace."

"No. That's not what you meant. What you meant was, 'I changed during a state of intense emotional stress, and I don't want them to try to replicate that.' Correct?"

Ally decided to stick to the lie. "No."

"All right. We may have to go from a no-cavities scenario to a root canal. Have you ever had a root canal?"

"No."

"They're not so bad. Of course, your dentist would use Novocain. And when he removed your front teeth, I doubt he'd use a claw hammer. I need you to take this seriously, Ally."

"I am."

"Make me believe it."

"I don't know what you want from me."

"The truth."

"I gave you the truth."

"You're not a good liar. Fortunately for you, if this does come down to torture, we won't be starting with you. We'll be starting with your friend Lou."

"He's not my friend."

"Still holding a grudge? That's reasonable, I guess. Friend, enemy ... the point of having him here is that once we start opening up his face with the claw end of the hammer I mentioned before, you're going to wish you had cooperated back when this could have been a nice and simple Q&A session."

Ally felt so sick to her stomach that she was surprised she didn't just throw up right there. It was too late to not cry, but hopefully she could avoid turning into a complete blubbering mess.

"I'm sorry," she said.

"You're forgiven. Let's skip the questions and get right to the meat of the matter." Mr. Dewey stood up. "I want you to bite me."

"Where?"

Mr. Dewey pulled up his sleeve. "Right here. A good bite on the arm. Break the skin."

Ally couldn't believe that he was serious. Why would anybody *want* to become a monster?

Still standing, Mr. Dewey placed his arm in front of her mouth. "Bite hard. Stop when I tell you to."

What if she lied and said that she was HIV-positive? Would he abandon the whole idea, or would he see right through that and take out the claw hammer?

Better not to find out.

"Okay." Ally noticed that the henchman was now pointing a gun at her. Did it have silver bullets? If she changed into a werewolf during the bite, would he shoot her in the head, to make sure she didn't chew off Mr. Dewey's entire arm?

Ally opened her mouth. Mr. Dewey pushed the back of his arm against it, just below the elbow.

The henchman looked amused. Mr. Reith looked slightly appalled. Ally was terrified; she could handle biting the guy, no problem, but would he retaliate if it hurt more than he was expecting?

"Do it," said Mr. Dewey.

Ally pressed her teeth against his skin, then slowly bit down. If Mr. Dewey made any sounds like he was getting a thrill out of this, Ally was going to kill herself.

So far, he wasn't reacting, though she didn't like the way he was staring into her eyes as she bit.

"You're holding back," he said. "Just bite me. It's okay."

Ally bit down harder. Not as hard as she could, but hard enough that she could feel his skin giving way beneath her teeth and taste the first hint of blood.

He still didn't flinch.

She could feel two trickles of blood running down her chin.

"That should do it," said Mr. Dewey. "Thank you."

Ally opened her mouth and he pulled his arm away. The wound glistened. He looked at the bite mark as if admiring a beautiful painting in a museum, and didn't seem to be in any hurry to apply a bandage or antiseptic.

"Is that it?" Ally asked, not daring to be hopeful.

"Sadly, no. I'm covering all of my bases here. Your bite *may* have worked, but it would be ridiculous to set you free after you've only given me a human bite. I need a wolf bite. So we're going to be here for as long as it takes you to change. Hopefully it won't be long."

"I don't know how."

"You'll learn."

Ally had never stopped trying. She had no idea how to turn back into a wolf. She certainly didn't feel less frightened and stressed out now than she had in the van.

"I'm not lying. I don't know how to do it."

"You may just need a little push. Something to get the adrenaline flowing. Something extremely painful."

Lou spoke up. "Hey, Reith, are you gonna let him get away with this?"

Mr. Reith looked surprised by the question. "I beg your pardon?"

"He's threatening to torture a teenage girl. You into that?"

Mr. Reith smiled. "I'm into whatever measures are necessary to accomplish the end result."

"Is that so? Because you totally boned us on this job. It's a freaking miracle that we were able to nab her. Does Dewey know how you set us up to fail, even when his life was at risk if we didn't catch her? What would you have done if she'd escaped from us, or if we'd gotten arrested?"

Mr. Reith shrugged. "Right now we're exactly where we want to be, so it's irrelevant."

"He wouldn't even tell us her name," said Lou to Mr. Dewey. "You know what would've helped? Her name. We could've been waiting for her at her house instead of following her in a van, attracting everyone's attention."

"I admire your attempt to try to turn us against each other," said Mr. Dewey. "It's almost smart. But it's not going to work, so think of something else."

"I'll let you know what I come up with."

"Julian, get the drill."

The henchman broke into a wide grin as he walked over to the closest shelf. He picked up a dark blue power drill, held it up as if posing with a handgun, then brought it to Mr. Dewey.

Mr. Dewey inspected the drill, then removed the bit. "You know what? I've changed my mind. Bring me the smaller bit."

Julian got him a narrower bit. Mr. Dewey snapped it into the drill, then waved it in front of Ally's face.

"I was originally going to use this on Lou, to let you see first-hand how messy this process can be. When a big, tough man like Lou was shrieking in agony and pleading for me to stop, you'd understand that this was not a bluff. Unfortunately for you, I've decided that we don't need a pre-show. This drill is going into your ankle. To start."

Mr. Dewey touched the drill bit to Ally's ankle.

She frantically shook her head. "No! Please don't!"

"I'm going to give you ten seconds to transform. And then I'm going to press the button, and this spinning metal drill will start to bore its way into your foot."

"Don't do it!"

"Leave her alone!" Lou shouted.

"Is that really in your best interest, Lou? I'd keep quiet, if I were you."

"Please don't do it," Ally begged. "Please don't. I lied to you, okay? I lied. I can control the change." Her heart was racing and she was drenched in sweat and her voice was so off-kilter that she wasn't sure if anybody could even understand what she was saying.

"Then that's very convenient," said Mr. Dewey.

"I—I've been able to do it for a couple of years now," said Ally, praying that Mr. Dewey couldn't tell that she was lying again.

"Interesting. So do it now."

"I can't."

"Why not."

"I can't do it with Lou in the room."

Mr. Dewey raised an eyebrow, confused.

"He touched me," Ally explained. "In the van." They couldn't possibly know the full timeline of how things played out between her two abductions, could they?

"What do you mean?"

"Do you need me to touch a teddy bear? What do you think I mean?"

Lou, apparently playing along, looked down at his feet as if mortified.

"Hmm," said Mr. Dewey.

"I can't think about anything else while he's here. I can't focus. I need to be able to focus."

Ally began to sob. She wasn't much of an actress, but she'd been struggling to keep her emotions under control all of this time, so releasing them was easy.

It actually felt good to let it all out.

"That true, Lou?" Mr. Dewey asked.

Lou didn't respond.

"I asked you a question."

"No," said Lou. "She's full of shit."

"Is that so?"

"Yeah. She's trying to pull something over on you."

"Hmm." Mr. Dewey hadn't removed the drill bit from Ally's ankle. "Those kinds of tendencies would be news to me, but maybe you just don't have a lot of opportunity to indulge in them, huh, Lou?"

Lou looked up and held Mr. Dewey's gaze for a couple of seconds, then looked away.

Lou got what she was doing, right? He seemed to be giving a brilliant performance.

"Please," said Ally, "just take him out of here. Take him away. Then I'll change, I promise."

Mr. Dewey kept the drill pressed against Ally's ankle. "Lou, Lou, Lou, you sick little pervert. I guess when you're stuck for months with only George for company, stuff builds up, huh? Can't control the ol' impulses? Well, it's not my thing, but I'm not one to judge."

"I am," said Mr. Reith. "It's disgusting. If we do abide the young woman's request and remove him from the room, I think he should be castrated."

Mr. Dewey grinned. "You heard the man, Lou. Say farewell to your manhood."

"I didn't do anything!" Lou insisted. "She's a liar!"

"I can only believe one side of the story, and too bad for you, I'm believing the side where you're a very naughty boy." Mr. Dewey pointed to Julian. "Get this deviant out of here."

Julian walked over to Lou's chair. He kept a gun pointed at Lou's head with one hand, while unfastening the straps with the other.

Ally desperately wished that Mr. Dewey would remove the drill.

It was kind of awkward for Julian to unfasten the straps using only one hand, but he got most of them done without too much apparent difficulty. Before he unfastened the strap on Lou's hand, Julian tapped the barrel of his gun against Lou's temple.

"I've got permission to blow his brains out if he tries anything, right?" Julian asked Mr. Dewey.

"Of course."

"You hear that, tough guy? You're lucky I don't put you out of your child-molesting misery right now."

"Don't talk to him," said Mr. Dewey. "Just take him away."

"Sorry, sir." Julian unfastened the strap. Then he crouched down, pointing the gun between Lou's legs, and began to unfasten the straps on his feet.

Lou did not look happy about the gun placement.

Ally was just trying to get Lou a single instant where he could do something. There was a good chance that this instant might involve a bullet to the crotch, but they were going to torture and kill him anyway, right?

Julian unfastened the final strap.

This was the instant.

Ally threw her head back and let out the loudest, most agonized-sounding shriek she possibly could.

CHAPTER SEVENTEEN

Glorious Chaos

Lou had been a professional criminal for all of his adult life, and most of his teenage years. He'd had many guns pointed at him. They didn't scare him much anymore. Unless, of course, they were pointed at his dick.

His genitals had retreated to the best of their ability, as if he'd spent hours in a swimming pool, but that wouldn't protect them if Julian pulled the trigger. He couldn't go out like this. Not shot in the dick. Please, no.

He wasn't one hundred percent sure what Ally was intending with her accusation. He thought, and hoped, that her plan was to buy him an opportunity to escape. He'd have to take out three men, one of whom was currently pointing a gun at his junk, but it was flattering that she had so much faith in him.

Or maybe she'd just figured that if she accused him of being a pedophile, they'd focus all of their attention on him for a while. Postpone the drill-through-the-ankle for a while longer. Around guys like these, it was a dangerous plan; they could've said, "Hey, that's a *wonderful* idea! Why didn't we think of that?"

Lou would be optimistic and assume it was the former.

What was he going to do?

His one option seemed to be: punch Julian in the head once the last strap was unfastened, and pray to every freaking concept of God that existed in the history of humanity that Julian didn't pull the trigger.

Don't. Shoot. Off. My. Dick.

Lou didn't know if Mr. Reith was packing a gun or not. To keep himself sane, he was going to assume that the old man would not be a major factor in his escape attempt. Mr. Dewey and his drill would be a problem, as would the several heavily armed men that were hanging out elsewhere in the warehouse.

Okay, his primary focus would be not getting his dick shot off, and then a very close second would be trying to get Mr. Dewey into some sort of hostage situation.

He could do this.

He hadn't contributed much so far, thanks to the tranquilizer darts, but he could do this.

What he'd do is, as soon as Julian unfastened the last strap, he'd knee him in the face. Break his nose. Hit him so hard and so unexpectedly that he'd let go of the gun instead of pulling the trigger and sending a bullet deep into Lou's shaft.

As soon as Julian unfastened the last strap, Ally threw back her head and screamed bloody murder.

Julian flinched, startled.

He flinched even more as Lou kneed him in the face.

Both of Julian's hands went to his mouth. Lou had missed his nose but delivered one hell of a knee to Julian's jaw, possibly breaking it.

Julian was still holding the gun, so clutching at his jaw with both hands created a slapstick moment involving smacking a gun into his own injured face that would probably be amusing in retrospect, although right now Lou was concentrating too hard on getting the weapon away from him to enjoy it.

Lou stood up.

Ally's scream changed, getting much higher in pitch. Lou was focused on Julian, but in his peripheral vision he thought he saw the drill boring into her foot. There was definitely some blood.

Lou stomped on Julian's foot and grabbed for his gun.

This was another slapstick moment that would, if he lived to recount this adventure later, be delightfully amusing. It wasn't so amusing now, because Lou was a big guy, and he had big feet, and he was putting every ounce of strength into this stomp, so instead of a wacky sound effect, Julian's foot shattered with a grotesque *crunch*.

Now there were two people screaming in the room.

Lou ripped the gun out of Julian's hand, snapping Julian's trigger finger in the process.

Mr. Dewey stood up. Droplets of blood flew off the drill bit as it spun.

Ally was screaming and thrashing around in the chair. She did not, unfortunately, look like she was changing into a wolf.

Lou shot Julian in the forehead. Before the poor guy's body even collapsed, Lou dove at Mr. Dewey. Lou didn't *want* to take a drill to the side if he could help it, but it wouldn't be fatal, and this was not the time for cautious, timid behavior.

Mr. Dewey thrust the drill at Lou.

Got him in the chest.

Julian had stopped screaming immediately after the back of his head exploded, but now they were back to two people screaming in the room.

Lou pointed the gun at Mr. Dewey's face.

Almost pulled the trigger.

No!

He needed Mr. Dewey as a hostage.

Mr. Dewey backed away a step. Lou's chest hurt like hell, but blood wasn't spraying, and until he discovered otherwise Lou was going to pretend that no internal organs were punctured.

Lou wasn't sure what Mr. Reith was doing. He hoped to not become the kind of person who would bash an old man unconscious with his own cane, but if it came to that...

Having Mr. Dewey at gunpoint wasn't enough. If his men burst into the room—and they would, any moment now—they could just fire a few rounds into Lou's back without putting their boss or the werewolf at risk.

Sure, he could eventually get Mr. Dewey where he needed to be through the process of threatening him with the gun, but there was no time for any kind of conversation. So Lou lunged at him again.

Mr. Dewey jabbed at him with the drill, which tore across Lou's chest like a rock skipping across a pond, while Lou twisted himself around, trying to get Mr. Dewey in a headlock.

He did, just as the door flew open.

"Stay back!" Lou shouted, pressing the gun against Mr. Dewey's neck. "Stay back or he's dead!"

"Do what he says," said Mr. Dewey.

This still wasn't a great position. Lou shifted a bit, to make sure that Mr. Dewey's body was mostly in front of his, and that the gun was clearly visible.

"Drop the drill."

Mr. Dewey dropped the drill.

One man was in the room, pointing a gun at Lou. Another man stood in the doorway, also with a gun, and Lou could see Sean and Brent, the guys who'd driven him from Ontario to Tropper, standing behind him.

"Everybody lower your guns or I swear I'll kill him," said Lou. "I've got nothing to lose! Don't test me!"

Lou was telling the truth. If they didn't listen, he would indeed put a round into Mr. Dewey's skull and then take out as many of the others as he could before he went down in a flurry of bullets.

The closest man seemed to see this in Lou's eyes, although he kept his gun arm extended.

Mr. Dewey shouted, "I said, do it!"

The man lowered his gun.

"Good work, good work," said Lou. "Keep listening to me and nobody has to die. We just want to get out of here."

Mr. Reith hadn't gotten up from his chair, though he did look extremely unhappy about this turn of events.

"Reith! Get up!"

Mr. Reith shook his head. "I don't think so."

"I said, get up! I'm not gonna hurt you!"

Mr. Reith stood up, using his cane to assist him.

Lou felt like the old man was probably exaggerating his need for the cane, just a little, but Lou suddenly decided that his logic behind calling out Mr. Reith (he was less likely to try any sudden attacks when unstrapping Ally from her chair than the other men) was faulty, since Mr. Reith would be really frickin' slow. He needed somebody else to do that. But he didn't want them to think he wasn't in full control of the situation.

"Against the wall!" he shouted at Mr. Reith, even though he had no particular reason for Mr. Reith to be against the wall. "Facing it! Do it now!"

"I'm not going anywhere."

"I'll kill him!"

"I don't care what you do to him, quite frankly."

Okay, fine. Lou didn't have time to argue. That Mr. Reith would be killed immediately after Mr. Dewey met his demise was implied, but either the stubborn old fuck was at peace with his own mortality, or he didn't think Lou could kill him before the whole "flurry of bullets" thing. He was probably right.

"You then," said Lou to the closest man. "Get her out of that chair. Do it fast."

The man looked at Mr. Dewey as if for approval.

"Do it," said Mr. Dewey. "He'll suffer later."

The man nodded and walked over to Ally's chair. She'd stopped screaming, though she was still sobbing and gasping for breath. The hole in her ankle was bleeding but, without inspecting it closely and without any medical training, it didn't look *that* bad to Lou. Maybe it didn't drill into the bone. Lou desperately hoped that it hadn't hobbled her, because though he could carry her easily under different circumstances, he couldn't really do it while he was trying to hold a gun to a crime lord's head.

To his credit, Mr. Dewey's underling didn't seem to be trying to pull anything over on Lou as he unfastened the straps. "Faster!" Lou told him, even though the underling did legitimately seem to be unfastening them as quickly as he could.

"Here's what's going to happen," said Lou. "The three of us are going to walk out of this room, and none of you are going to try to be heroes. We're all lowlife criminals here; nobody needs to show off. Then we're going to collect George, and then we're going to get into a truck, and once we've driven out of this building we're going to dump your boss's ass onto the street, and after that if you want to chase us you're more than welcome. Nice and simple. Everybody got that?"

Nobody actually answered, but Lou was pretty sure they all got it.

"May I offer a different suggestion?" asked Mr. Dewey.

"Sure."

"Leave the girl. If you take her, we will never stop hunting you. Never. You know that. If you leave her with us now, we'll let you and George go, free and clear."

"Why should I believe that?"

"Because I want the girl more than I want you dead."

"Sorry."

"What kind of life do you want for yourself, Lou? Hiding out again? Living in a shack? All you have to do is leave her, a girl you were going to bring to me anyway, and we'll call it even. If our paths accidentally cross again I won't hesitate to kill you, but you have my word that we won't try to find you. I'm *done* with you."

"Can't do it. Maybe before you went all Driller-Killer on her, but, no, I can't leave her with you to be tortured to death. No deal."

"You're dooming your partner as well. Would he agree with your decision?"

"Yep."

"I doubt it."

"We'll ask him. In the meantime, shut the fuck up. Your mouth might jostle my trigger finger."

"She's done," said the man, unfastening the last of the straps.

"Step away," Lou told him.

The man stepped away from the chair.

"Can you walk?" Lou asked Ally.

Ally stood up, then her injured foot immediately twisted beneath her and she had to brace herself against the chair. Her foot slid a bit on the blood.

"Shit," said Lou.

"No, I can walk, I think," Ally insisted. "I just need you to ..." She trailed off.

"She's going to slow you down," said Mr. Dewey. "Nobody would blame you for abandoning her."

Lou wanted to whack him in the head with the gun, to discourage further comments, but with his luck he'd knock the guy out.

Having George around would be extremely helpful right now. He didn't want to send any of the men to go retrieve him, though, because there wouldn't be anything stopping them from just killing him. Assuming somebody hadn't already.

"Okay," said Lou. "Just put your hand on my shoulder."

Ally did so. Lou stepped toward the doorway, and she stepped along with him, and Mr. Dewey didn't resist too much to being dragged forward that one step. This was not the most graceful way to make their exit, but it would have to do.

"Everybody get out of the way!" Lou shouted. "Against the walls! I mean it!"

The men didn't quite move against the walls, but they did get out of Lou's way.

As they crossed through the doorway, Ally momentarily lost her grip on Lou's shoulder and he thought she was going to fall to the floor, but she steadied herself in time. For somebody who'd had a goddamn hole drilled into the side of her foot, she was doing remarkably well.

There were a couple of other men in the main area of the warehouse, watching them closely as they emerged but not risking their boss's life by pointing guns where they shouldn't be pointed.

"Where's George?" Lou demanded.

The man who'd been shot in the stomach, who was no longer wearing his snowsuit but was still wearing his bulletproof vest, pointed to a closed door, right next to the room Lou and the others had come from. At least *that* was convenient.

"Bring him out," Lou said.

"I need the keys for the locks," said the man.

"Who has them?"

"I don't know."

"Okay, I'm really not going to play this game. Whoever has the keys had goddamn well better get in there and set George free, or I swear I will just go on a killing spree."

"Do it!" said Mr. Dewey.

For a second Lou thought that he was referring to the killing spree, which seemed odd considering how cooperative Mr. Dewey had been so far, but then he realized that Mr. Dewey was referring to setting George free, which made a lot more sense.

A short guy with thick sideburns walked over to the door and punched a code on the keypad. The door popped open.

"No surprises," Lou warned him.

The short guy walked inside the room.

When he came back out, there was a surprise.

CHAPTER EIGHTEEN

Overstuffed Transportation

George was not typically one to promise people that they'd get out of messes. He tended to be more of a matter-of-fact, "Sorry, but the chances of surviving this are almost nil" kind of guy. Why give false hope? So it surprised him to hear himself vowing to get him and Eugene out of this, especially since neither one of them were real werewolves and thus the chances of them suddenly acquiring the superhuman strength necessary to snap their bonds was woefully low.

The door opened. A short guy walked in, looking nervous instead of sadistic. He took out a pocketknife and quickly cut George's hands and feet free, then, after a moment to find the right key on the key ring, unlocked the chain around George's foot.

"Come on," he said.

"Where are we going?"

"You're free."

"Seriously?"

"Yeah."

"Unlock Eugene. He's coming with me."

The short guy hesitated, as if considering how he was going to explain that George was lucky to be free at all and really wasn't in any kind of a position to start making demands about who he'd be bringing with him. Then he walked over and crouched down next to Eugene's foot.

George had only just met Eugene, owed him nothing, and didn't much enjoy looking at him, but this whole thing had gone so badly that maybe if he helped rescue the poor bastard from an existence that was almost literally worse than death, it could help balance out what they'd done to Ally.

As the short guy unlocked the chain, Eugene said, "I'm not leaving."

"What?"

"This is where I belong."

"What?"

Eugene grinned. "I'm kidding, kidding, kidding. Let's go."

It was clearly painful for Frankenwolf to walk, but there was almost a spring in his step as they left the room.

Outside, Lou was standing there with a gun to Mr. Dewey's head. Ally stood on the other side of him, one foot covered with blood, bracing herself against Lou's shoulder as if using him to keep her balance.

"I missed some shit, didn't I?" asked George.

Lou didn't reply. He was too busy gaping at Eugene.

"Don't worry, he's cool," George assured him.

Lou continued to gape.

"You're not taking him," said Mr. Dewey.

"I disagree," said George.

"Can we go now? Please?" asked Ally.

The van that had transported George and Lou from Canada was still parked in the warehouse. "Give the van keys to George," Lou told the man who'd unlocked the chains.

The man took a key off the ring and tossed it to George. George caught it and hurried over to the van, with Eugene limping behind him, and the Lou/Ally/Mr. Dewey trio behind them.

George opened the rear door. The cage took up pretty much all of the space back there, which was inconvenient, since there was only room for two people up front.

George pointed to Mr. Dewey. "You. In the back."

Mr. Dewey shook his head as well as he could with a gun pressed against it. "Absolutely not."

"You don't have a choice."

"If you put me in the cage, I have to assume that you're not planning to keep Lou's promise to release me as soon as we drive out of here."

Crap. With only one hand, Lou couldn't drive the van and keep a gun pointed at Mr. Dewey's head. Unless Mr. Dewey sat on Lou's lap—and that wasn't going to be acceptable for anybody involved—George was going to have to drive, and Lou, Ally, and Eugene would have to go in the cage.

George quickly helped Ally into the back of the van, noting with some anger that there was a hole in the side of her foot, as if somebody had jabbed her with a meat thermometer. His anger was hypocritical, since he'd been personally responsible for the many bruises on her body, but her new wound didn't look like self-defense.

Then he helped Eugene into the back, not oblivious to the fact that Ally, not knowing Eugene's tragic backstory, would think she was being caged up with some sort of horrific and possibly murderous lab experiment. "Don't worry, he's harmless," George assured her. Ally was pretty much in a state of shock now, so she didn't have any particular reaction as Eugene climbed into the cage and scooted all the way to the back.

"Trade me," George said to Lou, reaching for the gun.

Lou gave him the gun, then got into the cage with the others. George shut the rear door of the van with one hand, keeping the gun pointed at Mr. Dewey's face with the other.

"I'm going to make you the offer that your partner declined," said Mr. Dewey. "Leave the werewolf with me, and we'll call it even."

"Which werewolf?" George asked. "The real one, or your third-grade science project attempt at making one?"

"Eugene was a way to keep my frustration level under control. Some people use alcohol or drugs, some people take long walks, and I express my creativity."

George walked Mr. Dewey over to the passenger side of the van and opened the door. "Get in."

Mr. Dewey turned to his men, all of whom were pointing guns at them and carefully watching the situation. "I've been promised that I'll be released as soon as we leave this building. If that does not happen, open fire. Kill everybody in the van, including the girl and Eugene. I authorize use of whatever force is necessary."

George wished that Lou had negotiated for a slightly further release spot, like the end of the block, but this should be okay. You couldn't just go blowing people away in the middle of the street of downtown Tropper.

"We're going to let him go," George promised the men, a little surprised that none of them had taken a shot at him. "You'll get your boss back, don't worry."

Mr. Dewey climbed into the passenger seat of the van. George told him not to worry about buckling up, and not to bother shutting the door all the way. He wouldn't be in there long.

George hurried around the front of the van, keeping the gun pointed at Mr. Dewey the entire time. If any of Mr. Dewey's men were going to risk a kill shot, now's when they'd do it, so George was even more tense than he had been during the other bad moments today.

Nobody tried to shoot George as he opened the driver's side door and got inside, which was a relief. He stuck the key in the ignition, trying to simultaneously watch Mr. Dewey to the right of him and whatever he could see happening in the side-view mirror.

Lou, Ally, and Eugene had all ducked down beneath window-level, just in case.

"I'm offering you one last chance," said Mr. Dewey.

"And I appreciate it."

"We don't have to be enemies."

"I feel like we kind of do, at this point."

"You're making a terrible mistake."

"Listen, we're letting you go as soon as we're clear of this place, so be happy about that. If you decide that you're going to hunt me and Lou down to the ends of the earth, fine, but all we ever wanted to do was be left alone. We never did anything to harm you, or disrespect you. A job went bad because we didn't have enough information. This job went bad because we also didn't have enough information. Data is useful. When we have data, jobs go well. Lou and I had a perfectly good reputation before the whole Ivan the Werewolf thing; that's why you hired us."

"I didn't hire you. Mr. Bateman hired you. And that's why I had him killed."

"Is somebody going to raise the door for us or what?" George asked. He honked the horn.

One of the men—the guy in the bulletproof vest—walked toward the sliding door. He was still holding up his gun. George didn't care that all of the other men were, too; he didn't like this guy getting so close with it.

"Lower your gun," said George.

The man lowered his gun, but only a little. Not down to his side. It was at about a forty-five degree angle to the floor. He could still pop off a shot at George pretty easily. Whether he intended to shoot George or not, it was obvious that he was at least keeping his options open.

This was too much to keep track of.

Mr. Dewey moved.

It wasn't necessarily an aggressive move. George was too focused on the approaching man to also devote enough attention to Mr. Dewey, so he might have simply been shifting in his seat. He'd definitely leaned toward George.

Perhaps it was an innocent lean.

Perhaps not.

Either way, George shot him in the forehead.

CHAPTER NINTEEN

A Tinge of Regret

Before the first chunk even began to slide down the window, George wished he hadn't done that.

He hadn't *completely* done it on purpose. There was an element of having an overly nervous finger on the trigger involved. Still, the man walking toward the sliding door was clearly hoping for an opportunity to take George out, and Mr. Dewey had (probably) tried to take advantage of him being distracted.

George had no choice.

He had to defend himself.

That said ... this was extremely, intensely, mind-bogglingly bad.

Ally screamed.

At least now things were simplified. Whereas before George had to figure out the best course of action, and weigh the consequences of his decisions, now everything could be conveniently distilled into: *get the hell out of here, fast.*

No other gunshots had started firing yet. Apparently everybody needed a moment to process the fact that Mr. Dewey had just taken a round to the head.

George couldn't just plow through the metal sliding door without building up some momentum. He put the van into reverse and slammed his foot on the gas pedal.

Now the men started shooting.

George ducked down and braced himself for the pleasant *thunk* of one of Dewey's men getting struck by the van, but it didn't happen.

None of the windows had shattered. The men were shooting through the body of the van, either trying to get at those in the cage or trying to hit the fuel tank. There were no screams of pain coming from behind him, so as far as George could tell, nobody had been hit.

After backing up about twenty feet, George put the van into drive. He floored the gas pedal and the van shot forward. A bullet fired through the driver's side window, leaving a hole and a spider-web pattern, but the window didn't shatter.

If the van didn't break through the sliding metal door, they were all essentially dead.

The van struck the sliding metal door, broke *most* of the way through, then stopped.

The man in the bulletproof vest was right next to the van. Sadly for him, he wasn't wearing a vest over his head, so when George squeezed off a shot, it put another hole in the driver's side window and then went through his left eye.

George put the van back into reverse.

This time, as he sped backwards, he did hear the *thunk* of somebody getting hit, although the sound wasn't as satisfying as he would have hoped.

Ally screamed again. She was entitled.

George put the van into drive, slammed the gas pedal, and smashed into the sliding door (which would never slide again) a second time. This time the van plowed right through it, and George pulled out onto the road, took a sharp right turn, and sped away from the warehouse.

It was dark out already. Wow. Today had just flown by.

"You killed Dewey!" Lou shouted from the cage.

"I know!"

"Why? Who does that?"

"It wasn't completely on purpose!"

"We're screwed!"

"We're not screwed!"

"We couldn't be more screwed!"

George eased up on the gas pedal a bit. It was still snowing and this would be an abysmal time to get into an accident. He made a right turn to help lose any of the men who might pursue them, which was probably all of them.

"Are we really worse off now that he's dead?" George asked.

"Yes! Yes, we are!"

"What if this means our problems are over?" George asked. "Maybe with Dewey dead, we can finally relax?"

Mr. Dewey's corpse slumped over and hit the dashboard.

"Have you lost your mind?" Lou asked.

"A little, yeah."

"Why did you shoot him?"

"I told you! He moved aggressively! Don't blame me! If you had both hands then you would've been up here driving and keeping him covered at the same time just like I was, and you would've done the exact same thing!"

"No, I wouldn't have!"

"I guess we'll never know!"

"Couldn't you at least have shot him in the leg? That would've stopped his aggression."

"I'm not saying that I weighed every option."

"You said I would've done the same thing!"

"You would have! In my place, you would have made an equally poor decision."

George checked all of the mirrors. There was not, at the moment, any sign of anybody chasing after them. That wasn't going to last.

Just ahead there was a tiny Mexican restaurant that looked dumpy enough not to have security cameras. He pulled into the parking lot, drove around to the back of the building, stopped the van, reached across Mr. Dewey's body, opened the door, and shoved his corpse out onto the ground. Then he rolled down the window to hide the blood on the glass, and drove away.

"I can't help but feel that somebody will find him," said Lou.

"We can't drive around with a dead body in the front seat. Who cares if they find him? It'll be something to distract the police. We probably should have dumped him right in the middle of the road."

Damn. They really *should* have dumped him in the middle of the road. Oh well. Too late now.

Okay, yeah, he wished he hadn't killed Mr. Dewey. When you killed somebody with Mr. Dewey's power, a lot of vengeance came your way. But, technically, they were already on his shit list, underlined and in boldface. Would Mr. Dewey have ever stopped seeking his own revenge?

The answer to that was: yes. Because Mr. Dewey was dying of brain cancer. Once his expiration date passed, they would've been more or less fine.

Out of the frying pan, into the fire, then into the volcano.

"Well, what's done is done," said George. He said stupid things like "what's done is done" about as often as he reassured doomed people that everything was going to be all right, but it seemed appropriate in this case. It was done. Mr. Dewey wasn't coming back. They were dealing with werewolves, not zombies.

"Yeah, our *lives* are done," said Lou, who was also not bringing his A-game to this particular conversation.

"Can you two please stop arguing?" asked Ally. "It's not accomplishing anything."

She was right. She was also thirty years younger, had a hole in her foot, and was in a cage with one of her kidnappers and a ghastly freak, so the fact that she was the one proposing rational discussion was kind of embarrassing.

"Yes, we can," George announced. "Thanks for getting us out of there, Lou."

"Anytime."

In the rear-view mirror, George could see that Eugene was pressed tightly into the corner of the cage, chin against his knees, covering his face with his hand and paw.

"That's Eugene," said George. "Dewey messed him up bad."

"Yeah," said Lou. "I was going to ask about that."

"I don't want to talk about it," said Eugene.

"I can respect that."

"Where are we going?" Ally asked.

George continued to carefully watch their surroundings. Obviously, it was going to be much more difficult to watch for cars full of gun-toting criminals speeding toward them in the dark, but so far things looked okay. It was entirely possible that Mr. Dewey's men *wanted* to riddle the van with thousands of rounds of ammunition, yet felt it was more prudent to just abandon the warehouse and worry about George and Lou later, since the police would be on their way to investigate the gunshots.

Or they might be right around the corner, ready to fling dynamite at them.

"We're going to get you someplace safe," George told Ally.

"Just pull over and let me out. I'll be fine."

"No. It's got to be a hospital or a police station or something. Well, preferably not a police station. But we can't let you out until we know for sure that we've lost these guys."

"We're closer to my house than a hospital. Just take me there."

George considered that. Right now, as far as the police knew, Ally was just a fourteen-year-old girl who was a few hours late getting home from school. Even if her mom reported her missing, the house wouldn't be crawling with cops. Sure, somebody might have said that they saw the van outside her house, and maybe somebody noticed that the wolf-girl in the pictures was wearing the same dress as the missing girl, but it should be safe enough to drop her off near her home.

There was the issue that Mr. Reith probably knew her name and where she lived, and the whole werewolf element was something that she'd have to figure out how to deal with, but that wasn't George and Lou's problem. They'd get rid of her and get the hell out of town.

Shane tilted back his head and breathed deeply, taking in the cold night air.

"Anything?" Robyn asked.

"Nope. Crabs?"

Crabs closed his eyes as he inhaled. Shane could catch the scent of another werewolf from at least a mile away, but Crabs had an even more finely tuned sense of smell. If they kept driving around Tropper, they'd eventually find her.

"I can't smell your daughter yet," said Crabs.

Shane could only smell another werewolf when they were actually in wolf form, but Crabs could smell her even if she was human. In fact, he'd been the one to assure Shane that Ally had inherited his gift.

"Okay. Let's go talk to her mom."

————

"What happened to you?" Ally asked Eugene.

"Nothing you need to hear about."

Eugene should've been terrifying to her—okay, he *was* terrifying—but he also looked so *sad* that he was more heartbreaking than scary. She couldn't quite bring herself to place a reassuring hand on his knee, but she wanted to.

"At least you're free now."

Eugene nodded. "Yeah. Maybe I can be fixed, a little. They can do amazing things with plastic surgery, right? I think my ribs have healed like this, so they'll have to be re-broken. Do you think doctors have a rib-breaking machine, or do they just ... you know what, you should talk to Lou instead."

"Really," said Ally, "you look kind of bad-ass."

"Think so?"

"Definitely."

Eugene smiled. "It's sweet of you to lie to make me feel better. So why are you here?"

"I'm a werewolf."

Eugene's smile disappeared. "Don't tell me you believe that, too."

"I am. I found out this afternoon."

"Come on."

"How do you think George got all ripped up?"

"No offense to George, but it seems like lots of people want to rip him up."

"Maybe, but I did it."

"Can you change now?"

"Please don't," said Lou. "Seriously."

"Well," said Eugene, "if you are a werewolf, then I wish you the best of luck with it."

————

There were no police cars at Peggy's house. Shane was simultaneously relieved, because it meant that he could talk to his ex-wife in person, and annoyed, because it meant that she wasn't taking their daughter's disappearance seriously enough.

"Both of you wait in the car," he said, as Robyn pulled into the driveway.

"Crabs will wait in the car," said Robyn. "I'm coming with you."

"Peggy hates you."

"She hates you, too. I need to be there to make sure things don't get out of hand."

"Robyn Miles, keeper of the peace," said Crabs.

"Okay," said Shane. "But you can't be antagonistic."

Shane and Robyn got out of the car. The yard needed mowing and Peggy *still* hadn't gotten that dent in the mailbox fixed. Why the hell did the judge give her the house?

"How about I do the talking?" said Robyn, as Shane rang the doorbell.

"I don't need you to do my talking for me. I'm perfectly capable of speaking to her about this matter. I'm going to find out what she knows about Ally, and then leave. No big deal. Quit acting like it's going to be the apocalypse."

The front door opened. Peggy didn't look happy to see him.

He wasn't happy to see her, either. Her face didn't look great—her makeup was streaked and her eyes were puffy from crying—but her post-divorce body pissed him off every time he saw it. Did it occur to her that if she'd kept herself in shape while they were married he wouldn't have slept with other women? (She only knew about Robyn, but there'd been six or seven, not counting prostitutes.)

"Shane," she said, as if he didn't know his own name. She glared at Robyn. "You're not supposed to be here."

"Ally is missing, and you're going to wave a restraining order in my face? Is that what kind of mother you are?"

"I'm sorry, Peggy," said Robyn. "Obviously we're worried and we wanted to find out if you had any information. May we come in?"

"No. You can't. We can talk out here."

"Fine," said Shane. "Be a bitch about it. Let's talk out here instead of inside like civilized human beings."

"Shane! Knock it off!" Robyn gave Peggy an apologetic look that made him want to puke. "I'm sorry. He's really upset about Ally. We all are. You've talked to the police, right?"

Peggy nodded. "They've filed a report. I've been calling all of her friends but nobody knows anything, except that Trista walked most of the way home with her. That's it. That's everything I know so far. She's a teenager; she could've just gone to see her boyfriend and lost track of time."

"She has a boyfriend?" Shane asked.

"Not that I know of. I'm just saying."

"You don't think you'd know if she had a boyfriend?"

"What I'm saying, Shane, is that she is a teenage girl, and teenage girls sometimes do things like go off with boys without thinking to call their mothers to let them know where they are. I'm saying that, yes, I'm worried, but it's too soon to think the worst."

"Fine. So basically you have no useful information whatsoever. I'm going to look in her room real quick, and then we'll let you get back to all of the helpful stuff you've clearly been doing to aid in finding Ally."

"I told you that you can't come inside."

"And if you're going to stop me from doing a two-minute search through my own daughter's room to see if there are any clues about where she's gone, then you're putting our differences before Ally's safety, and I don't have to tell you what kind of a parent that makes you."

"The police already looked."

"And they know Ally better than I do?"

Peggy rubbed her forehead as if suffering from a migraine, then stepped out of the way. "Two minutes. Then leave."

"Thank you," said Shane, moving past her. He didn't expect to find any clues in Ally's room. What he needed, and what he would never admit even to Robyn, was to get a fresh scent. He hadn't seen Ally in a few weeks, and though he was sure he could find her if they got close enough, a deep whiff of an article of clothing she'd wore yesterday would be extremely helpful.

It would be even more helpful if Crabs did it, but no way in hell would Robyn or Peggy allow him up in her room, and some things weren't worth fighting over.

He hurried up the stairs and into Ally's room. Wow. It looked like it had actually been cleaned within the past couple of weeks. Incredible.

Shane opened the lid to her clothes hamper and looked inside. There was a pair of light blue cotton panties on the very top, and it was tempting, but he could hear Peggy's footsteps coming up the stairs and she'd have an absolute meltdown if she caught him. He supposed he couldn't blame her.

Instead, he grabbed a nightgown, pressed it to his face and inhaled deeply, then tossed it back into the hamper.

He paced around, pretending to look for clues, as Peggy entered the room.

Seriously, would it have killed her to hop on an exercise bike a couple of times after Ally was born and before their marriage crashed and burned? As far as Shane knew, she wasn't getting any, so obviously her toned body was just to make him jealous about what he couldn't have. As if he cared. If Peggy knew the things that Robyn let him do to her, she wouldn't bother trying to compete.

"What exactly are you looking for?" Peggy asked.

"I don't know. Anything."

"I'm sure she's fine."

"I'm sure you're right."

"I need you to leave now, Shane. I promise I'll call you the second I hear something."

"When did she quit playing the violin?"

"Excuse me?"

"Ally quit, right? Isn't that what you told Robyn? Why didn't you ask me what I thought?"

"We can't micro-manage every aspect of her life."

"Apparently not, since you can't even keep her safe."

"This is absolutely not relevant or appropriate right now. We can discuss it later. For now, I need you to leave before I call the police."

"You're gonna call the cops on me?"

"I don't want to."

"Did I really hear you right? I'm here out of concern for our daughter, who could be in somebody's basement with duct tape over her fucking mouth, and you're threatening to call the cops because I'm lingering too long? Is that what I heard?"

Peggy sighed and turned away. "I don't care what you do. I'm going back downstairs. Stay as long as you want."

That bitch *was* going to call the cops on him. Shane couldn't believe it. He wanted to change right here and start scattering her body parts all over Ally's room.

He wouldn't do it, not really, but, oh, he would enjoy every second of it.

———

No police cars were outside of Ally's home. Perfect. But there was another car in the driveway that hadn't been there before. Plainclothes cop? Private investigator? Concerned friend, relative, or neighbor?

"You recognize that car?" George asked, stopping the van about three houses away.

Ally crawled to the other side of the cage to get a better view. "Yeah! It's my dad's!"

"All right. I'll let you out."

CHAPTER TWENTY

Father/Daughter Reunion

George put the van in park but left the engine running as he got out and walked around to open the back door. If Ally didn't have an injured foot, he would've done this several blocks away, to avoid witnesses, but he'd have a complete meltdown if he released Ally only to have Mr. Dewey's men nab her again before she made it home.

"Lou, come on up front," said George. "Eugene, we can't risk anybody seeing you, and there's no room up there for you anyway, so you're going to have to stay in the cage until we get a new ride."

Eugene shrugged. "Okay with me."

Lou got out of the van, quickly followed by Ally. George didn't expect a hug or an "I'll miss you most of all, George," but he couldn't help feeling weirdly betrayed as she limped off toward her home without a word.

George shut the rear door, then he and Lou got back into the van.

"So ... New Zealand?" Lou asked.

"In a minute. I want to make sure she gets inside."

"You're not dropping off a date."

"Yeah, yeah, fine, you're right. Let's go."

Every step hurt and she might be causing permanent damage to her ankle, as well as getting frostbite from walking in her bare feet, but right now Ally didn't care. She was free! She couldn't believe it. She'd thought she was going to die a horrible death at the hands of several different madmen today, but she was finally free!

Though she had a lot of new issues to work out in her life, for now she wasn't going to worry about anything but seeing Mom again. And Dad.

The back door of Dad's car opened and somebody got out. Ally stiffened a bit but kept walking.

Crabs.

Why had Dad brought him?

She'd only met Crabs once before, and that was plenty. He'd looked at Ally as if he wanted to lick her face. If he'd stopped by again, Ally would've asked Dad to keep him away during her visits, but fortunately he hadn't come back. She suspected that this was at Robyn's request (though she hated Robyn for stealing Dad away, she also couldn't deny that Robyn had always been nice to her) but hadn't wanted to bring up the issue.

"Hello there, young one," said Crabs. "I know some people who are concerned about you."

"I'm okay," she said, stepping up onto the curb with a wince.

"That's a lot of blood. I don't like to see a little girl bleed like that. Let me take you inside to see your mommy and daddy." Crabs reached out his hand.

Ally didn't take it. "I'll be fine."

"I guess you're a big girl now." Crabs walked ahead of her and opened the front door. She stepped past him and called out to Mom that she was home.

"Is it just me," George asked, "or was that guy seriously creepy?"

"He was a little creepy."

"Did you notice how Ally avoided him?"

"Maybe she's got a creepy uncle. C'mon, George, it's time to go."

"I don't like it. My gut tells me that something's wrong."

"My gut tells me that we're sitting here in a van filled with bullet holes outside the house of a girl we kidnapped today. This is not a good place for us to linger."

"I'm not sure if I get a vote," said Eugene from the cage, "but if I do, I'm voting with Lou. This is a bad, bad, bad place to linger."

"I'm telling you, there was something wrong with that guy."

"So what? He has nothing to do with us. She said it was her dad's car. Do you want to get recaptured? Do you want to go to jail?"

"I thought you were the one who was all concerned about her safety? You were the one who didn't want to kidnap her in the first place."

"I know!" said Lou. "And maybe that's why I'm feeling less guilt about the whole thing than you are! We've taken her back home. We're done. It's completely insane to still be here."

"As somebody who is teetering on the edge of insanity, I agree," said Eugene.

"Here's what we're going to do," said George, driving past the house. "We're going to drive around for five minutes, only five, and then we're going to drive past her street one more time."

"And what do we expect to see?" asked Lou.

"One less car. Mr. Dewey drilled a hole in her ankle. They'd take her straight to the hospital, right?"

"Yeah."

"So if we drive by and both cars are still there, we can agree that it's suspicious, right?"

"And then what? We walk up and knock on the door?"

"If we have to. I just murdered a psychopathic crime lord. I'm not so concerned about a mom, a dad, and a creepy uncle."

Lou shook his head. "No. This is stupid. I always go along with what you want, but we're in too much danger to hang around because of your gut. Eugene agrees with me. Let's go."

"Eugene doesn't get a vote."

"Well, I do. And I say we go."

"All right."

They drove in silence for a moment.

"We're going back there in five minutes, aren't we?" asked Lou.

"Yeah."

"Why do you even ask my opinion on things?"

"Ally ...?"

Robyn wanted to rush over and embrace her, but she was unwelcome enough in this house as it was, and she didn't want to make things worse by being the first one to hug Ally.

It was definitely the dress from the pictures, and it was torn as if the wearer had suddenly increased in size while it was on. No question about it—Ally was a werewolf.

This was *fantastic* news.

Robyn couldn't have children herself, a fact about which she occasionally found herself locked in the bathroom, silently weeping. Ally had always been somewhat cold toward her, for obvious reasons. But if she had just found out she was a werewolf, she'd be scared, confused, and seeking help.

Robyn would be there to help her.

They'd become far closer than even blood relatives.

Shane and Peggy came down the stairs. Peggy looked momentarily surprised to see Crabs standing there (did she even know who he was?) but then ran across the room and squeezed her daughter tight.

"Oh, thank God!" she said, bursting into tears. "Thank God you're home!"

"Who bruised you up?" asked Shane. "What happened to your foot? Who did that to you?"

"I'll tell you everything, I promise," said Ally. "I'm not sure we're safe, though. Can you take me to the hospital?"

"Of course, sweetheart, of course," said Peggy. "Let's go right now."

"Who did it?" Shane demanded. "Describe them. Did one have a thick black beard?"

Robyn almost let out a gasp. What was he doing? They couldn't talk about Lou and George right there in front of Peggy! There'd be plenty of time for questioning and vengeance later.

"None of that matters right now," said Robyn. "All that matters is that Ally is safe."

She opened the front door, and this time she did gasp.

Even though they were wearing facemasks, Ally recognized both of the men.

One of them, who she recognized from his jacket, was a guy with red hair and cruel eyes. The other was the man formerly wearing a white snowsuit—the one George hadn't killed.

The redhead pushed Robyn to the floor and pointed a gun at her. "Do not scream. Do not make a sound. If anybody tries anything, you're all dead, do you hear me?"

The other man waved his gun around at the rest of them. "*Did you hear him?*"

"Yes," said Robyn. "We hear you. We all hear you."

"We're only here for the girl. Nobody else gets hurt."

Dad stepped in front of Ally, shielding her with his body. "You're not going to get her."

The redhead pulled the front door closed behind him. "We don't have time to dick around. If we have to drag her out of here past everyone else's dead bodies, that doesn't bother me a bit. There are four other men waiting in a truck right outside, so if you think you're going to get out of here, you're wrong."

"I don't care if there are four hundred men waiting outside," said Dad. "You're not taking her. It's not going to happen. It's just not. So you can take your little toy guns and head right back to your trucks."

The redhead laughed. "You're heroic as fuck, aren't you? If somebody pointed a gun at me, I'd let them take my daughter and throw in my baby son free of charge."

"Just leave," said Dad.

"Everybody except the girl, get down on the floor. Anybody who isn't on the floor in three seconds dies."

"Please, don't!" said Ally, stepping out from behind Dad. "Don't hurt any of them. I'll go with you."

"The hell you will," said Dad. "You know that we called the police as soon as Ally walked through the door, right? They're on their way. You're going to get caught either way, so do you want to get caught with a kidnapped girl in your truck?"

"Her foot looks pretty bad," said the redhead. "I'm surprised you didn't call an ambulance, or tell the cops to meet you at the hospital. That's what I would've done."

"I don't care what you would have done."

"That's more than three seconds." He pointed his gun at Mom. "Why aren't you on the floor?"

"Mom, get down," said Ally.

Mom dropped to her knees.

"Flat on the floor."

Mom got all the way down.

"So that's one of you who doesn't die today." The redhead pointed his gun at Robyn. "You, down all the way."

Robyn also lay stomach-down on the floor, though she was leaning up enough to continue to watch the men.

The man in the bulletproof vest jabbed the barrel of his gun into Crabs' chest. "Why aren't you down yet? What are you, simple? Got nothing to live for?"

"I live in the moment."

Now the redhead pointed his gun back at Dad. "You're going to force me to make some noise, huh?"

Dad nodded. "I'm surprised you didn't invest in silencers."

And then, just like that, all at once, Dad transformed.

His clothes split apart, his body grew, and fur sprouted from his flesh like time-lapse photography of a plant growing. Within seconds, the process was complete.

It didn't matter that Ally had suspected that her own powers were inherited. Seeing that Dad was an actual werewolf surprised the hell out of her.

Mom shrieked.

The redhead shot Dad in the chest.

"Silver bullet, asshole," he said.

Dad walked toward him, snarling.

The redhead frowned. "Silver bullet, right?" he asked, looking over at his partner. "Weren't these supposed to be silver bullets?"

He shot Dad three more times before Dad stood right in front of him.

And now ... wait, *Crabs* was a werewolf, too?

And Robyn?

The redhead dropped his gun.

Brent glanced over at the house at the sound of the gunshot. "Idiots couldn't get her without shooting somebody," he muttered. "I told you we should've gone."

Sean stuck a couple of fingers under his facemask and scratched his neck. "Should we go in?"

Brent shook his head. "Not quite yet. Maybe they just killed her mother."

"You should go in after them," said Mr. Reith, who sat in the back seat.

"We don't know what's happening in there. There's no need to panic just because we heard one shot."

"I am your boss now," said Mr. Reith. "And I say that the girl is still extremely valuable, and that if we lose her again, I will take all of my anger out on you."

"What are you gonna do, whack me with your cane? I worked for Mr. Dewey, not you. You're lucky your old slow ass is even in here with us."

"That's a very foolish attitude."

Three more gunshots came from inside the house, one after the other.

Sean scratched his neck again. "Damn it."

"All right, *now* we'll go in," said Brent. He looked back at that short little shit Glenn, who sat next to Mr. Reith. "All three of us, let's go."

Under other circumstances, Brent would've left Shawn or Glenn here, in the driver's seat in case they needed to make a quick getaway. But he didn't know Mr. Reith, and didn't trust him not to order the driver to speed off if things got crazy.

"Sean will remain here," said Mr. Reith, apparently reading his mind.

Brent shook his head. "Nope. Sorry." He didn't care if Mr. Dewey respected that shriveled old fossil; Brent had no idea who the hell he even was, and until Mr. Reith coughed up some credentials, Brent wasn't going to let him decide the course of action in a dangerous situation like this.

Brent took the keys with him as he, Sean, and Glenn got out of the truck and ran toward the house.

The redhead let out a soft whimper.

Dad looked over his shoulder at Ally and gave her the most frightening smile she'd ever seen, including scary dolls and clowns.

He swung his clawed hand all the way back, as if preparing to deliver a knockout punch, and then bashed it into the side of the redhead's skull.

His head didn't come off, completely. The blow ripped off most of the skin from his ear to his chin, snapped his neck, exposed most of his throat, and caused his head to flop to the side, but it remained attached.

That was not true after the second blow.

CHAPTER TWENTY-ONE

An Untidy Home

Ally and Mom both screamed.

Ally was glad the man was dead, but as when George had killed the men in the woods, she didn't like seeing it happen right in front of her. And watching Dad do it, even if he wasn't recognizable as her father right now, was far worse.

Dad grabbed the headless body before it fell and hoisted it into the air, letting blood rain down upon his fur. Then he flung the body against the staircase, snarling as the redhead's spine snapped.

This was not simply a case of "kill or be killed." Dad had enjoyed that murder. Loved it. Unlike Ally, he could control when he changed, but like her, he apparently couldn't control his bloodlust when he was in wolf form.

The other man fired a shot at Crabs, then he fired another shot at Robyn, then another shot at Crabs, and then before he could squeeze off a fourth shot they were both upon him. He didn't last long.

By the time the man landed on the floor, it was obvious that he stood no chance whatsoever of surviving, but that didn't stop Crabs from shoving his elongated mouth deep into the man's now-skinless stomach and slurping up a treat. Then he dug in with his jaws and pulled away, stretching something thick and red until it snapped.

He swallowed whatever it was, then reached in with his claws, scooping up a handful of something else and flinging it at Dad. Dad batted it away with his paw, knocking it to the floor in a thin red mist.

A food fight. Crabs and Dad were having a food fight.

Ally wanted nothing more than to pass out. Instead, she screamed some more.

"Dammit!" George shouted, as three men hurried toward the house. They were all wearing facemasks, but he could tell who they were: Sean, Brent, and the short guy with the thick sideburns. Checking up on Ally was just supposed to be a token gesture!

The men immediately split up: Sean running to the front door, Brent to a window, and the short guy around the back of the house.

"They're doing this fast and messy," said Lou. "We need to just run right in after them and take 'em out."

George nodded. "I totally agree."

Sean went inside, gun raised, leaving the door open behind him.

"Is there anything I can do?" asked Eugene from the back.

"Yeah, you can be our getaway driver."

"Is there anything *else* I can do? My hands aren't equipped for driving anymore."

George stopped directly in front of Ally's house. "If anybody comes out and it's not us, scare the shit out of them." He put the van into park. "No offense."

"None taken."

George and Lou got out of the van and rushed to the front door.

Desmond Reith remained hunched over until George and Lou had gone inside. At his age, ducking down like this was not an easy process, and if the thugs had bothered to pay attention they probably would have seen him back here. But they didn't.

The sound of more gunshots came from the house.

Desmond smiled. He didn't know what exactly was happening inside, but he liked the idea that Ally might have changed into her true form and started slaughtering Mr. Dewey's former employees. The men had chuckled amongst themselves when Mr. Dewey handed out the silver bullets. They wouldn't be laughing now, since of course Mr. Dewey had been lying to them. He couldn't risk having one of those idiots kill Ally.

Poor delusional Dewey Decimal. The man who believed that he could turn himself into a werewolf. Sorry, Dewey Decimal—even if George hadn't blown your tiny brain out, you couldn't change. You were either born a werewolf or you weren't. Getting bit by one meant nothing.

Desmond hadn't planned for Dewey to die, but it didn't bother him. He'd already served his purpose by unwittingly thumbing his nose at the Wolves. It was probably best for him that he'd received a relatively painless bullet to the head.

Brent had left him in the truck without keys, like a child. How helpless did he think Desmond really was? Desmond had never made a legal dollar in his life. Did Brent think that he couldn't hotwire a truck and leave him behind?

George stepped through the doorway, and immediately took a bucket of blood to the face.

Not from a literal bucket, but the quantity of blood that splashed over him was just like if somebody had flung a bucket's worth at him. It took him a moment to blink it out of his eyes, and when he did he saw that both of Sean's arms had been torn off. In fact, his shoulders were gone, too.

Ally had changed again.

No, wait, she hadn't. She was huddled on the floor with an older blonde woman. George was looking at a different werewolf.

Two different ... *three* different werewolves.

Shit.

The werewolf closest to George, which was the largest of the three, cocked its head to the side as it saw him. It dropped Sean's not-dead body to the floor, pointed at George, and then beckoned.

George felt that, all things considered, it would be in his best interest to decline that invitation.

Instead of wasting any bullets on these hell-beasts that were almost certainly invulnerable, he spun right the fuck around, almost knocking Lou over.

He felt a clawed hand on the back of his jacket, and suddenly he was flying across the living room, not actually in mid-air but without anywhere near as much foot-carpet contact as he'd like. He fell to the floor before he struck the wall.

Seconds later, Lou joined him.

The biggest werewolf pointed to Sean's body, then leapt as high into the air as it could without hitting the ceiling. It curled into a ball, and landed with all four feet, claws extended, directly on Sean's torso. Then it jerked its arms and legs far apart, scattering Sean to both sides.

This was clearly done for George and Lou's benefit.

Where the hell were the police? A neighbor had to have called the police, right? There were gunshots and screaming and stuff; help had to be on the way!

Sean was unmistakably dead now. George fondly remembered the time when Sean had been one of the larger problems in his life.

Brent burst into the living room from whatever room he'd snuck into in the back. His presumed plan to open fire was abandoned as he saw the three werewolves and the condition of his buddy's body.

From the scraps of clothing that hung off his body, one of the werewolves was the creepy guy who'd been waiting in the car. He did a menacing walk across the room toward where George and Lou lay, but didn't pounce. He just watched them, grinning, as if daring them to try to get away.

The third werewolf, who was either a woman or a man who'd been wearing a bra, was standing in front of Ally and her mother. George couldn't tell if it was trying to protect them, or just save them for last.

Since George had tried to turn and run a mere few moments ago, he didn't judge Brent for doing the same. It wasn't cowardly to flee from a situation where you were completely screwed. Brent made it maybe three steps. His next few steps just consisted of frantic kicking as the largest werewolf lifted him into the air, holding him by the back of the neck with one hand.

The werewolf turned so that Brent was facing George and Lou, and then raked the talons of its free hand down Brent's body, opening him up from just below his neck to his waist, shaking his body so that more would spill out.

Then it did it again.

And once more.

The werewolf jiggled Brent around like a ragdoll, then snapped him over his knee. It was the first time George had ever seen an exposed spinal column.

A window broke in another room.

The werewolf guarding George and Lou ran out of the living room to investigate. For a split second George considered shouting out a warning to the short guy, then decided that there was no compelling reason to do that.

On one hand, George was happy to not be dead yet. The murders of Sean and Brent were clearly meant to terrify him and imply that he and Lou were next on the mangling block. He didn't know why Mr. Dewey's men were considered more disposable, but George was glad of it. On the other hand, it was very likely that he and Lou were being saved for a much worse fate.

With Sean and Brent dead, and the short guy probably soon to meet his demise, George decided that it didn't make sense to save rounds that could, if his aim was perfect and the werewolf wasn't expecting him to suddenly shoot, take out an eye or two.

As soon as George made his move, Lou seemed to understand his plan and they both opened fire.

They had a moving target before they squeezed off the first shot, and most of the rounds punched uselessly into the werewolf's chest. One nicked its ear, and one shattered a back tooth, which had to hurt like a son of a bitch even if you were a ferocious beast.

The werewolf howled in pain, though not as much as George would've howled if one of *his* teeth had been shot off, then dove at them.

"Dad! Don't!" screamed Ally.

Dad? Seriously?

George and Lou both hurled their empty guns at the monster. George hoped to hit the werewolf's eyes and send up a spray of eyeball jelly, but instead both guns bounced off the werewolf's skull, neither one cracking it open like an egg.

It was enough, however, to cause the werewolf to cease its attack for just a moment, which was in turn enough of a delay for the werewolf to absorb Ally's message of "Don't!"

It looked at Ally, then back at George and Lou, and then it smiled, tilting its head a bit to make sure that the grin they saw favored the side with the shattered, bloody tooth.

In another room, the short guy screamed.

The werewolf pointed at George, and then held up its hands, curled into fists in a "Put up your dukes" gesture.

"We'll pass," said George.

The werewolf gestured more emphatically.

"Ally, could you tell your dad that if we don't clear out of here, we're all going to prison?"

"Dad—"

The werewolf put a finger to its lips. Shhhhh.

Ally's mom, sobbing, put both arms around her daughter.

George reluctantly got to his feet and put up his own fists. The werewolf pointed at Lou, telling him to do the same thing. Well, at least it was going to be an unfair two-on-one fight. Lou stood up, with equal reluctance, and the two thugs stood there, fists in the air, in the proper position but not really ready to rumble.

The werewolf grabbed George by the shoulders and slammed him into Lou, almost but not quite knocking Lou off-balance. George delivered a vicious head-butt, bashing his forehead against the werewolf's snout just as Lou kicked the creature in the side.

It let go of George and stumbled away a couple of steps. Its facial expression seemed to say, "What the hell? You weren't supposed to put up a *real* fight!"

George and Lou rushed it.

It was a big scary creature, but screw it, they were big scary criminals. The average person, upon seeing George and Lou walking toward them in a dark alley, would crap their pants. Yeah, it helped that the werewolf was apparently not intending to simply rip them apart the way it had Sean and Brent, but still, George and Lou weren't going to go out like helpless victims.

Lou's tackle was somewhat more effective than George's. Lou was actually able to slam the werewolf against the wall, cracking the plaster, while George took a fist to the head and crashed into a recliner.

Better a fist to the head than talons.

The third werewolf strode back into the living room, dragging the short guy by one of his legs. Mr. Dewey's man was crying and pleading and unsuccessfully trying to dig his fingers into the carpet.

"Stop it, Dad!" Ally wailed. "Just stop it."

The werewolf pointed down at the short guy, then made a gesture that resembled snapping something in two. The other werewolf nodded.

The female werewolf suddenly transformed back into her human form. As with Ivan, George couldn't believe how quickly she could do this. If this had been a movie, George would've had a good chuckle over the cheesy special effects. In real life, it was more than a little freaky.

Before the change was complete she'd already put an arm over her breasts, as if anticipating that her clothing would not have survived the process. She was an attractive woman, probably in her late thirties. Maybe she was Ally's mother and the other woman was a babysitter or something.

Nah. The wolf-lady didn't look anything like Ally, while there was a distinct resemblance between Ally and the blonde who was still holding her tight.

"No time for games!" said the woman.

"Robyn, please, make them stop!" Ally shouted. "Just let us go! We won't say anything, I promise!"

"Can't you hear the sirens?" Robyn asked the other werewolves. "Kill them quickly so we can go!"

Next to the recliner was a tall but very small glass table with a metal frame. Kind of looked like IKEA furniture. There was a drink coaster on it but no drink.

George picked it up by one of the legs and wielded it like a club. The werewolves might kill him, but it sure as hell wasn't going to be quickly.

CHAPTER TWENTY-TWO

An Even Less Tidy Home

Desmond Reith smiled as he drove past the two police cars with their lights flashing and sirens blaring.

C'mon, you motherfucker, thought George. *Change back. Just for a second, change back so you can talk to the pretty lady in the shredded clothes. Do it. One second. That's all I need.*

The werewolf didn't change, so George bashed it with the table anyway, swinging it so hard that he thought his arms might pop out of their sockets, which had happened to him before and which was not pleasant. He could feel at least one of his chest gashes opening up even wider.

It was, George had to say, one hell of a good hit. Any non-wolfman who'd taken that hit would have a snapped neck right now. And Lou immediately followed with another kick to the chest that sent the werewolf careening backward into the wide-screen television set, knocking it off the stand.

The woman changed back into a wolf.

George wasn't watching the other werewolf and the short guy, but he heard a disgusting wet ripping sound and a cry of pain that was abruptly silenced.

This was no time to take a defensive approach. George hoisted the table, which no longer had the glass surface and thus no longer technically qualified as a table, over his head and charged.

This hit was nowhere near as effective as the first one. Ally's Dad blocked it with his hand, then tried to yank the table out of George's grasp. They stood there, playing tug-of-war for a few seconds, until it popped free of George's sweaty hands and the werewolf flung it aside.

The werewolf who'd murdered the short guy pounced, leaping across the room and knocking George to the floor. Its claws dug into his arm.

Ally's dad lunged at George, too.

No, he was lunging at the other wolf. Ally's dad dragged the other creature off of George.

Saving him for himself?

Lou frantically looked around the living room for something *he* could use to bash in the skull of a werewolf. There was no fireplace (and thus no fireplace poker), no really heavy books, no candlesticks...

There was, however, a goldfish bowl.

Lou hated to create collateral damage of the twin goldfish swimming in there, but one sometimes had to sacrifice the innocent when doing battle with the supernatural.

He picked up the bowl, sloshing water over the side. This was definitely a two-handed job, but, hey, you worked with what you had. The largest of the werewolves, obviously their leader, was still focused on George, and though Robyn growled out a warning, it came too late.

Lou didn't smash it against the back of his head like he'd intended, but the thick glass bowl did shatter against the werewolf's right shoulder blade. The werewolf let out a loud sharp cry, like a dog getting hit by a car.

And Lou still had a long jagged piece of glass in his hand. He thrust it at the other werewolf, jabbing it deep into his snout.

The werewolf pulled back, the glass still lodged in its face. It had no visible reaction. It plucked out the piece of glass and stared at it, almost quizzically.

Robyn, meanwhile, had a very strong reaction. She snarled with rage and went for Lou's throat. He blocked her with the stump of his missing hand, and he thought the pain of Robyn's claws digging into it might have been even more intense than the pain of having his hand bitten off in the first place.

Robyn slapped Lou with the back of her hand. He fell to the floor, landing on some of the shards of glass and at least one of the goldfish. His re-injured stump had already gotten blood all over his jacket.

He couldn't do this shit for much longer. He really wished he'd kept in better shape during their months in hiding. Push-ups, sit-ups ... something.

Ally felt an instant of intense horror as Lou's ass came down on Finny. But only an instant, then she returned her attention to all of the other horrible things happening around her.

Three dead human bodies in her living room. Not just dead—mutilated. It was a complete gorefest in here. How was she supposed to cope with this?

George smacked the metal table frame against Dad again, buying himself enough time to get back to his feet. George backed away and held up the table as if he were a lion tamer.

The sirens were much closer now. Definitely on their street.

Robyn pulled Lou to his feet, then shoved him toward George. George moved out of the way, and Lou struck the recliner and fell once again to the floor. These guys spent a lot of time on the floor.

Robyn changed back to human. This time she apparently didn't care if everybody could see her boobs. "Stop," she said. She didn't shout this, but instead hissed it like a schoolteacher who is one tiny step away from a meltdown. "Change back so I know that you understand me."

Dad reverted to his human form. A moment later, so did Crabs. Dad had blood gushing out of the side of his mouth, adding to all of the gangster blood that was already on him. Crabs was also covered in other people's blood, but in human form you could see that Lou's piece of glass had done serious damage to his nose.

Neither of them seemed bothered by the pain, though. If anything, Dad seemed more exhilarated than Ally had ever seen him, like he was having the best day of his life.

Robyn looked out through the open door. "There are two police cars out there," she said. "Four cops. Shane, you and Crabs need to go out there right away, and you need to kill them. Do not play with them. Kill them. If you do it right now, when they don't know what to expect, you can get all four of them. Kill them quick and come back. Then we'll leave with Ally. If you keep acting like we're at an amusement park, this will end badly for everyone. Do you understand?"

Dad and Crabs both nodded. Then they transformed back into wolfmen and ran out of the house.

Robyn turned toward Ally. "You're coming with us. I hope you realize that it's in your best interest."

Ally shook her head. "No."

Glass shattered outside.

George stood there, still holding the metal table frame, clearly unsure what to do. He traded glances between Lou, who hadn't gotten up, and Robyn. Then he rushed at Robyn.

She changed, just her arm, and grabbed the frame out of his hands as he swung it at her. She swung it back, bashing George in the side. He stumbled backwards, struck the recliner that kept getting in his and Lou's way, and landed on the cushioned seat.

"Get back up," said Robyn. "I dare you. Shane will be furious if I kill you, but he'll get over it."

George didn't get up. Ally didn't know if he was heeding Robyn's warning, or if he just wasn't physically able to stand right now.

"You need to be with your dad right now," said Robyn.

"No!"

"If you try to take my daughter from me," said Mom, "I'll kill you."

Robyn sighed. "I'm not going to be the one who does that. If you want to get in the way of Shane and Crabs when they come back, be my guest, but this is one of those deals where if you really love someone you'll let them go."

"Go to hell," said Mom. She patted Ally's shoulder and began to stand up. "Come on, let's go."

Gunshots outside.

"Do *not* move," said Robyn. "I'm not a thrill-killer like your ex, but I've done it, and I won't lose a second of sleep if I do it to you. Get *down*, Peggy. Don't make me ruin you."

Mom crouched back down.

"Thank you."

More gunshots and shouting outside.

George realized that this was a very good time to run.

He was no coward, but he believed in the wisdom of an occasional retreat. Though George didn't want to leave Ally with her psycho werewolf father, there was no evidence that Shane meant to do her any harm.

Ally's mother might be in deep shit if she tried to stop them from taking her, but as heartless as it was to say, that wasn't George's problem. He and Lou needed to get out *now*, while Shane and Crabs (*Crabs*? What the fuck?) were busy murdering police officers.

It wasn't a chivalrous plan, but these were not chivalrous times, and George and Lou wouldn't do her any good lying in pieces on her living room floor next to the other thug corpses.

George stood up and pulled Lou to his feet.

"Sit back down," Robyn warned him.

George ignored her. Instead, he and Lou hurried toward the kitchen. There was definitely a door to the outside, since that's how Brent had come in. George's guess—and his desperate hope—was that Robyn wouldn't try to stop them, because if she did, that would give Ally and her mother an opportunity to escape, and "keep Ally from escaping" was probably more important than "keep George and Lou from escaping."

They made it to the kitchen. Robyn shouted that she was going to kill them, but she didn't follow.

"What about Eugene?" asked Lou.

"He'll be better off without us," said George. "The next wave of cops will help him. Poor guy could use a trip to the hospital."

"So could I."

George grabbed a dishtowel off the refrigerator handle as they made their way toward the still-open back door. "Nah, you'll be fine. You're a tough guy, Lou."

"You're saying that while we're running away."

George had no response to that.

As they left the house and stepped into the fenced-in backyard, George suddenly changed his mind. Not in a "We can't abandon this poor girl at her time of need," way, and not quite in a "How the hell are we going to get over this fence?" way. It was a "We look suspicious at the best of times, and right now we're covered in blood; maybe wandering around a suburban neighborhood trying to find a new vehicle isn't the best idea."

A slightly better plan, though still kind of a shitty one like all of today's plans, would be to hide around the side of the house. Once they were done killing the cops, the two werewolves would go back inside. If they both went, that would give George and Lou a very, very short opportunity to run to the van.

Though George was no fan of cops, he didn't like that these poor bastards were doomed (or possibly already dead and shredded). But he couldn't think of any way to save them that wouldn't put himself and Lou in much worse jeopardy. To make himself feel better, he'd just assume that these were corrupt cops with no families who hated babies, kittens, and burgers.

They reached the front corner of the house just in time to see the last of the four cops being dragged from his vehicle. The other three cops were dead, but the werewolves had obviously followed instructions and done it quickly and efficiently, with no unnecessary flinging of limbs.

Crabs bashed the last cop against the side of his car, apparently to make him stop struggling. Then he grabbed the cop's head with both hands and gave it a sudden sharp twist, snapping his neck. He continued to twist until blood started to pour, then dropped the body as Shane waved him back toward the house.

As soon as Shane and Crabs went inside, George and Lou half-ran, half-stumbled over to their van. The truck that had brought Mr. Dewey's men was gone; had somebody else been in there?

George and Lou got into the van. Eugene sat up as George started the engine.

"So, werewolves, huh?" he asked.

"Yep."

"Okay. Okay. I just, okay."

"No need to say anything," George assured him, as they drove away from Ally's house.

"I was going to go inside. I thought, hey, I have less to live for than anybody in there, why shouldn't I try to help out? I have no skills but I can at least take a bullet for somebody, right? Then the police showed up and I thought, oh, good, law enforcement is here, there's nothing more to worry about. Then these ... these ... these ..."

"Werewolves."

"These *werewolves* came out of the house and started murdering the police officers! Smash, rip, smash, rip, smash, rip! I just ... I just, I want to say that they're men in wolf costumes, but people in costumes can't jump around like that, and, oh, man, I know I've got to be drugged but I don't feel drugged and don't remember taking any pills or getting any shots, but ... where's Ally?"

"We had to leave her."

"You left Ally?"

"Yeah."

"Why?"

"Because things got out of hand! Didn't you hear all the shooting and screaming? You just watched four cops die. Why do you *think* we left her?"

"I didn't see the fourth one die," said Eugene, "although I guess I knew it was coming." He sniffled. "I don't like that you left her. She seemed like a good kid."

"She'll be okay. One of the werewolves is her dad."

"Oh. That's not something I expected you to say. I don't know how I feel about that. Is Lou okay?"

Lou certainly didn't look okay. He'd gone completely pale and was sweating like crazy. George handed him the dishtowel. "Hey, buddy, tie this around your hand. Try to stop the bleeding."

"I can't tie it with one hand."

"Then hold it against it."

Lou pressed the towel against his stump. It turned red right away. This was bad. George was in awful shape himself, but they really needed to stop that bleeding or Lou's life could be in danger.

"Stay with me, Lou. As soon as we get out of this neighborhood, I'll find a place where we can lay low, and we'll get you patched up."

Lou let go of the towel so that he could wipe the sweat off his forehead. "This is kicking my ass," he said. "And we're leaving a girl to die."

"She's with her dad!"

"Her dad is in the middle of a killing spree."

"Maybe the killing spree is over! Dewey's men are dead and the cops are dead, so maybe that's all the killing they needed to do this evening! Do you want me to turn around so we can get ground up some more? On the way there you were saying that you didn't *want* to go, and now that it went badly, you want to go back? Make up your frickin' mind!"

"I wasn't saying that I wanted to go back. I was just saying that we were leaving her to die. I'm sad about it but not saying that we should do otherwise."

"Fair enough."

"Where'd they go?" demanded Shane, changing into his human form as soon as he walked back into the living room. He spat out some blood. Though his molar hurt, he had to admit that it was a good kind of pain, an electrifying pain that let him know that he was more alive than he'd ever been. Good thing his mouth had been in wolf-form when the bullet hit, or it would've gone through his cheek first.

Robyn pointed to the kitchen. "That way."

"And you let them go?"

"I'm guarding Ally!"

"Crabs, go after them!"

"Can they be my victims?"

Shane didn't answer right away. Finally, he nodded. "Yeah, you can kill them if you absolutely have to. Try to save them for me, though."

Robyn shook her head. "Crabs, no. You listen to me. You go after them, and you kill them both. Do *not* save them for Shane. Kill them. We've got Ally, and that's what's important, so we need to drop the revenge and just get out of here."

It kind of surprised Shane that he didn't want to slap the shit out of her for saying that. But he was on a high right now, better than anything he'd ever felt in his life. He couldn't believe that he'd sustained himself for so long with the occasional murder of a filthy, reeking vagrant. His whole body tingled. He didn't even care about the pain, or the fact that later he'd have to spend some time digging bullets out of his flesh, or the fact that he'd almost surely have to leave his old life behind forever. Why had he ever cared about his ridiculous job? He felt absolutely fucking great.

So great that he didn't even need to kill George and Lou himself. As long as they died, who cared?

Okay, as long as they died *horribly*, who cared?

Crabs changed back into a wolf and ran into the kitchen.

Shane licked some blood off his fingers, resisting the urge to burst into hysterical laughter. God, this felt fantastic. This is how they were going to live from now on. Free. No supervisors, nobody clucking their tongue because he'd taken a forty-seven minute lunch instead of forty-five, no tedious meetings or smokers or mandatory baby showers. They'd live as wolves, hunting prey whenever they felt like it. No rules. No responsibility.

He reached out his hand to Ally. "Come with us. It'll be great, I promise you."

Ally shook her head.

"I understand that this is all kind of overwhelming right now, but you belong with us. Do you think your mom is going to be able to help you figure this all out? This will all work out, I swear to you, but we really need to get going."

"No."

Shane clenched his fists. He suddenly realized that he had a great big erection, right there in front of his daughter. Luckily, what remained of his pants was covering the actual skin, and she'd just have to get over this kind of thing.

"Ally, I know you're scared," said Robyn. "That's totally normal. I was scared out of my mind when I first discovered my power, and I didn't have my dad to help me understand it. We can train you."

"Get out of here," said Ally. "Just go."

"We can't do that," said Robyn. "So let me explain this another way. Four police officers, good men with families of their own, are dead. More of them will be on the way. If they show up here before we're gone, they will die. Are you okay with that? Are you okay with more innocent people dying?"

Ally began to sob again, but she stood up.

"No!" Peggy stood up as well. "You touch her, and I'll—"

Robyn only changed her index finger, enough for it to sprout a talon. With a quick flick of her hand, she slashed it across Peggy's neck. Peggy's eyes went wide and she grabbed at her throat, blood spurting between her fingers.

"She doesn't need you any more," Robyn told Peggy, as she fell.

CHAPTER TWENTY-THREE

Crabs Unleashed

Blood.

Bloody blood.

Georgie and Louie had leaked on the kitchen floor. It smelled delicious. But Crabs could not lap it up right now. No. Not now. He would get more blood from the source. Right from their wounds. Would he drink from their existing wounds? Or make brand-new ones? Perhaps he would do both. Lick the existing blood until it was all gone. Then make more blood appear with his teeth.

He would think of Ally while he was doing it.

That was not a good thing to think about. Shane might be mad if he knew. These were his own thoughts. Thoughts for his own mind. And what Shane did not know would not hurt him. It might hurt Ally.

Shane knew. Crabs thought he knew.

Crabs would not do anything to Ally while Shane was there.

He was only joking with himself about Ally. He would not hurt her. He would not want to hurt her. If she was bleeding from the belly he would not kiss her to make her all better.

The men were not in the kitchen, so Crabs left the kitchen.

They were not in the back yard.

He knew which way they had gone.

Crabs ran around to the front of the house. A van was driving away. They were in it.

He could not outrun a van on the highway. But he could outrun a van that was on a street lined with pretty houses. The van was not driving as fast as a van could go. He could catch it.

The people inside were all filled with blood. He would drain them like a million mosquitoes.

It would not take long to go back into sweet Ally's house and tell Shane. They could chase the van together. It would not take long, but it might take long enough that Crabs would lose them. He did not want to lose them. He would go alone. And get all the blood for himself. And the meat. And the bones. He liked to gnaw on bones. He liked to imagine that the bones were still attached to a skeleton woman, who screamed and screamed as he gnawed on her leg.

Crabs had already started chasing the van before he even decided that he would not go back for Shane.

He wished he could fuck Robyn.

Shane would let him. They had talked about this. Robyn would not. He had not talked about this to her. He believed Shane when he said that she would not.

He had almost caught up to the van.

He was not hungry. But he could eat.

"George! Werewolf!"

George checked the rear-view mirror. "Where?"

"Right behind us," said Eugene. "Drive faster!"

George accelerated. He wasn't much concerned with witnesses at this point, but he definitely did not want to careen off the street and crash into somebody's home. "How close?"

"He's right here!"

"Is he running on all fours?"

"No! Up like a man! But he's fast!"

George slammed on the brakes.

Nothing happened.

"Why did you stop?" asked Eugene. "You're supposed to be driving faster, faster, faster!"

"He was supposed to smack into the van!"

"He didn't!"

There was a loud thump as something, most likely a werewolf, jumped onto the roof of the van.

"That's him! That's him!" shouted Eugene.

Lou quickly rolled up his window. A streak of Mr. Dewey's blood remained on the glass.

"It's okay! This isn't the first werewolf I've had on the roof of a van!" George accelerated again, then slammed the brakes, trying to dislodge the beast. He tried that a couple more times, but it wasn't working.

"They can break windows with their hands!" Eugene said. "I saw them do it!"

"Shut up! I'm trying to hear if it's moving around up there!"

George did the brake-and-accelerate thing again. No werewolf tumbled off the roof.

"Screw it," said George. "Let's see how well it hangs on when I'm doing eighty."

George floored the gas pedal, building up speed for the next couple of blocks, then took a super-sharp right turn at the corner.

There was a scraping sound on the roof, then the wolfman fell off and struck the pavement, landing on its side.

"Ha!" shouted George. "Suck it, Crabs!"

"He's getting back up," Eugene said.

This would probably be a good time to drive away. But it was an even better time to try to squish a werewolf under the tires of the van. George slammed on the brakes, put the van into reverse, then floored the accelerator again.

The van shot backwards, headed straight for Crabs. The werewolf stood there, unmoving, as if daring them to try to run it over.

Right before the van would have smashed into him, Crabs leapt up.

Another *thump* on the roof.

"He's on the roof again!" Eugene shouted.

"I know!"

"Why'd you let him do that?"

"I wasn't trying to let him do that!"

"Why didn't we just drive away?"

"Because if he hadn't leapt back onto the roof, he'd be dead! We'd have one less werewolf to deal with! Do the math!"

George braked, put the van into drive, and then accelerated again.

"I'm not trying to be ungrateful for what you did for me," said Eugene. "You saved my life. All I'm saying is that the werewolf had stopped being on the roof, and now he's on the roof again."

"You shut the fuck up," said George. "You do not have permission to question my choices! If Lou wants to yell at me because the werewolf is back on the roof, he's allowed to do that. But I just met you and I pulled you out of a hellhole, so all you get to do is sit back there in your cage and keep your mouth closed no matter what I do! Got it?"

"I don't like that you called it *my* cage."

"*The* cage. Now stop talking. If you see one of the other werewolves coming at us, you can alert me to that, and if you see a cop car that I didn't notice, feel free to otherwise speak up, but if you have criticism about what I'm doing here, even if you think it's constructive criticism, keep it to yourself. If you really need to get it out of your system, whisper it to yourself, or make a mental note so that we can discuss it at a later time, but right now, in this van, your right to make any comments about the way I'm handling our escape from this peril has been revoked. Understand?"

"Yes, sir," said Eugene. "You're really verbal when you get upset, did you know that?"

George slammed on the brakes again. This time the werewolf did not tumble off the roof. George floored the gas pedal. He was paying more attention to dislodging the werewolf than to the route he was taking, so they were still in Ally's neighborhood. He probably deserved some criticism for that.

"Lou, here's what we're going to do," said George. "Roll down your window. Be ready for him to reach inside, and when he does, you grab his arm and yank him off the roof."

Lou nodded, but he didn't actually reach for the window handle. His whole face was drenched with sweat. Even his beard looked soaked with perspiration. And he was pale, even by the standards of a guy who'd spent a lot of time hanging out in a shack in Canada. He looked absolutely horrible, like he might just keel over at any second.

"Lou? Lou, you still with us?"

"Yeah," said Lou. "I'm okay."

"You look like crap."

"Do I?" Lou pulled down the sun visor. He glanced at it, then pushed it back up. "There's no mirror on that one."

"Trust me. You look awful."

"I feel awful."

"We'll get you help. If we have to take you to a regular hospital, screw the consequences, that's what we'll do. Just stick with me, okay. Think non-bleeding thoughts."

"Yeah."

"But my idea about rolling down the window and yanking the werewolf off the roof when he reaches inside, that's still workable, right?"

Lou smiled and closed his eyes.

George suddenly felt violently sick to his stomach. This was not the kind of situation where Lou should be closing his eyes without having been hit by a tranquilizer dart. George knew that his partner was in bad shape and that they needed to get the bleeding under control soon, but this seemed to be far more serious than he'd thought. Lou wasn't bleeding *that* bad from his stump.

"Lou! Eyes open! Don't fade on me!"

Lou opened his eyes. They were glassy and unfocused. "I'm not going to die on you, George."

"If you do, I'll kick your—" George slammed on the brakes. "—ass!"

The werewolf fell off the side of the van.

It wouldn't take much to run him over. A good three-point turn and he'd be smushed underneath the tires. Or George could at least run over his leg. Let's see him jump back on the van with a crushed leg.

No. George floored the accelerator yet again and the van sped off.

"He's not on the roof anymore!" said Eugene.

"I know!"

"Nice work!"

"Is he following us?"

"Yeah."

"Close?"

"Not as close as before. I think you're losing him. Yeah, you're losing him. Just keep driving fast. He stopped. Yeah, he's done chasing us. I think we're clear!"

Crabs stopped chasing the van.

Damn them to Hades.

He could have had all that blood to himself. Now he had to share.

He had been frightened while on top of the van. He had not expected to feel this way. He was a werewolf. Werewolves were not afraid to be on vans in motion.

But he had been. He had felt unsteady. Instead of leaping onto the front hood and smashing through the windshield, he had only focused on trying not to fall off.

It was a waste.

Now he would have to return to Ally's house and tell Shane that he had let them get away. Shane would be furious.

Crabs noticed that a woman was standing in her front yard. She was staring at him. Her mouth hung open.

Shane would not want Crabs to leave witnesses.

Crabs got the woman before she could run back into her house, and, oh, she was scrumptious.

———

"I'm sorry I was a jerk about the werewolf on the roof," said Eugene. He sniffled. "I don't know what's wrong with me sometimes."

"It's totally fine," said George. They'd finally left Ally's neighborhood. George could hear sirens, but as long as none of them were directly behind him, he was feeling confident about their ability to get out of Tropper.

"How's Lou?"

"He'll be okay. We've been through some insane shit together, and he'll be ..."

The van was dark, so George refused to be terrified by the fact that Lou didn't seem to be breathing. He was breathing just fine. George simply couldn't see him in the dark. C'mon, how often could you actually see people breathing?

"Lou?" he asked, poking his partner in the side. "Lou, wake up. You don't get to sleep while the rest of us work. Hey, Lou! Wake your lazy ass up! Seriously, Lou, you're embarrassing yourself in front of our guest. Wake up."

George kept his eye on the road, but reached over and pressed his fingers against Lou's neck.

The lack of a pulse didn't mean anything, because George's fingers were cold and even if there *was* a pulse, he might not be able to feel it. Or even find it. What was he, a doctor? He didn't know how to find a pulse.

He pressed his thumb against Lou's wrist.

"Is everything okay?" Eugene asked.

"*You shut the fuck up!*" George shouted. "Just shut up! Stop talking! You're going to drive me out of my fucking mind! I should've left you to be sliced up some more, you fucking freak!"

And then, for the third time in his adult life, George began to cry.

CHAPTER TWENTY-FOUR

Loss

Peggy lay on the floor in a quickly growing pool of blood. It wouldn't take her much longer to bleed out. Seconds, maybe. At this moment, Shane realized that he was completely in love with Robyn.

Because he should have been pissed at her. Insanely pissed. He would have *loved* to slash Peggy's throat like that. It would have been one of the highlights of his existence. He'd fantasized about killing Peggy in all sorts of different ways, fantasies that often occurred while he was having sex with Robyn, and if he could watch Robyn slash Peggy's throat and be just as satisfied as if he'd done it himself, this had to be true love.

Maybe there was a ring in her future.

Shane would have really enjoyed watching his bitch ex-wife continue to stain her poorly vacuumed carpet, but they had to get out of here. No matter how invulnerable he felt, there was a limit to how many police officers he could murder before they finally became outnumbered, so they had to flee.

Ally hadn't screamed. In fact, she hadn't reacted at all. It was as if her mind was still processing the idea of her dead mother, and rejecting it. Good. She'd be easier to deal with if she was in a semi-catatonic state.

Shane stood there just long enough to watch Peggy's final death twitch. He wanted to kick her in the face, open her throat up wide, but, no, for Ally's sake he had to maintain the illusion that Peggy's death hadn't been fun for anybody.

He transformed and scooped up his daughter. She didn't resist. He hurried out of the house, followed by Robyn, who didn't change.

Several of the neighbors were standing on their front porches, and Shane was amused by the thought of them seeing a wolfman carrying a teenage girl, followed by a mostly-naked bloody woman. Robyn had great tits, but Shane was pretty sure that the neighbors were watching him instead.

Should he throw Ally in the trunk or in the back seat? She'd be a lot less trouble in the trunk if she decided that she needed to escape from them, but the more awful things he did to her, the more difficult it was going to be to reconcile later.

Still, if she changed while she was in the back seat, it would be problematic. Better to go with the trunk, just in case. Once the neighbors had seen a werewolf walking out of the house, it didn't really matter if they reported a young girl going into a car trunk. If any of them tried to be heroes, well, another few corpses wouldn't make a whole hell of a lot of difference at this point.

None of them tried to be heroes.

Pathetic cowards.

Though Shane stood at the rear of the car, Robyn didn't seem to realize that he wanted her to open the trunk. She got into the driver's side, closed her door, started the engine, then opened the door again and looked out, annoyed. "What are you doing?" she asked. "Get in!"

Shane rapped his knuckles against the trunk lid.

"No. We need to talk to her."

Shane knocked again. If she made him change back to yell at her...

She popped the trunk lid. He opened it. Damn it. The trunk was full of all kinds of crap. When was the last time Robyn had bothered to clean this out? There wasn't room to put Ally in here, and there wasn't time to start emptying it, so she'd just have to go in the back seat.

Shane slammed the trunk closed, then opened the back door and shoved Ally, who seemed barely aware of her surroundings, inside the car. He got in after her just as he noticed Crabs running back toward them.

"Why is that idiot running right in the middle of the road?" Robyn asked. "Everyone's going to see him!"

Shane chuckled. "Sweetheart, we're long past that."

"Really? You think we're past the point where we have to be cautious?"

"Yes, actually. Admit it. This is awesome. I can't even explain how great I feel right now. We should've done this a long time ago. Think about how much of our lives we've wasted by not embracing what we truly are."

Robyn shook her head. "The only good thing to come out of this is that we've got Ally back."

"What are you talking about? Hell, you're the one who slashed Peggy's throat."

"And I did it because we were out of time. I didn't *want* to do it."

"You can't tell me you didn't enjoy that," Shane said, leaning across Ally so that he could open the opposite door for Crabs. Crabs started to climb into the back seat, until Robyn turned around.

"What are you doing? Change first."

Crabs changed back into a human, then got into the back seat. Robyn started driving before Crabs could even close the door.

"Robyn killed Peggy," said Shane.

"Did she?" Crabs grinned. "Was it a transcendental experience?" Crabs was always a little difficult to understand when he spoke, and it was even harder now that he had blood running out of his split nose. He didn't even bother to wipe it off. Shane admired that.

"It needed to be done to get us out of there," said Robyn. "There was nothing 'transcendental' about it. You two psychos need to get yourselves under control, or you're going to wind up in prison."

"Or a zoo," said Shane.

"Go ahead and joke. This is really hilarious. That's fine. I don't have a problem with being the party-pooper, because you'll thank me when you're not sliced up and being studied under a microscope."

"Don't worry about her," Shane told Crabs. "She's more excited than we are. You can see it in her eyes."

"May I see your eyes?" Crabs asked.

Robyn, not surprisingly, did not look back to let him see her eyes. But Shane knew the truth. Her pupils were dilated just like they were when he was giving it to her really good, and if Crabs and Ally weren't in the car with them, she'd probably be looking for a place for them to pull over. Hell, maybe she'd try to figure out an excuse to leave Crabs and Ally alone for a few minutes, so that they could transform and get it on, still covered in blood.

"George and Lou," said Shane. "Dead?"

Crabs inspected some blood underneath his fingernail. "No."

"They got away?"

"In a manner of speaking."

"What manner of speaking? They either got away or they didn't."

"Then they got away. They drove off into the sunset of their lives. But I smelled a lot of blood. Where do kidnappers go to treat their wounds?"

"Robyn did get Lou pretty bad. My baby's killing all kinds of people today!"

"Mom?" asked Ally, in a soft voice.

"Mom's not here," said Crabs with a giggle.

"Don't make jokes about the death of her mother," said Shane, punching Crabs in the shoulder, hard. "The hell's the matter with you?" Shane placed a reassuring hand on Ally's knee. "Honey, your mom was holding you back. I know you loved her, but if she loved you, she wouldn't have tried to stop you from coming with us. We know what's happening with you. She doesn't."

Ally seemed to become aware of her surroundings, all at once, with a violent shudder. "Let me out."

"Can't do it, honey."

"She killed Mom."

"Mom brought it on herself. Someday you'll understand that. Why didn't your mom tell you what you really were? Did you ever wonder that?"

"She didn't know!"

"Of course she did. How could a mother not know that?"

"Mom was one, too?"

"Yeah," said Shane, hoping that Robyn wouldn't call him out on his lie. "She was. And she didn't say a damn thing to you."

"Neither did you."

"She made me promise not to! Believe me, honey, if your mom weren't so paranoid, I would've told you long ago."

Shane could see in the rear-view mirror that Robyn was glaring at him. Like, *really* glaring at him. He could legitimately be in deep shit with her, in a nookie-withholding manner, if he didn't set the record straight. And having watched her murder Peggy, he wasn't inclined to try to take the nookie without permission.

"Okay, that's not true," said Shane. "Daddy's just a little mixed up by all that's happened. Your mom was not a werewolf and didn't withhold anything from you. I didn't tell you, because I didn't think those genes had passed on to you, and would you have believed me if I told you?"

"Yes," said Ally. "If you'd changed into a werewolf, I would have believed you."

"All right. I can buy that. Look, you're going to go through a grieving process, and that's completely understandable. You may even hate me for a while. But I think you'll realize very soon that you're much better off. You don't have to worry about bullies at school, or anything."

"Dad, you work in a cubicle. You hate your life."

"Not anymore. Not anymore, honey. Everything changes tonight. We are going to roam free!"

"We're going to sleep out in the snow? Kill deer for food? What kind of fucked-up fantasy world are you living in, Dad?"

"Watch your mouth!" said Robyn. "I don't care what we've all been through, I will not have you using that kind of language in my car."

"You murdered my mom and you care if I say the f-word?"

"That's right. I do. And that's something you're going to have to accept, because you live with us now, and you're going to follow our rules, and quite honestly I'm getting sick of hearing about your mother. She's dead. We can't change that. Let's move on."

"Whoa," said Shane. "That's harsh."

"I was safer with George and Lou, and they're the ones who kidnapped me!

You're all insane!"

"Sanity is in the eye of the beholder," said Crabs.

"What the hell does that even mean?" asked Ally. She began to sob. "Let me go, just let me go, let me go, let me go, let me go!"

"Nope," said Shane. "Sorry, but you're clearly in a state of shock right now, and you don't know what's best. Just relax. Go to sleep. Dad will take care of everything."

"Where are we going?"

"Out of town before they start putting up roadblocks."

"Where after that?"

"Does it matter?"

"Yes, it matters! How could it not matter?"

Shane hated to admit it, but he kind of wanted to slap the shit out of his daughter right now. Why couldn't she see that this was the best thing for her? How the hell did somebody discover that she was werewolf and not want to be with other werewolves? And she said that *he* was insane?

He could hear police sirens, and loved the fact that he didn't really care. What were the cops going to do to them? Launch a missile at their car?

Crabs finally wiped some blood off his face. "A loose end remains untied."

"It wouldn't, if you'd caught them," said Shane.

"I don't have wheels or a motor. But now we're in something that does."

"Let it go," said Robyn. "We'll never find them."

"I have the scent."

"Seriously?" Shane asked. "You can track them down?"

"I make no promises. I doubt they're lingering."

"But you think you can do it? Even after getting that chunk of glass in your nose?"

"I do."

Shane rubbed his hands together in glee. "I love it. We'll hunt down the scumbags who stole Ally, and then we're off to do whatever we want, whenever we want! Unless *somebody* has a problem with that idea."

"We can't stay in this car," said Robyn. "We have to get another one, quick, and then you have to swear to me that if Crabs can't pick up the scent right away, we'll leave George and Lou for another time."

"I swear," said Shane.

Crabs held up three fingers in the Boy Scout salute. "Honor."

Robyn sighed. "Fine."

Shane would not be picky—they'd murder the driver of the first car that they could find in a reasonably isolated area. But he hoped it would be a beautiful woman. Preferably a blonde, long hair, well-endowed. Not too much makeup. If she looked like Peggy, all the better. But he wouldn't be fussy.

CHAPTER TWENTY-FIVE

Demise

George pulled the van over to the side of the road. This place wasn't secluded; they were on a two-lane highway with a bit of traffic, but right now George didn't care.

"Lou! Lou!" George slapped him in the face. "Come on, Lou, don't do this to me! Don't do this to me!"

George was blubbering like a goddamned baby, with snot and everything. He knew that Lou was dead. No amount of shouting and slapping and praying was going to change that. His friend was dead.

He heard the rear door of the van open, and for a second he thought that somebody was coming inside, but he glanced in the rear-view mirror and saw that it was Eugene, getting out.

"Please, Lou, you can't leave me like this. This is bullshit, Lou. You're not going to leave me alone. That's a dick move. A dick move, Lou. Please, c'mon, open your eyes. Open your fucking eyes."

Lou wasn't breathing. There was no trace of a pulse. He wasn't coming back.

Eugene opened the door. He was already shivering in the cold, since he remained dressed only in his boxer shorts. "What happened to him?"

George wanted to say something hostile. Instead, he just wept.

Eugene pressed his fingertips against the side of Lou's neck, being careful not to scrape him with his talons. Then he held his palm over Lou's mouth.

"Okay, no pulse, no breathing ..." Eugene reached for Lou's jacket, batted at the zipper, then gave up. "Can you unzip this for me?"

George unzipped Lou's jacket and pulled both sides open. Eugene pressed his pointy ear against Lou's chest. He squeezed his eyes shut as he listened for a heartbeat.

"There's nothing," said Eugene. "Oh, Jesus, George, I'm sorry. I know CPR but I can't do it by myself. I'll put his seat back." Eugene opened the side door, then reclined Lou's seat as far back as it would go before it hit the cage.

Eugene pressed his mouth over Lou's and gave two quick breaths. Then he tapped Lou's chest with the hand that was a paw. "Right here. Both hands. Push with your palms. Sharp upward pushes. Fast ones. Thirty times."

George put his hands on Lou's chest as instructed. He wasn't really at the right angle, but he contorted his body so he could do the pushes correctly.

"Count them off," said Eugene.

"One, two, three, four ..."

"A little harder."

"... five, six, seven, eight, nine ..."

At thirty, George took his hands away and Eugene pressed his ear to Lou's chest. "Still nothing." Eugene gave Lou two more breaths. "Again."

George did thirty more pushes. Nothing. Two more breaths from Eugene. "Again."

"Don't die on me, you asshole," said George. "I mean it. I will kill myself and hunt you down in hell if you leave me. I don't have any other friends, you selfish piece of shit. I've got nobody. I swear, Lou, I will find a gun and shove it right in my mouth just to kick your ass in hell. Don't test me."

Eugene listened to Lou's chest. "I ... I don't know what to tell you, George. There's just nothing there. I don't know what happened."

George knew what happened. Blood loss, two tranquilizer darts, stress, violence, and a body that was already high risk for cardiac arrest. The only surprising thing was that he didn't have a heart attack sooner.

A car pulled up behind them and stopped. There were no flashing lights, so it wasn't a police car. Just a Good Samaritan.

Eugene nervously looked back at the car. "I need to know what you want to do. Are we going to keep running?"

George punched the dashboard.

"George! Listen to me! If we're done, that's fine, but I'd like to know."

"We're still running."

"Okay. I'm getting back in."

Eugene hurried to the rear of the van. George heard a loud expletive as the Good Samaritan saw him. Then Eugene climbed back into the van, and the cage, and pulled the door closed behind him.

Lou was dead.

In a day where very little felt real, this was the most surreal moment of them all. How could Lou be dead? They'd spent virtually every waking moment together, driving each other crazy, for the past few months. Been a team for ten years. Neither of them were destined to live long, healthy lives, but it simply didn't seem possible that Lou was gone.

A heart attack. He'd died of a frickin' heart attack.

George wanted to swerve the van into the other lane, smash into something head-on, but with the way today had gone he'd survive the crash and end up as a limbless vegetable in a hospital ward.

He didn't believe in sentimental crap like, "Lou would have wanted me to go on and live a happy life," but Lou certainly wouldn't want him to commit suicide, go to prison, or get killed by those other three werewolves. The urge to smash up the van would pass.

His hand hurt. He'd really bashed it on the dashboard. Not a good idea to be injuring himself at a time when there were plenty of non-self-inflicted injuries available.

Eugene crawled to the end of the cage closest to George. "Will you be okay?"

"No."

"How long did you know him?"

"Don't talk to me."

"I'm just trying to help."

"Well, don't try, all right? You didn't just lose your best friend, so don't act like you're going to magically wave your werewolf wand and ease my misery."

"Sorry."

Aw, crap. Yeah, George was hurting right now, but Eugene had lost his son, his daughter, his wife, *and* been turned into a scientific art show experiment gone horribly wrong. If they wanted to play the game of Who Got Screwed Over Worse By Life, Eugene had him beat, big time.

"No, I apologize," said George. He blinked tears out of his eyes and wiped his nose on his sleeve. "It doesn't matter what I'm going through right now. That's not okay."

"It really is, though. I understand."

George looked over at his dead friend, hoping that he would somehow spring back to life. *Ha-ha, fooled you! Sucker!*

"Ten years," George said, his voice quivering as he returned his attention to the road. "I guess that's not so long in the grand scheme of things. There are a lot of people I've known longer. But we were partners. We trusted each other with our lives. It's like how a cop's bond with his partner can be stronger than the one he has with his wife, except that instead of catching bad guys we *were* the bad guys, and, you know, instead of protecting society we'd break people's thumbs."

"Probably more dangerous than police work," said Eugene.

"I know, right? At least if you're a cop you know that most of the people you work with aren't going to leave you for dead as soon as a job goes wrong. We had each other's backs. We might not have had anybody else's backs, but we had each other's."

Maybe this would be a good time for the cops to find them. George looked so pathetic right now that they might let him go instead of having to listen to this big tough guy bawl like a teenage girl whose boyfriend just broke up with her.

Crying time was over. He'd cry over Lou's grave after he buried him. Until then, he needed to focus. Mr. Dewey's death would definitely be a problem in the near future, but for right now all of the people he would have immediately sent out for vengeance were also dead.

He wished he knew how Ally was doing. Maybe once he had time to rest, heal, and try to gather some resources, he'd do some kind of rescue mission.

Yeah, right. Like he had any resources. He was about as useful to Ally as he had been to Lou.

George honestly didn't know if Mr. Reith's lack of being dead should be a concern. Was he the kind of person who would send men to Mexico or Canada to hunt George down? He had, as far as George knew, *wanted* the werewolf-kidnapping job to go badly, so maybe he was completely satisfied and George would never hear from him again.

So, if he took the optimistic view that he was in no current danger from Mr. Reith or Mr. Dewey's associates, and the cynical view that there was nothing he could do to save Ally, then the only thing he had to worry about right now was acquiring a new vehicle, and then getting someplace safe where he could hide out for a good long while.

Or he could hunt and kill those fucking werewolves.

"What do you want to do?" he asked Eugene.

"Right now?"

"Short term."

"Clothes would be great. Not Lou's. I hope you didn't think I meant that I wanted to take Lou's clothes."

"I didn't."

"Thank God. That would've been a horrible thing to suggest. I can't even imagine that you would've thought of me if I'd said that."

George took a moment to compose himself so that he wouldn't snap at Eugene again. "What I meant was, outside of the obvious need to get some clothes, what do you want to do? Do you want me to drop you off somewhere? Do you have any friends or relatives?"

"I do, yeah, but I can't just show up at their doorstep like this. They'd scream and hit me with something. That's what I'd do, if somebody like me just showed up after dark on my front porch. I'd set him on fire. Whoooosh, buuuuurn, crisp, crisp, crisp." Eugene cleared his throat. "I feel like I act more sane when you're acting insane. Maybe you should act more insane."

"Look, I apologized for what I said earlier, but I can't have you going whack-nut on me. I may be getting out of town, or I may be going Charles Bronson. Are you coming with me, or am I getting rid of you?"

"Which do you recommend?"

"Me getting rid of you. Because I'll be honest—right now I'm leaning less toward self-preservation and more toward revenge."

"I'm going to stay. Not trying to be contrary; I just think that, right now, I don't want to have to explain myself to anybody else."

"It's your funeral," said George. "And by that I mean a shallow grave with no funeral."

"I'll take it."

CHAPTER TWENTY-SIX

Romantic Interlude

The driver of the red sedan was not blonde, attractive, or even female. He was, in fact, a potbellied loser with dull, intelligence-free eyes. But he'd pulled over when Robyn waved to him from the side of the road, and he'd been fun to kill even if he was unpleasant to look at.

Ally had shouted out a warning to the poor bastard, even though Crabs was supposed to be keeping her under control, and she totally freaked after Shane tore out his heart. Okay, after Shane *exposed* his heart—it didn't actually rip out like he'd hoped.

So now she was in the trunk. Too bad.

They'd changed into their last set of spare clothes, then rubbed snow on their arms and faces and gotten off the most noticeable of the blood. If anybody looked at them up close or in the light, they'd know something was weird, but driving around they should be okay. To help even more, Shane was currently lying in the back seat, so that people would only see a man and a woman in the car, not two men and a woman.

Crabs had his window down, which Shane supposed was kind of suspicious in Minnesota in November, but not enough that people would point and scream, "Werewolves!"

"Keep driving in a straight line," said Crabs.

"Are you positive?" Robyn asked.

"I'd bet on me."

"That's not what I'm asking. If we're putting ourselves at this much risk, I need you to be positive."

Crabs said nothing.

"Should I take that as a no?"

"The science of smell is not exact."

"Then we're not doing this. How are you even smelling anything but your own blood? We're done. George and Lou will still be there to kill some other time."

"She's right," said Shane. "Abort."

"That would be a mistake."

"Then where are they?" asked Robyn.

"Close."

"How close?"

"Sixty seconds."

Shane sat up. "Seriously?"

Crabs inhaled deeply. "Yes."

"They're off the beaten path. But not far off. If we give up now, our life will be a thick ocean of regret."

"What is a thick ... you know what, I don't even care," said Robyn. "Just tell me where to go."

"Turn right when you can. Not that one. The next one."

Robyn turned right. There were no streetlights on this small, narrow road, but the tire tracks in the snow indicated that, yes, somebody had driven down here recently.

They passed a small brown home. A dog chained on the front porch barked at them.

"I hate dogs," Shane muttered. Some werewolves could control them, but it wasn't a skill that he, Robyn, or Crabs had ever been able to figure out.

They drove for another minute before they got to the next house. Shane kind of liked it out here. Secluded. They could do a lot of stuff without worrying about the neighbors seeing them. He'd have to look into property prices in this area.

"There," said Crabs.

He was right. The van with the bullet holes was parked in the driveway.

Shane laughed. "See? Why would anybody ever doubt your gift?"

Robyn pulled up right behind the van. Its engine was off. There were no lights on but it looked like somebody might be sitting in the front passenger seat.

"Think it's a trap?" Robyn asked.

"How would they know we're following them?" Shane asked. "Nah, they're probably ditching their vehicle just like we did. They could already be long gone."

"No," said Crabs.

Ally, inside the trunk, began to pound or kick on the lid again. It was annoying as hell, but Shane would have done the same thing in her place, so he couldn't really blame her.

"Robyn and I will check out the van, and then the house. You stay here. Make sure nothing happens to Ally."

"May I quiet her down?"

"No. You may not. Don't open the trunk."

Shane and Robyn got out of the car and cautiously approached the van. Shane peeked in through the back window. There was a large, empty metal cage in there.

Those sons of bitches had put Ally in a *cage*.

Shane's rage did not blind him to the fact that his daughter was currently locked in the trunk of a car. But that was different. It was for her own good. There was something symbolic about a cage that pissed him off to a degree that he couldn't even describe.

"Hey," said Robyn. "Come up here."

"What is it?"

"It's Lou Flynn. He's dead."

"Are you sure?"

"Look at him."

Shane peeked through the window. "He could be faking." Shane opened the door, transformed his right hand into a werewolf claw, then raked his talons across Lou's neck a few times. "Or not."

"So where's George?" asked Robyn. "Do you think he'd leave his friend behind?"

Shane shrugged. "They're not really honorable men."

"Looks like two sets of footprints leading to the house. Was anybody else with them?"

"Not that I know of."

"Maybe Lou walked to the house, then came back here before he died. No, there'd be blood on the ground. We'd better be careful when we check it out."

Shane and Robyn walked toward the house. It had a nice big yard, but the home itself was a dumpy little one-story hovel that was desperately in need of a new coat of paint.

The front door opened.

Shane froze, ready if necessary to transform and pounce.

Somebody walked out of the house.

Shane squinted, not sure exactly what he was seeing. "What the hell is that thing?"

"I have no idea."

The ... thing waved as he walked toward them. The fact that he was in a pair of boxer shorts in Minnesota in November was the least weird thing about him. He kind of looked half-human and half-wolf, but the wolf parts were badly stitched onto him. One of his ears looked like it was going to fall off. He was a complete mess.

"Stop," said Shane. "Don't come any closer."

The man blinked in surprise. "Sorry. I assumed I was the one in danger, not you. I won't make any sudden moves. It hurts me to move anyway."

"Get down on the ground."

"Come on, show some heart. I'm freezing to death. There's no reason to be antagonistic. We're all werewolves here, right?"

Shane walked closer to the man. Robyn followed. "What do you mean, we're all werewolves?"

"I was there for the massacre. George and Lou had me in a cage. Didn't you see me? No, I suppose you didn't, or you'd remember me. One of the few things I have going for me is that I'm memorable."

"I don't know what you're talking about."

"Why are you playing stupid? We're werewolves! We're supposed to be brothers!" He gestured to Robyn. "And sisters! Brothers and sisters! Family! We're all family! Maybe whoever is pounding inside of your truck is family, too!"

"You're not my family," said Shane. "I'd have put you in a garbage bag and thrown you in the Dumpster."

"There's no reason to be cruel," said the man. "My name's Eugene." He tapped his forehead, where the word 'WOLF' was carved. "Look what they did to me! Marked me! Sliced me! Mixed and matched parts that didn't go together!" He began to weep. "They messed me up so badly that I can't even morph anymore! I can't morph! Can you imagine how empty your life would be if you couldn't morph?"

"So what happened to you, exactly?" Shane asked.

"Lou and George captured me. Threw a net on me while I was leaving my house. Took me to a lab. Told me that I was being 'modified' to get the werewolfism out of me. Took away my dignity. Look at what those butchers did to me!" Eugene held out his arms and turned completely around in a slow circle.

"Is that a *tongue* on your back?" asked Robyn.

Eugene nodded. "There was no scientific merit to what they did. They just wanted to humiliate me!"

"Where is George now?"

"He stole a car and left."

"Leaving you behind?"

"His friend died. I think it hit him pretty hard. Good riddance, I say. They were both evil. I'm not saying that I haven't killed in my wolf state—I have, lots of times. But that's all instinct. These guys are just demons."

"Where did he go?"

"I don't know."

"What kind of car is he in?"

"Blue. Light blue."

"What model?"

"I don't know cars very well. One of those small ones. The boxy ones. From those commercials. Do you mind if I go back inside? As you can see pretty clearly, I'm not dressed for the weather, and I don't think I can handle getting frostbite on top of everything else that's wrong with me."

Shane punched Eugene in the jaw, knocking him to the ground.

"No, you may not go inside yet. I feel like you're holding out on me, man. That's not very nice to a fellow werewolf."

"What more do you need to know?" Eugene wailed. "George thinks he's some big werewolf hunter! He wants to kill us all! Wipe us off the face of the earth!"

"George and Lou are hired guns."

Eugene frantically shook his head. "No way. Maybe that's how it is on paper, but you didn't hear them talk. George is on some kind of holy quest, I swear I'm not making that up, the guy isn't right in the head. He wants us all in pieces floating in jars!"

"Your ear looks like I could pluck it right off."

"You don't have to be disrespectful like that," said Eugene. "I'm trying to share information with you."

Shane almost kicked him in the head to see how many teeth he could knock out, but, no, until they figured out what was going on, he should keep Eugene alive. *Then* he'd kick out his teeth. Shane didn't care if he was a fellow werewolf (and he seriously doubted it). Eugene was weak. Shane hated weakness.

Shane looked back at his new car. "Hey, Crabs!"

He heard the door open, and then Crabs walked up. Crabs wouldn't have been able to see Eugene with the van blocking his view, but he had no particular reaction to seeing him, as if he encountered people who looked like Eugene on a daily basis.

"Take a whiff. Is George still around?"

Crabs closed his eyes and inhaled deeply. "Yes."

"Good. Go check out the house."

Crabs nodded and stepped forward. Robyn held up her hand.

"No. Crabs, you make sure Eugene doesn't go anywhere. Shane and I will check the house."

Shane thought that was kind of odd, but he didn't care who did what as long as somebody went in there to flush out George, if the chickenshit was hiding.

"Don't you dare open the trunk," said Robyn.

"Your trust in me will be validated."

Shane and Robyn walked over to the house. It could still be a trap, but what kind of trap could George set with so little time? Was this his winter home where he kept a stockpile of silver bullets? Just to be safe, Shane changed right after opening the door. Robyn did so as well, and they walked inside.

The inside of the house showed a little more self-respect than the outside, but still, there was plenty the owners could have done to fix it up. When wallpaper starts to peel, you glue it back up or replace it. This wasn't brain surgery.

The TV was off. The house was silent. There was a bit of melting snow on the inside doormat, but that could have come from Eugene's feet.

"What do you think?" asked Shane, after they both changed back.

"Let's check out the bedroom," said Robyn.

"Seriously?" Shane was delighted. "Is that why we're here?"

"It's going to be fast and dirty," Robyn told him. "I can't wait anymore or I'm going to lose my mind. I'm giving you permission to be quick."

"What if George sees?"

"Then he'll get a nice little show that he can tell his friend about. Oops, no, his friend is dead. George isn't in here. And if he is, we'll search when we're done." She walked over to the king-sized bed. "Remember: quick."

"But not *too* quick."

"I promise you I'll finish first."

Shane stepped up behind her. "As wolves, right?"

"Of course as wolves! Why would you even ask that? Why would I take this kind of risk if we weren't going to—"

"All right, all right, relax. I was just making sure."

Shane bent Robyn over the bed, and then they both transformed.

George, watching through the slots in the closet door, thought, *They're not really going to have werewolf sex right there, are they?*

Yes, they were indeed.

No foreplay. No lube. Within seconds of changing, Shane was thrusting away inside of her, while she snarled and writhed and ripped up the blanket with her claws.

Though George was all in favor of getting right down to business, this looked painful. It was the grossest thing he'd seen in a day that had been filled with one gross thing after another, but he couldn't look away.

Right now, Lou was lucky to be dead.

To make things even more awkward, George was sharing this closet with Tom and Betsy, an elderly couple who'd been kind enough to let an injured man into their home. They couldn't see what was happening and didn't know that there were werewolves involved, but they *did* know that there was violent fornicating happening right on the other side of their closet door, on their bed, and they both looked suitably horrified and appalled.

George hoped like hell that they wouldn't make any noise, although he was uncertain that he'd be able to remain silent himself if this nightmare didn't stop soon.

Robyn climaxed, unless she was faking it at an extremely high volume.

Shane followed immediately. He did it internally, thank Christ, or George would have reached up, grabbed a coat hanger, straightened out the hook, and used it to stab his eyes. In fact, if they didn't quiet down in the next few seconds, he might use one to pop his eardrums.

CHAPTER TWENTY-SEVEN

Eyeball Bleach

George couldn't help but wonder what would happen if Robyn changed back into a human before Shane withdrew. This was not information he wished to acquire in any form, whether a first-hand sighting or a second-hand anecdote, but he couldn't stop his mind from going there.

Fortunately, they separated before they changed back. Their clothes were in terrible shape. Which was a point of concern, since George was currently hiding in a closet, which contained clothes that they might want to steal.

Instead, with their scraps of clothes barely hanging off of them, Shane and Robyn left the room. They didn't even cuddle. Hell, Shane didn't even give her a quick, "Hey, thanks, babe," kiss.

George glanced over at Tom and Betsy. He'd done a lot of terrible things in his life, but never had George felt that he owed somebody an apology more than at this moment.

But he shouldn't speak. Alerting the werewolves to his presence because he wanted to apologize would not be the brightest thing he could do.

He heard the front door close as they left the house. They weren't even here to look for him. They just wanted a place to get it on.

"I am so very sorry," George whispered to the elderly couple. "I had no idea that was going to happen. I truly thought they were just coming in here to kill me."

Tom and Betsy had nothing to say.

"Don't leave the closet for at least a couple of hours," George told them. He figured that the werewolf danger would be over long before that, but he didn't want them calling the police.

"Yes, sir," said Tom. He'd looked nervous when George first knocked on his door, and he looked quite a bit more nervous now. He would be forever haunted by what he'd heard.

George slowly opened the closet door, which of course creaked loud enough to make George worry that Shane might have heard it from outside.

"Any chance you two have anything silver?" George asked. "A knife?

Crucifix? Fork?"

Betsy shook her head. "Only my earrings."

"That probably won't cut it. I'm going to steal some of your stuff before I leave. Is that okay?"

———————

"Did you kill him already?" Crabs asked.

"He wasn't in there," Shane said. "We looked."

Crabs narrowed his eyes and licked his lips. "You did other things."

"Shut up, Crabs," said Robyn.

"You went in there and had intercourse. Intercourse. We heard it, and I can—"

"I'm serious, Crabs," said Robyn. "If you keep talking, I will rip your jaw off. I mean that literally. Literally. I will literally tear your jaw off if I hear one more word about what you think we might have done in there."

Crabs shrugged. "I was not defining you by your choice. I am not fortunate enough to have a partner, or I would have done the same thing, sooner. But George still lurks."

Eugene, who was still on the ground, looked absolutely miserable. Shane thought it would be kind of funny if, after everything this poor bastard had obviously been through, his ultimate fate was to freeze to death. He could've been saved by a jacket.

"I already told you that George is gone," said Eugene. "He stole a car and drove away. He's getting further and further and further and further away with every second we don't go after him. You're standing around talking about intercourse while he gets away."

"That's not your problem," said Shane.

"It *is* my problem! It's my problem, big-time!" Eugene slowly and shakily got to his feet. He wobbled a bit but remained upright. "I need revenge. The only reason I haven't slashed my own neck with these surgically attached fingernails is because I need revenge before I die. You three are keeping me from that. Right now. Right now at this moment you're keeping me from revenge. *I need revenge!* Vengeance! Payback! Retribution! Eye for an eye! Tit for tat!" Eugene swung the hand that was a wolf paw menacingly in the air. "Death to George and Lou! I'm halfway there, but I didn't get to kill Lou myself, so it only barely counts! Death to George! Death to George!"

"What the hell is the matter with you?" asked Shane.

"For real? You can really look at me and ask that question? You're not taking this seriously! None of you are taking this seriously! Let me explain this in single-word sentences so that you can follow the message I'm trying to convey: George. Is.

Getting. Away. Right now he is in a boxy light blue car, in motion. Are any of us in motion? I'm not in motion, I can tell you that much. Let's go, go, go! Let's get in your car and go! I've said all of this and yet we're all just standing here! What's the deal with that? Car! Go! Now! He's on his way to Melville Park right now!"

"Melville Park?"

"Yes, Melville Park! Why are you always three steps behind me in this conversation? You need to take me to Melville Park!"

"I'm not taking you anywhere."

"Except Melville Park, right?"

"What's he doing there?" Shane asked.

Eugene sighed with exasperation. "That's where he's answering for me and the girl getting away. You have to answer for that kind of thing when you're dealing with your superiors. That's where the money drop-off is going to happen. That's where everything is going to happen, but is that where we are? No. I'm looking around, hoping to see that I'm in Melville Park, but instead I'm still at the house where George stole the car that he could drive to Melville Park. This is bullshit, bullshit, bullshit."

Shane gave him a not-so-light shove. "Watch the potty-mouth. My girl doesn't like cursing."

"And she's right not to. It's the sign of a small, simple mind. I should have found another word. Come on, you have to take me there, I can't stay here, I have to get him, I have to get George, I have to get George, I'm a werewolf who can't morph, I need revenge, can't you see that, can't you see that, can't you see that?"

The freak was about to have a complete meltdown right there. No way was he riding along with them, even if his body weren't so messed up.

"Sorry," said Shane. "You can just hang out with Lou here. He looks lonely."

"Oh, that's funny. That's a jolly funny laugh. You know, that's how people end up going to hell. Do you think God wants to hear you say things like that? Do you think he's up there giggling at that witty thing you just said, or is he judging you? I think he's judging you. And I think that when you're sizzling in that pit of lava, you're going to look back and wonder if it really was just a great idea to—"

"Enough," said Shane. "Everyone back in the car."

"Thank you," said Eugene.

"Not you."

"You know what? Fine. I forgive you. You have my forgiveness."

Shane, Robyn, and Crabs got into the car. "Are you sure we shouldn't bring him along?" asked Robyn. "He may know more than what he's said."

Shane shook his head. "No. I'll kill him if I have to be trapped in a car with him. And, I'm not sure if you noticed, but he's the kind of guy who would attract attention."

Eugene placed his hoof on the side window. "Please?"

"Get back in the warmth, you jackass," said Shane. Robyn started the engine and backed out of the driveway. Eugene started to follow them, and Shane wondered if he might have to start throwing rocks and shouting "Shoo! Get out of here! Shoo!" But then Eugene turned and sadly walked back to the house.

"You do have to feel sorry for him," said Robyn.

"I don't. I think it's hilarious."

"He's a fellow wolf."

"*Was* a wolf. Now I don't know what he is, but he's not one of us, that's for sure."

"Are we going to the park?"

"Hell yeah. I haven't killed somebody in a park since this afternoon." Shane grinned, trying to show off his shattered molar. "It's all over for George."

George walked out of the house, holding an aluminum baseball bat in one hand and a heavy winter coat in the other. He had a small bottle of superglue in his pocket, as well as a wad of about two hundred dollars in cash.

"The plan worked," said Eugene. "They wouldn't take me. I'm relieved but I'm also kind of insulted. I was pretending to be insane, but I wasn't pretending all that hard."

"You did great," said George, who hadn't heard any of the conversation and didn't actually know how well Eugene did, but, hey, he should be supportive of his new buddy. "So are they going to the park?" They'd passed a sign for the park earlier. The town seemed pretty dead now that it was dark, so hopefully the park would be, too.

"As far as I know."

"Good. So let's hurry." He tossed the coat to Eugene, who wasn't able to catch it. Eugene picked it up off the ground, tried to put it on, then looked embarrassed. "Could you ...?"

"Sure." George set down the bat and helped Eugene into his coat.

"I'm sorry, I just haven't had a chance to practice. I've been chained to a wall. I know that once I get used to it, I'll be able to do stuff for myself again."

"You're not going to live the rest of your life with a wolf paw sewn where your hand used to be," George assured him, picking up the bat and then walking toward Tom and Betsy's car. "We're going to get you fixed up as well as ..." He trailed off as he saw Lou's body.

"What?" Eugene asked. "Oh ... wow. I'm sorry. I guess they wanted to make sure he was dead."

George clutched the handle of the bat so tightly that it almost felt like he could crush the metal. He didn't mind the pain. He liked it. Relished it.

"Which one did it?" George asked.

"I don't know. I didn't see them do it. I would've tried to stop them, George, I swear."

George had been pretty bored while he and Lou were hiding out, but when he went into hiding this time, he wouldn't be bored at all. Because he was going to bring at least one of them with him, and his new hobby was going to be finding ways to make them suffer. Maybe Mr. Dewey had the right idea. Maybe he'd turn one of them into his own personal Eugene project. Never let them die.

He needed to get over this. Oh, he'd keep the rage going—the rage was productive right now—but he couldn't just stand here thinking gruesome thoughts. "We've gotta go," he told Eugene.

"I'm really sorry," Eugene said. "I mean that."

They went to Tom and Peggy's car. The idea of leaving Lou behind hurt George's soul, especially now that those monsters had defiled him, but it would take too long to get his body into the other car by himself. Continuing to drive the van would be suicidal. And Lou was dead. Giving him a respectful burial would make George feel better, but it wouldn't do shit for Lou. Lou was gone. Putting himself at risk for a Lou-shaped pile of meat would mean that his best friend had died for nothing.

Okay, Lou *had* died for nothing either way. There was no point to this. No noble sacrifice. If the world was a better place with him gone, it wasn't because Lou had died for any sort of cause, it was because George and Lou were scumbags.

They got into Tom and Betsy's car. "Are we going to return their car when we're done?" Eugene asked.

"I doubt it."

"I feel bad that we're stealing it."

"We also stole their bat, some money, and some glue. And probably their sanity."

"What's the glue for?"

"A werewolf-killing tool."

"Nice."

"Where's your nearest Goth club?"

"Goth club?"

"A club where Goths hang out. Or punks. It doesn't matter. Where would I find somebody with lots of rings and piercings?"

"I don't live in Tropper."

"Oh, that's right."

"I was never really into the club scene. I pretty much just spent time with my family."

"I guess small-town Minnesota isn't the best place for Goth clubs, but any club aimed at college kids would have to have at least one heavily pierced person, right? We'll find it."

As they drove away, leaving Lou behind, George tried unsuccessfully to stop the tears.

"It's okay to cry," said Eugene.

"No. It's not."

"It really is."

"If you want to be a crybaby, that's fine." George wiped his eyes. "Knock yourself out. It's not my thing."

"All I'm saying is, cry if you want to. I won't tell anyone. And if you need a hug, all you have do is ask."

"Thanks," said George, sarcastically. "That makes me feel ever so much better."

He would never admit this to anyone, but it actually did make him feel better, a little.

CHAPTER TWENTY-EIGHT

Precious Metal

George came very close to crapping his pants as they passed a parked police car, but it didn't pull out after them. He came even closer to crapping his pants a second time as they passed a pair of police cars that were driving in the opposite direction. But apparently Tom and Betsy had not yet reported their vehicle as stolen. Hopefully they were still hiding in the closet.

They stopped at the first place that looked remotely promising. It was called M.K.M. and the sign gave no indication of what that might stand for. But it had a skull in the logo and there was loud music blaring from inside.

The bouncer looked a bit taken aback as George walked through the door. "Hey, you okay?" he asked.

"Yeah, it's fake blood," said George. "Looks badass, huh?"

"Can I see your ID?"

George patted at his pocket. "I don't have my wallet with me. C'mon, I'm way beyond twenty-one."

"You can't drink without an armband, and I can't give you an armband without an ID."

"I wasn't going to drink. I'm just here to see a friend."

The bouncer shrugged and let George pass.

Not many people were in the tiny club. A few kids stood and nodded their heads in time to the beat of the band that was on stage, but it was clearly the opening act for the opening act and there wasn't a ton of enthusiasm.

George quickly scanned the club, hoping to find one of those kids who went absolutely berserk with the piercings, where you worried that they might accidentally get them caught on something and rip half of their faces off. There were none like that, but a couple of girls sitting at a table near the back, dressed in lacy black outfits, did seem to be wearing plenty of jewelry. They were both college-aged, so there was nothing George could do about the "creepy old man hitting on young women" vibe that he'd no doubt give off, but hopefully he could charm them enough to let him buy some of their stuff.

"Hello," he said, walking up to their table. "I promise I'm not trying to hit on you."

"Uh-huh," said one of the girls. She wore blood-red lipstick and her hair was a shade of black that didn't appear in nature, but she wasn't wearing any makeup beyond that. She took a sip of her beer and gave George a look that said that she'd really appreciate it if he would fuck off.

"I'm not, I swear. This is going to sound crazy, and that's fine, but I have to kill some werewolves tonight, and I really need to buy any silver jewelry you've got."

The other girl leaned across the table. "Are you Lou Flynn?"

"Uh, no. I'm his partner."

"George Orton? So that stuff that's on the news is true?"

"I haven't had time to watch TV today so I'm not sure what's on the news, but if they're talking about werewolves, yes, it's true."

"Oh my God! This is so cool! My boyfriend updated your Wikipedia entry a few months ago! Yeah, people have reported walking wolves, and there's this house full of dead bodies, and my mom barely let me go out tonight! So you're hunting them?"

George nodded. "Yeah. But I need silver. Rings, bracelets ... whatever you've got. I've only got about two hundred bucks."

The girls began taking off their rings. "Will you do an interview with my boyfriend for his blog?"

"You bet."

The first girl stuck out her tongue, revealing a large stud. "Thith too?"

"That would be great."

After they dropped Crabs off, Robyn kind of looked like she wanted to have sex again, but that would have been irresponsible. So they drove a few blocks from Melville Park, which was a decent enough park with a slide, swing set, jungle gym, and all of the other prerequisites except for playing children, and parked in the lot of a large grocery store. The parking lot wasn't very well lit and Shane figured they'd be anonymous enough. Better than taking the risk of driving past the wrong cop.

He'd released Ally from the trunk and sat with her in the back seat, while Robyn remained up front. He didn't like warning his daughter that he'd be forced to inflict physical harm upon her if she caused a commotion or tried to get away, but he really had no choice in the matter. She seemed to take the warning seriously.

He hated seeing his daughter's face all blotchy, her eyes all swollen from sobbing. Now that the high of the previous slaughter had faded, he really wished that Robyn had at least not murdered Peggy right in front of her. Lots of teenagers lost their mothers and got over it, but having her mother murdered right before her eyes was a wound that might stick around for a while.

Nothing he could do about it. Still, the next time they were alone he'd let Robyn know how badly she'd screwed up.

"We need to find out what made you change," he said. "We can't leave town as wolves if you're stuck as a human."

"I don't know what made me change," Ally insisted. It was hard to understand her while she was crying. "I can't do it."

"Yes, you can. We'll figure it out. It's a little different for everyone, but once you find the trigger, with some practice you can change whenever you want." He changed his hand. "See? When you get good enough, you can change whatever part you want."

"Why would I want to just change my hand?"

Shane glared at her. "Maybe you want to slash somebody's throat, but you don't want anybody to see you turn into a full wolf. How about that?"

Slashing a throat? He'd really said that to her? Wow. Shane felt like he should apologize, but didn't.

Ally didn't seem to catch his faux pas. "I'm not going to start killing people."

"Nobody said you had to. Where were you when you changed?"

"In the back of the van."

"By yourself?"

"With George."

"What was he doing?"

"He was holding me down."

Shane let out a snarl. "And how did you feel about that?"

"How do you think I felt?"

"I don't know. That's what we're trying to sort out. We've got to analyze the shades of emotion. I'm sure you weren't happy about it, but how exactly did you feel?"

"I was scared."

"That's a start. How did you feel when you got the drill through your foot?"

"Scared."

"And it hurt, right?"

"What do you think?"

"Did George hurt you when he was holding you down?"

"No, not really."

"So, fear without pain, maybe? It could be that the intense fear makes you change, but the pain counter-balances it and prevents the change. Maybe not counter-balances it, that sounds stupid, but if the pain is stronger than the fear, that could be why you can't change. Think about how you've felt today. All day. Have you hurt more, or have you been more scared?"

"I've hurt more."

"All day? So all day, the pain has been stronger than the fear?"

Ally nodded.

"Then maybe we're on the right track."

They weren't on the right track. Ally was in a lot of pain, but even when the actual drill bit was boring through her flesh, the terror had been worse.

She hadn't been trying to examine her emotional state before the transformation, but now that Dad was trying to talk her through it, she realized the difference.

When George had held her down in the back of the van, she'd been frightened, but she'd also been more mad than anything else.

Since then, she'd been scared, and she'd been horrified, and she'd been devastated, yet she hadn't actually been furious, even at Robyn.

At the moment before the change: rage.

That was it. That was the secret.

What she didn't know was how to make herself angry. Or at least, more angry than scared. Because right now, she was positively terrified, and she didn't think she could turn that into fury.

She wouldn't want to change now, anyway. Not with Dad and Robyn right there. Two werewolves who knew what they were doing in their wolf form would catch her easily, and she truly believed that Dad would hurt her. Maybe he wouldn't kill her, but he'd make sure she didn't try to get away again.

Still, if she was able to lose them, for only a moment ...

———

Crabs liked being in this tree.

Wolfmen could not climb trees. So he climbed as a human. Almost all the way to the top. From here, he could watch everything that was happening in the park.

Nothing was happening now. Maybe nothing would.

It was peaceful up here in the tree. It should have been too cold, but Crabs never felt cold. Other people would complain about the cold and Crabs would silently laugh at them.

If George actually did show up, Crabs would kill him.

He was not supposed to kill him. He was supposed to run back and let Shane know that he was here. And perhaps he would decide to do that. But for right now, his plan was to leap down from the tree. He was so good at changing that he could do it in mid-air, so that was what he would do. Leap down, change in mid-air, and then pounce on George and rip him apart.

Poor George.

If that other man was there, Crabs would kill him, too. Crabs knew he wasn't a werewolf. The man thought he could fool everybody else, but he could not fool Crabs. Crabs was the one who had told Shane that the woman in the bar was a werewolf, and if it were not for that, Shane and Robyn would never have met. Never would have fucked.

But people did not always listen to Crabs. He did not care.

He would have a lot of fun ripping strips of flesh off George's body, starting at the bottom and working his way up. Maybe he would alternate taking bites between George and the man who had had a terrible life. There were so many possibilities. Crabs wanted to hug himself.

A car approached. Crabs recognized the car. It was the car from the house. Had the other man stolen it, or was George with him?

George got out of the car.

Crabs was very happy.

The park was empty.

George hadn't expected the werewolves to be there, just waiting around for him, but he couldn't help but be a little disappointed. He was pumped with adrenaline and anger, and ready to take it out on somebody, even if he didn't survive the experience.

Eugene was hanging out a couple of blocks away, huddled in his new coat. If the werewolves saw him, they'd know that he and George had planned this together. And since this was a reckless, insanely dangerous scheme that essentially came down to beating the crap out of a supernatural beast, it was best not to get Eugene killed for revenge that wasn't his own.

If this were a real meeting with somebody who was part of a criminal empire, George would have remained in the car until they arrived, instead of standing outside in the cold, looking suspicious. He didn't think the werewolves would know that, though. He didn't want to be in the vehicle if they showed up, because his weapon was a baseball bat, and you couldn't easily swing those within the confines of an affordable car owned by two elderly people who drove it once a week for church and groceries.

He strolled through the park, trying to be subtle about his bat. He didn't expect anybody to not notice that he was carrying a bat, but he didn't want them to see that it had several silver rings, a tongue stud, and other assorted pieces of jewelry, including a necklace in the shape of a coffin, super-glued to it.

He'd assured the girls that he would return their jewelry, and though it might be damaged, it would have serious street cred.

If his experience with Ivan was typical of the way things worked, just touching them with silver wouldn't do anything. The silver only worked from the inside. Which meant that if one was, say, wielding a baseball bat with silver rings glued to it, one needed to hit the werewolf really frickin' hard to penetrate the skin.

George thought he could handle that.

Some branches rustled.

A werewolf leapt from the trees.

Crabs landed right next to the slide, about twenty feet from George.

Instead of pouncing immediately, Crabs cracked his knuckles. If he could speak as a wolf, he obviously would have said something sinister, like "Well, well, well, what a tasty treat I have in store."

George raised the bat.

Crabs cocked his head, a bit confused.

George could speak, so he said, "My name is George Orton. You killed my partner. Prepare to die."

From a pure technical standpoint, it was possible to argue that the werewolves had not officially killed Lou. But in a situation where he wanted every possible speck of an advantage, he thought it made sense to have his enemy think, "Did he really just kind-of quote The Princess Bride?"

Claws and baseball bat raised, they ran toward each other.

CHAPTER TWENTY-NINE

George Smash

It was, George believed, the most powerful swing ever made with a baseball bat, one capable of sending the ball soaring out of the stadium and into the heavens.

Except that he missed.

Crabs ducked underneath the bat, dropping to all fours just long enough to avoid being struck. George did a not-quite-as-powerful backswing, which also missed.

Crabs jumped to his feet. It was hard to discern a wolfman's facial expressions, but George thought it translated as "mildly amused."

The werewolf leapt at him, its front claws aimed at George. This was a poor strategic move on Crabs' part, because this time George's swing with the baseball bat *did* hit him, bashing Crabs in the arm.

Half of the rings popped off.

There was no evidence that any silver had broken through fur and skin, but still, getting hit with a baseball bat was painful, even for a werewolf.

He didn't make a sound, though. Crabs rubbed his arm, which sadly had no protruding bone, was not twisted at a weird angle, and did not hang uselessly at his side. His arm looked fine. Crabs just stood there, staring at George as if he were an odd scientific specimen. He flexed his claws.

George had known that super-gluing rings to a bat was not going to create the ultimate werewolf-killing weapon, but he was kind of concerned that he'd lost half of the rings on the first swing. He still had two more werewolves to beat to death after Crabs.

"Make you a deal," said George. "Just lie on the ground and I'll smash open the back of your head. Quick and easy."

Crabs might have laughed. Again, it was hard to tell when he was a wolf.

"You liked that?" George asked. "I've got more jokes where that came from? Why did the werewolf—?"

Crabs knocked George completely off his feet and against the slide. George mostly hit the flat surface, but he also struck the raised metal on the side, so it was not a pleasant feeling.

Before he could swing the bat, Crabs pinned his arm down. George head-butted him. His forehead smashed against werewolf jaws, so this hurt George a lot more than it did Crabs. He could tell there was blood involved, even before Crabs licked it off of him.

"Don't lick me, you asshole!" he said, trying to pull his arm free. Crabs licked George's forehead again, as if trying to get the last bit of ice cream out of the bottom of a cone.

George really didn't need this in his life right now.

He spat in Crabs' face. He wasn't expecting Crabs to recoil and shriek, "It burns! It burns!" but George hoped that he'd take sufficient insult to the gesture to lean back a bit. Or he'd bite a huge chunk out of George's face. One of the two.

Crabs had no reaction. The spit dangled from his chin and he didn't even seem to notice. To be fair to Crabs, there was a lot of blood on his face, so it wasn't *too* weird that apparently the saliva was no big deal.

George did another head-butt. The first one had simply been a random move to hit whatever was in front of him, but this one was more targeted. He'd see how Crabs liked having George's rock-hard skull smash into his injured snout.

Crabs did not like that at all. An extra bonus spurt of blood came out, getting in George's left eye, and Crabs howled with pain. George's bat-wielding arm was still pinned, but he used his other hand to grab Crabs' nose and give it a vicious Three Stooges-style twist, though without the accompanying sound effects.

Crabs bit down, nearly taking off two of George's fingers. George tried to jab his index finger into Crabs' eye, while blinking blood out of his own eye. It wasn't the finger-plunging-into-the-juicy-orb result that he was going for, but he got him *next* to the eye, which probably didn't hurt much but definitely startled the werewolf.

Then George grabbed Crabs' ear, crushing it in his hand while he tried to rip it right off the werewolf's head. He dug his fingernails in deep and squeezed as if he were making a ball out of tin foil.

Apparently that was as much agony as Crabs could handle at all once. He moved away from the slide, clutching at his nose with one furry hand and his ear with the other. He was still behaving in a relatively calm manner—no thrashing around in pain—but he was clearly hurting.

Time to go on the offensive and make one-third of his werewolf problem go away.

George raised the bat as if waiting for a pitch, then swung, bashing Crabs' in the side. Crabs let out a yelp of surprise and pain.

Blood dripped from one of the rings, and a small spot on Crabs' side was sizzling. George had broken the skin.

This time, Crabs' expression seemed to say, *What the hell did you just do to me? This isn't fair!*

George bashed him again, hitting him on the other side. More sizzling. A blow to Crabs' shoulder didn't seem to break the skin, but still, it was a very violent baseball bat hit to the shoulder.

The next swing missed, as did the one after that, but Crabs held up his arm to defend himself against the next one and took a hit directly to his right elbow. The tongue-stud came off the bat and remained imbedded in Crabs' arm.

His attempt to pluck out the stud was hampered by George smacking him in the head.

Smoke was billowing from three or four different spots on Crabs, and now his arm *was* hanging limp at his side. If that stud stayed in there long enough, maybe it would burn all the way through and his arm would fall off.

George raised the bat over his head, prepared to deliver the killing blow. Or maybe the dozens of blows leading up to the killing blow—George was cool with it either way.

He was no stranger to anger, and in fact his happiness level rarely rose above a level of moderate annoyance, but this was the kind of rage where it felt like he had stepped outside of his body, where he didn't care how much damage he was doing to himself with each blow. The only thing that mattered was getting revenge for what they'd done to Lou.

Unfortunately for Crabs, Lou would have been the one to tell George that he'd gone far enough.

He brought the bat down as hard as he could.

This was not as hard as he could even a minute ago, but it was still pretty goddamned hard.

Crabs blocked the swing with his hand, pulverizing his palm. Yet he still was able to yank the bat out of George's hand and fling it aside.

Fine. Whatever. George didn't need a weapon.

He rained blows upon the werewolf with his fists, aiming for the smoking spots. Crabs fought back, getting in a couple of savage swipes with his claws that George couldn't even...no, wait, he definitely felt that one.

George punched him in the face and chest, over and over. He couldn't even imagine what he was doing to the hand that had already been injured. It would probably have to be amputated. He didn't care.

Now Crabs' eyes were wide with panic. Fucker probably never though a human could beat him in a one-on-one fight. His wounds from the silver had stopped sizzling though, except for the elbow that still had the stud in it.

George threw a punch that hit Crabs directly in the center of his nose, splitting the two halves completely apart.

That seemed to take the homicidal urges out of Crabs, all at once. He simply stopped fighting and walked away, stumbling, looking as if he might fall right over with any step.

George kind of felt sorry for him.

Not really.

Crabs staggered over to the teeter-totter, which was like a gift from the Gods of Wanting To See Werewolves Get The Shit Beaten Out Of Them Even More, because he was at the down end.

Was that end the teeter or the totter?

Didn't matter.

George couldn't run, but he got over to the other end with amazing haste for a guy who was so messed up, and pushed it down to the ground.

Perfect.

The end of the teeter-totter struck Crabs so hard that his head *should* have been jettisoned off his body like a rocket.

It didn't, though. Didn't even break his neck. That Crabs was one resilient son of a bitch.

He stumbled back in the direction from where he came, headed toward the slide. His arm changed back to human, then one of his legs, then his head.

"You done?" asked George.

Crabs walked right into the slide but stayed upright. He looked over at George, appearing disoriented and confused. "That was immature."

George walked over and picked up his bat. "Where's the girl?"

Crabs spat out a thick blob of red mucus. "No."

"That wasn't a yes or no question."

"My last words will not be betrayal."

"Then maybe they don't have to be your last words."

Crabs smiled. "Ah. The dealmaker arrives."

"I'm not trying to cut a deal. Just trying to give you a chance to make things right."

"By turning her over to you?" Crabs spat out another red blob. "That feels morally unsound."

"Okay," said George, walking over to him. "I didn't want you to live anyway."

Crabs changed his arm back, grabbed George by the throat, then bashed him against the slide. He bashed him against it again, and then once more, and George started to worry that he might actually be paralyzed.

"Drop the bat," said Crabs, digging his claws into George's neck.

George dropped the bat. His blinding rage disappeared almost instantly, replaced by the most intense fear he'd ever experienced. He'd been close to death before, but this was *close*, and suddenly he didn't want to die.

"You do not get to kill me," said Crabs. "I am the killer. I will heal. You will not. My question is, do you want me to piss in your mouth before or after you are dead?"

George was too frightened to answer the question.

Crabs tightened his grip on George's neck. "Feeling less brave now? I have another question for you. When I lap up your sweet, rich blood, is it more disturbing when I'm a wolf or when I'm a human?" Crabs bent down and licked some blood off of George's chin. "What do you think?"

Human. Definitely human. But George didn't think he wanted an actual spoken answer to the question.

"For me, the flavor is better as a wolf, but I like the way you die inside when I do it as a human. Keep bleeding for me, George." George turned his head. Crabs continued to lick him, tracing a line down to George's ear.

"Shall I whisper sweet nothings into your ear?" Crabs asked. "You mangled my ear, but I will treat yours with love and caring."

"Go ahead, lick my ear," said George. "I don't give a crap at this point."

Instead, Crabs began to lick some blood that had gotten into George's hair. Or at least George thought that's what he was licking out of his hair. It didn't really matter.

"Your scalp is delicious," said Crabs.

Did thoughts like that actually flow through his mind, or did he just say weird shit to get a reaction?

George supposed it didn't make any difference. Either way, he was never going to be able to erase the sensation of this lunatic's tongue sliding down his hairline from his memory. This was "wake up in the middle of the night in a cold sweat" kind of stuff right here.

But, hey, at least he was concerned about horrible memories in the future, because if Crabs kept licking just a bit further, and didn't immediately choose to rip George's windpipe open when he moved...

George suddenly moved his head.

Crabs did not rip out his windpipe.

Instead, he accidentally licked the cold metal slide.

There was a split second where Crabs just looked annoyed that George had moved while he was being licked, but then Crabs realized that his tongue was stuck to the slide. He gave a quick gentle test tug before full comprehension dawned upon him.

If Crabs didn't still have his claws around George's neck, George would have loved nothing more than to sit back, point and laugh, and see how this all played out. Sadly, he was still in a dire predicament.

Crabs' creepy dead eyes went wide with panic.

George grabbed his wrist with both hands and pried his claws away from his neck, then rolled off the slide, landing on a patch of ice instead of soft snow.

This wasn't going to last long. The way to get your tongue unstuck from cold metal was to pour warm water on it, and Crabs had plenty of warm blood flowing to suit his needs.

George retrieved his bat.

Crabs transformed all the way back into a wolfman, which ended up just giving him a longer tongue stuck to the slide.

The werewolf yanked his head away. With all of the blood, it was difficult to say exactly how much tongue he left behind, but it was *some*, at least.

Tongue mutilation was clearly more disturbing to Crabs than nose mutilation.

George hit him with the bat.

Then again.

And again.

More of the jewelry flew off the bat, but at least a couple of the rings did their job, because there was some definite sizzling going on.

Somewhere around the tenth or eleventh hit, George realized that he was crying. Oh well. The only witness would be dead soon.

Crabs had stopped trying to defend himself.

And then, one hit with the baseball bat got him in the center of the forehead. The silver coffin necklace cracked the front of his skull.

Crabs didn't make a sound. He just pitched forward, dead.

"Yeah, that's right," said George. "Stay down."

George frowned. He really should have said something better after sort-of partially avenging Lou's death. If he'd believed that Lou was watching him from the afterlife, Lou would be shaking his head right now. *"Yeah, that's right, stay down?" Seriously? Screw you, George.*

He returned to the car, turned on the headlights, then looked around the battle zone for the silver rings that had fallen off. He only found one before giving it up as a lost cause.

He didn't feel particularly vindicated, but then again, there were still two werewolves left to kill.

CHAPTER THIRTY

A Bad Time To Be George

Being a werewolf was fantastic in every possible way except for the destruction of clothing. And because of that, you couldn't really carry a cell phone in your pocket, because the pockets might rip and you'd lose your phone. Therefore, Shane and Robyn couldn't text Crabs like civilized people, and instead had agreed to drive by the park if he hadn't returned with news in a reasonable amount of time.

They had not specifically defined "reasonable amount of time." It had only been half an hour, and Shane didn't want George to see them driving past the park.

"He probably fell asleep," said Robyn.

"I don't think Crabs sleeps."

"It's been too long. George isn't worth this."

"I disagree."

"You know that Crabs isn't going to report back, right? If he sees George, he'll kill him."

"Crabs wouldn't do that."

"Really?"

Shane shifted in his seat. "No, not really. You're right. Let's check on him."

Tom and Betsy's car was at the park. That emaciated lab rat had lied to them. He'd die for that, although he was in far too bad shape already to be any fun to kill. How could they torture him *more*?

So Crabs hadn't bothered to report back. Robyn glanced back at Shane. If she said a word about this, a single word, Shane might not be able to stop himself from going psycho on her.

But she didn't. She simply asked, "What's next?"

"I'm going to find out what's going on. If Ally tries to escape, take her down."

"You mean kill her?"

"No. But don't spare her legs." He looked his daughter in the eye. "You got that?"

Ally looked defiant, but nodded.

Shane hoped that Robyn knew that he didn't *really* want her to rip up Ally's legs. She probably did. He got out of the car.

He wished werewolves could see in the dark. He had to walk all the way over to the slide before he saw that it had blood on it.

A lot of blood.

And there was a path in the snow that led to the woods behind the park. Like a body had been dragged.

Lots of blood on the path, too.

Whose blood was it?

Shane changed, bent down, and sniffed the ground. Was it both Crabs' and George's blood? He couldn't tell.

If he went back to talk to Robyn, she'd tell him not to go into the woods after them, so he didn't go back to talk to her. He walked along the bloody path, watching closely and listening carefully, until he walked into the woods.

You killed my mother.

You killed my mother.

You killed my mother.

How did you get mad on purpose?

Oh, Ally was mad. She hated Robyn. Despised her. Would love to see her dead and dance on her grave.

But *trying* to be mad, madder than she was scared, simply wasn't working. She couldn't control her emotions like that. She wanted to become a white-hot ball of fury but couldn't do it.

With practice she could do it, but unlike the violin, she needed to be good at this *now*.

What if she just opened the door and ran? Would Robyn really hurt her?

Ally scooted an inch to the left.

"If you move at all toward that door, you're going back in the trunk," Robyn informed her. "Behave."

You killed my mother.

You killed my mother.

You killed my mother.

Crabs lay dead on the ground.

Shane couldn't believe it. Crabs was dead. George had murdered him.

How could Crabs be so weak? How could he let himself be killed by a human? Had he been careless? Had he fallen asleep and let George sneak up on him?

Shane had treasured their friendship, but if Crabs had been killed by an injured human, then he deserved to die.

The car was there, so George and the freak were still around. They wouldn't have just left their car and fled through the woods, so they had to be hiding.

Somewhere close.

Shane looked up in the trees.

There was George, right above him.

Getting closer.

Very quickly.

George didn't land on Shane, but the aluminum bat he was holding did. It got Shane right on the shoulder, which hurt like crazy. He cursed loudly, though it came out as a growl.

The thug was no Jackie Chan. He'd landed on his feet, but then crumpled. Snatching the bat out of his hands was easy enough. Shane tossed it to his other hand, so that he was holding it by the handle, then got ready to split George's skull open with it.

Oh, hey, look at that. He'd attached silver jewelry to it. How adorable. Shane pointed to the bat and gave George a thumbs-up.

"I figured it'll do the trick when I shove it up your ass," said George.

Shane jabbed the bat at him, getting George right in the gut. The oh-so-mighty werewolf hunter doubled over and vomited.

Poor guy. He was having such a bad day.

George's head was in the perfect bashing position. If Shane brought the bat down like a strength-testing hammer at a carnival, he figured he could split George's head all the way down to his chin. That should be the game. If he could splatter George's brain matter more than twenty feet away, he'd win a stuffed giraffe.

Shane felt kind of guilty. They'd both lost a dear friend, but at least Shane had gotten laid today.

He should turn Robyn loose on him. Give him one last ride before he died. She'd *shred* him, but what a way to go.

She'd never go for that. What a show it would be.

George groaned in pain and started to lift his head. Shane wasn't quite ready to pulp his cranium yet, so he swung the bat into George's leg, knocking him over. Home run.

He wasn't sure why it felt wrong to finish him off. Not that Shane was having any kind of second thoughts about this, but for some reason he felt as if there was some unfinished business. George was already starting to get up, so Shane bashed him in the other leg. It was nice that George had gone with a metal bat instead of a wooden one, otherwise this thing would have shattered.

If he'd known where the freak was, Shane would have changed back to human, because he desperately wanted to have one last conversation with George. Mock him. Laugh at him. Make him feel truly pathetic before he died. But even though George was no threat right now, and the freak was almost certainly no threat, either, Shane had to remain cautious until he at least knew where the freak was hiding.

So, no mockery. Life was full of sacrifice.

Then he figured out why he didn't want to kill George. He shouldn't be the one to do it. Ally had to make her first kill sometime, and what better first victim than the sleaze bucket who'd kidnapped her? If it wasn't for George and Lou, she'd still have her old life. Sure, Shane knew that the thugs had actually made things better for her in the long run, but she didn't know that yet.

Anyway, he liked the idea of George being killed by a fourteen-year-old girl. Even if she was a werewolf, it was still a pretty big blotch on his legacy.

Shane flung the bat like a baton. It was a good enough weapon to take out Crabs, so he probably shouldn't have it available to George once the real pain started.

Then he grabbed one of George's feet and dragged him out of the woods.

———

Eugene wished he had a good pair of snow pants.

Or any pants.

Or at least boxer shorts that were in better shape.

At least he was warm from the waist up. And, except for his feet, he'd been warm while he'd sat huddled on the ground, because he could tuck his knees underneath the coat and be reasonably toasty.

Then he'd decided that he needed to help.

Yeah, he was a mess, but he had to be able to contribute in a bigger way than just directing the werewolves to the park. It was three against one. If Eugene went over to help, he could make it three against two, or at least three against one-and-a-half.

If Ally got free, why, they'd practically be evenly matched. A totally fair fight all the way. Vegas odds makers wouldn't know what to do.

Eugene had started by walking off the road entirely, but trudging through the snow was too slow and too miserable, so he just walked on the edge of the road, figuring that if somebody drove by he'd see their headlights in plenty of time to hide.

George had saved him.

He had to help.

And the fact that he didn't entirely care whether he lived or died might make him a good ally.

————————

Shane dragged George into the center of the park. Then he crouched down beside him, jabbed a talon into George's upper thigh, and sliced all the way down his leg, not stopping until he reached the ankle. George was admirably brave about it. Shane did the same thing to George's other leg, this time starting from the bottom and working his way up. He wasn't slicing *too* deep; not severing tendons or anything, just cutting deep enough to make sure that George wouldn't get up and run away.

Shane walked back to the borrowed car, changed to human, and opened the back door.

"Come on," he said to Ally. "I'm about to give you the best present of your life."

Ally shook her head.

"That piece of human garbage that kidnapped you is right over there," said Shane, pointing to where George still lay. "You want to learn to use your powers? This will be a great opportunity. If you can't get mad at George, who *can* you get mad at, right?"

"Just leave him alone," said Ally.

"That would be ridiculous. When somebody does wrong by you, you no longer have to sit back and take it."

"You and Robyn did wrong by me."

Shane grinned. "And you know what? Maybe you'll make things right. But you can't do shi—" He caught himself in time. "—anything to Robyn until you've learned to harness your true nature, so why not take advantage of this lesson?"

"Let's just go," said Ally.

"She's right," said Robyn.

"No, she's wrong. George needs to die. I'd love to do it myself, but I think it'll be more valuable if Ally does it. If they've blocked off all of roads out of town, we may end up having to run off as wolves, so she needs to figure this stuff out."

"I'm not going to kill anyone," said Ally.

Shane changed his arm, grabbed Ally by the wrist, and pulled her out of the car. "Scream and I'll break your arm," he warned her.

She screamed. Shane twisted her arm until she stopped.

"That was stupid," he said. "You want to attract attention? Like it or not, you're a werewolf, and if they catch you, you'll end up like that freak. Is that what you want? You want to walk around school with 'WOLF' tattooed on your forehead and a useless paw sewn to your wrist?" He twisted her arm a bit more. "Is it?"

"No!"

"If I twist any more, a bone is gonna snap. You want that?"

"No, please."

"Then cut the crap, stop being such a spoiled brat, and walk with me. It's not that difficult, for Christ's sake. Your foot is barely even bleeding anymore."

She followed without further protest, though with a pronounced limp, as he led her over to where George lay. Now *his* legs were bleeding pretty bad. Throw this guy in the ocean and he'd draw every shark in a fifty-mile radius.

"Look at him," said Shane. "What do you see?"

"I see George."

"And what did George do to you today?"

"Nothing."

"Don't tell me 'nothing.' Don't lie to me. What did George do to you today? He put you in a cage, right?"

"No."

"No?"

"I said, don't lie to me, Ally. I mean it. I saw the cage."

"The cage was after he saved me. After Lou saved me. After we saved each other."

"Nobody saved anybody. They kidnapped you." Shane pointed down at George. "He's your enemy."

"I think your daughter likes me better," said George. He didn't sound like he was dying yet, though he certainly wasn't bothering to sit up. "That's gotta piss you off."

"You know what pisses me off?" Shane asked. "That you and your dead partner started a chain of events that led to the death of Ally's mom. Maybe you didn't kill her, but if you'd stayed in your cave or wherever the hell you've been cowering all this time, she'd still be alive."

"Robyn killed her," said Ally.

Shane slapped her across the face. "That's right. She did. And it was George's fault, not Robyn's."

"No, it's was Robyn's fault."

Shane slapped her again. "Honey, your trigger is either fear, anger, or pain. I'm happy to keep trying all three until we get somewhere."

"Maybe her trigger is you not being an asshole," said George. "I guess she'll never be able to change."

"Funny, George. It's all a bunch of great big laughs until somebody bleeds out. Wanna say something else?"

"No, I was just waiting for the chance to use the asshole comment."

"Here's one you can use: 'No, little girl! Please stop hurting me! I don't want to die!'"

"Nah. I'll think of something better than that."

Shane changed his arm and raked three talons across George's leg. George cried out in pain.

"Did you think of something better yet?" Shane asked.

"If you're going to kill me, then kill me," said George. "Don't just stand around jerking off in front of your daughter."

"I'll excuse you for not paying attention to the conversation Ally and I have been having, since you're gushing blood and probably not thinking clearly."

"It's not gushing. It's just leaking a lot."

"Either way, I'm not going to kill you. Ally is. Hopefully she's going to kill you as a wolf, but if not, she's going to kill you as a human."

"What are you talking about?" Ally demanded.

"I'm talking about bloodlust. I guarantee that if you rip his throat out with your bare teeth, that'll spark the change. That wasn't the way I wanted to do it, but clearly you're not making any effort on your part, so as your father I'm going to have to just throw you in the deep end of the pool."

Shane grabbed his daughter by the back of the neck and pulled her down with him as he crouched next to George. "Time to eat."

CHAPTER THIRTY-ONE

Red Robyn

Bullet to the back of the head.

Cement shoes on his feet before he was dumped in a lake.

Stroke. (There was a family history.)

These were but three of the many, many ways George would put on his list of ways he thought he would die that were more likely than a werewolf forcing his human teenage daughter to bite out his throat. In fact, if he'd been locked in a room for a week with nothing but a typewriter and instructions to come up with every possible method of his demise, he wasn't sure he'd ever arrive at that one.

There were worse ways to go, for sure, but this was pretty goddamn deranged.

He'd originally been hiding what little bit of strength he had left for the most opportune moment to strike. Now, after lying in the snow and bleeding, that strength was all but gone. He would not be suddenly springing to life and overpowering Shane.

He was basically finished.

It was a sad way to go, and maybe he'd be struck with a renewal of energy sometime before Ally's teeth reached his throat, but for now his biggest hope was that Ally would indeed transform into a werewolf in the next few seconds, so that she could finish him off with one big bite to the neck instead of what were sure to be lots of small, hesitant bites. Because that would really suck.

"What the fuck is the matter with you?" asked Ally. "I'm not going to bite his neck! Stop it, Dad! Stop it!"

"Quit struggling."

"No! You can't make me do this! You're insane! You're completely insane!"

"I'm your father, and you *will* respect me!"

"I have no respect for you! I hate you!"

Shane twisted the little brat's hair in his fist. "I said, do it!"

"Help!" Ally screamed. "Help me! Somebody!"

"Shhh!"

"Help me!"

"Shut up!"

"Help me!"

Shane wanted to break her spoiled brat neck. Rotten kids had such a sense of entitlement these days. They didn't think they had to do anything their parents told them.

He yanked on her hair until she cried out. "You wanna call for help again? Do it. See if I don't rip your hair out at the roots. You can be a werewolf with a great big bald patch on your head. I don't care. Do it. Call for help. Do it."

"Please, Daddy, just let me go ..." "

"You think that calling me Daddy is going to change anything? How stupid do you think I am? Don't try to play your own father. Bite his neck, now, or I'll kill him and then we'll continue this in the car. You don't want that. I promise you, Ally, you don't want that."

"Okay," said Ally. "Okay. I'll do it."

Ally opened her mouth wide, and George had his renewal of energy. Well, maybe not energy. Just a renewal of his desire not to have his throat ripped out. He tried to sit up, but his body wouldn't cooperate.

George tried to return to his earlier state of acceptance, but, nope, he couldn't summon it. He was just going to have to die in a state of unrestrained terror, damn it.

What on earth is Shane doing over there? Robyn wondered.

Never mind. She didn't want to know.

Ally's transformation was not physical. But suddenly it was as if a wild, rabid, crazed beast had been let out of a crate. And her entire animalistic outburst was aimed at Shane.

The girl just went berserk.

Screaming. Thrashing. Kicking. Slashing with her fingernails. George was very thankful not to be on the receiving end.

Could you change into a werewolf without actually changing? Had she suddenly gone feral on the inside? Or had she just had enough of her father's bullshit?

"What the hell, Ally?" Shane tried to keep her under control, but she'd gone absolutely insane. He could barely hold her.

If he transformed, he'd be able to hold her down, no problem, but Shane wasn't one hundred percent certain that he could stop himself from hurting her in his wolf state. He didn't mind hurting her a little, or even a lot, but as a wolf he might do permanent damage, or even kill her.

Killing her would not be okay.

"You need to knock this off right now," he told her, as she went for his eyes. "I mean it!"

He was actually becoming a little flustered.

Oh, for God's sake ...

Robyn got out of the car. This was exactly why she'd wanted to just leave town as soon as they got Ally. When she let the boys do what they wanted, things spiraled out of control.

––––––––

Running hurt, but Eugene ran anyway.

George was lying on his back in the snow while Shane struggled with the Tasmanian Devil that Ally had become. Robyn had gotten out of the car to help. So Eugene's best way to help would be to tackle Robyn.

She heard him before he reached her. The sight of a man in a winter coat and boxer shorts would probably be a strange one even without everything else that was weird about him, and it took her a second to process.

Unfortunately, Eugene was several seconds away from her, so she was more than ready by the time he reached her. He didn't care. Wolf-woman or not, he was going to tackle her and fight to the death.

He even let out a battle cry. Screw it, he had nothing to lose.

Eugene was ready for her to take a vicious swing at him, so he lowered his head right before impact.

He successfully ducked out of the way of her swing, which he figured was his one moment of good luck for this conflict. As he slammed into her werewolf chest, the snout that had been sewn onto his face popped almost all of its stitches at once. It flopped over and dangled by only one or two threads.

Robyn swiped at him. He put up his paw to block her. This time, all of the stitches broke, and the paw popped right off, falling into the snow next to his bare feet. There wasn't a fountain of blood, but there was definitely some blood.

Eugene hadn't been given the opportunity to look into the crater that used to be his nose after Mr. Dewey had it removed but before he'd sewn on the replacement. He wondered if he'd be alive long enough to recoil at the sight of himself in the mirror.

He thrust his other hand at Robyn's face.

Four of the five fingernails broke completely off as soon as they struck fur. They weren't his real nails, but they'd been on his hand for at least a couple of weeks, and they were well-stuck to the skin. So the pain of having four fingernails come off at once was, without question, the worst physical agony he'd ever endured. It felt every bit as bad as he might have imagined it would feel to have all four nails rip off at once, plus a little worse. He'd never had anything positive to say about Mr. Dewey, but at least he'd drugged Eugene before removing his real nails.

The fifth nail, the nail on his ring finger, plunged deep into Robyn's eyeball.

She did not react calmly to this.

The howl of pain from Robyn sent a genuine, literal shiver down George's spine. As in, his spine actually trembled from the sound that she made when, as George saw when he looked over, Eugene stabbed one of his long-ass fingernails into her eye.

Shane and Ally both turned to see what had just happened. Eugene pulled his hand away, and the fingernail snapped off. Eugene stepped back, blood dripping from his fingertips, while Robyn clutched at her eye and continued her wolfish shriek. The sound was so ghastly that, though it didn't make George feel sorry for her, it did make him wince at her plight. You never wanted to get a fingernail through your eyeball. Never.

Eugene knew that this was the moment to deliver his finishing blow, but he didn't really have a finishing blow. He was an emaciated, probably frostbitten, mangled mess whose only real offensive capability was the five fingernails that were now broken off.

Well, and the teeth that were stuck to his shoulders and jaw. Maybe he'd use the teeth.

He lunged at her, trying to get Robyn in a bear hug. She smacked him, but with the back of her hand instead of the claws, probably not intentionally, and he hit the ground.

Robyn wrenched the nail out of her eye.

Eugene looked up at her and tried to make peace with his death. It had been a fine life if you disregarded the past few weeks, and if this was how he went out, well, now George would be facing a one-eyed instead of two-eyed werewolf, and his odds of survival were that much greater.

George felt that it probably said something unpleasant about him that he couldn't work up the strength to move when Ally was being forced into attempted cannibalism by her father, but seeing Robyn with her eyeball spurting just brought him right back to life.

He sat up, hurting his back in the process, and somehow managed to wrap his arms around Shane's neck. Shane immediately transformed and stood up, but George maintained his hold, standing up along with the wolfman, hugging him from behind.

Ally punched him in the stomach.

Shane tried to shake George off of him, but Ally punched him again, and their combined efforts were just enough to keep Shane from ...

Nope, Shane backhanded Ally just like Robyn had backhanded Eugene, and she hit the ground. George, however, tried to squeeze even tighter. He'd strangle the son of a bitch. As long as Shane didn't know any wrestling moves that involved throwing your opponent off your back, George was not going to let go, no matter what.

Ally got back up and lunged at him. George couldn't quite see what she did, but it looked a hell of a lot like she'd grabbed a fistful of fur on his chest and yanked it, hard.

George tightened his hug even more. Break, you stupid neck, break. He tried to jam his knee into Shane's back, but he just got him in the ass, which the weirdo probably enjoyed.

Shane was thrashing around too much. Despite what he'd promised himself just moments ago, George wasn't going to be able to continue to hold on to him. If it were daylight, he would have told Ally to limp into the woods, find the bat, and bring it back to beat the shit out of her father, but since it was dark he was pretty sure this fight would be over before she returned.

Shane twisted around and George lost his grip, falling to the ground for what he was pretty sure was the hundred and fifty-eighth time that day.

Ally, undeterred, grabbed another fistful of Shane's fur.

They were losing anyway, so George wasn't happy to see that Robyn was headed toward them.

Eugene had to admit that he was happy when Robyn apparently decided that helping her boyfriend (husband? brother?) was more important than killing him. There was no part of his body that didn't hurt right now, but he could push through that.

Because Robyn clearly was not carrying anything, so the keys had to be in the car.

Robyn scooped Ally up in her arms. She wanted to crush the girl, fold her in half until she squirted from the sides like a jelly sandwich, but, no. Shane would be devastated if he lost his daughter, and quite honestly Shane was so far gone right now that he'd do something he'd regret.

Even with a horrific eye injury, she got stuck being the responsible one.

She hated her life.

But loved the sex.

With Ally out of the way, Shane could devote his full attention to George. He was over the idea that George should suffer a long, drawn-out death. Shane might seem to be a monster, but he really wasn't, and the sight of his beloved Robyn with blood streaming down her face was worse than a silver bullet to his heart. He'd finish off George, get Robyn and Ally back to the car, and then they'd get her patched up. She'd be fine. She had to be fine.

It hurt like hell for Eugene to use his raw, bloody fingers to turn the key in the ignition, but he did it.

The car engine roared to life.

He wasn't going to be able to control the steering wheel very well, but he could accelerate and brake just fine, even if he couldn't really feel his feet anymore.

The car shot forward.

George's first thought was that Eugene had gotten in the car and was speeding away from this whole mess. He had an instant of "That traitor!" before he remembered that he hadn't exactly been the most loyal companion today.

Then he saw that Eugene was, in fact, driving the car toward them.

Snow flew up behind the tires, but the car was making forward progress.

George quickly got back up.

What the hell was the freak doing?

Did he think he was George's rescue driver? That he'd throw open the door, George would hop in, and they'd speed away?

Shane wondered if he'd had experiments performed upon his brain, as well as his body.

This was the moment.

Perhaps not the moment George had been preparing for his entire life. Maybe not even the moment he'd been preparing for all day—a lot had happened today, and he couldn't remember all of it. It was, however, a huge moment, one where if George put aside every bit of pain that burned through his entire body, he could make something wonderful happen.

He leapt—actually leapt into the air—at Shane and shouted, "This is for—!"

He meant to say "Lou," but the breath got knocked out of him upon impact. Shane could figure it out.

They both hit the ground, George on top of him.

George moved out of the way of the car with half a second to spare.

As did Shane.

George bashed Shane's head against the side of the moving car twice, then shoved him back into the snow.

The rear tire ran over the werewolf's head with a satisfying crunch.

Robyn wailed, threw Ally aside, and rushed over to Shane's fallen body. The car kept moving forward, exposing her lover's crushed skull.

She threw back her head and howled in misery.

No. It wasn't a howl. Just a scream. She'd reverted back to human without realizing it.

She gasped as George wrapped his arms around her neck.

Her arms and legs started to sprout fur again, but George snapped her neck before she could change back all the way.

Whether her feelings for Shane were love, lust, or both, they'd really screwed her over.

Killing a woman made him feel like crap, even if she was a murderous werewolf, but he thought he'd get over it.

Eugene got out of the car. "Wow," he said.

"Yeah. Who needs silver bullets when you can commit vehicular homicide?"

Three dead werewolves. That officially counted as avenging Lou's death. He hoped the bearded bastard appreciated it, because George didn't think he'd ever fully recover.

"Should we celebrate, or should we get out of here?" Eugene asked.

"I'm thinking the latter."

"Yeah."

Dad was dead.

Robyn was dead.

She was no longer in danger.

Ally felt no fear.

Only rage.

CHAPTER THIRTY-TWO

Changes

George enjoyed a few seconds of hard-earned relief before he noticed that Ally had begun to sprout fur.

"Ally...?" he asked.

She looked over at him, eyes yellow, mouth extending, claws growing.

"I think we should get in the car," George told Eugene.

Eugene was way ahead of him. He opened the back door, wincing in pain as he did so, and got into the vehicle as George scooted into the driver's side. They both slammed their doors shut at the same time.

Ally, now fully transformed, dropped to all fours. She stood back up, as if still trying to figure out how to move in her new form, then stayed upright and ran over to the car. Apparently the hole in her foot wasn't an issue as a wolf.

"Can she get in?" asked Eugene.

Ally slammed her fist against the window right next to him. It cracked but didn't shatter.

George put the car into reverse and floored the gas pedal, running over Shane's crushed head again. There were going to be some nasty, difficult to explain surprises waiting for somebody, but that wasn't George's problem right now, though he did hope that the corpses weren't discovered by adorable children who just wanted to play at the park.

He got back onto the road. Ally chased after him. Then she stopped, sniffed the air, and began to run down the road in the opposite direction.

"Where's she going?" asked Eugene.

"Aw, no, no, no." George slammed his fist against the steering wheel, which was such a stupid thing to do that he couldn't quite believe he'd done it, even with all he'd been through. "What if she's going after easier prey?"

"You think that's what she's doing?"

"Shit!" If she was just fleeing from her former kidnapper, good, she deserved to finally get away from him, but though she'd suffered tremendous losses today, there was no figurative blood on her hands. She hadn't killed anybody. She hadn't done anything that would haunt her.

George couldn't let this night end with her taking an innocent life.

"We have to stop her," he said. "We can't let her kill anybody!"

His heart raced and his voice quivered with panic. He had to stop her. No matter what. Right now, the way things had worked out, it almost felt like a victory. He couldn't let it end in tragedy. Couldn't let Ally become a killer.

He turned the car around and sped off after her.

"How do we stop her without hurting her?" Eugene asked.

"I have no idea. Tranquilizer darts would be awesome."

"I don't have any."

"I know."

Ally was sprinting up ahead. George could run her down. There'd be one more victim of this awful day, but then he'd know that it was the last.

No. There had to be another way.

Ally looked back at him, let out a snarl that he couldn't hear, then ran off the side of the road.

George sped up. "Okay, we're going to try to cut her off."

He raced ahead of her, suddenly swerving as a goddamn deer decided to run across the road. He almost hit it, and in fact the front bumper might have grazed its tail, but the deer continued bounding onto the other side.

George glanced up at the rearview mirror. "Maybe she'll go for the deer. We can catch her while she's eating it."

"How?"

"I don't know."

It didn't matter. The deer ran off into the woods, out of sight, and Ally didn't go after it.

"Are you sure we can't talk to her?" Eugene asked.

"If you want to shout something encouraging out the window, be my guest!"

They were no longer in a secluded area.

In fact, a bunch of multi-colored Christmas lights declared that a few blocks ahead was the Tropper Holiday Festival. There was a huge, full parking lot. No wonder so few people seemed to be anywhere else in town.

"You have got to be fucking kidding me," said George.

There'd been several murders in town! Why wouldn't they cancel that shit?

It was a giant buffet.

How many people could Ally slaughter before the cops finally took her out?

A dozen? Twenty? Thirty? With that many people that close together, she could rack up a body count that would make her Dad's look pretty unimpressive.

"We have to run her down," said George.

"Are you sure?"

"Can you think of another way? Did you bring a net? It's going to be another massacre, Eugene!"

Eugene looked grim.

George slammed on the brakes, then he put the car into reverse. The tragic elements of what needed to be done had sort of overshadowed the fact that Ally wasn't just going to leap in front of the automobile.

"Roll down your window," said George. "Do that stuff where you try to appeal to the goodness inside of her. Hurry!"

Eugene rolled down his window, cringing with the pain of doing so, then leaned his head out. "Ally! Ally! Please! You don't have to do this!"

Ally changed direction, running right for the car.

"I think she wants to kill me," said Eugene.

George looked over his shoulder as the car raced backwards. She was running straight toward them, so as long as she didn't swerve at the last instant…

She didn't swerve, but she leapt up onto the rear of the vehicle. He heard her rapid footsteps on top, and then she leapt onto the front hood.

George slammed on the brakes again, and she tumbled off.

He could make a career out of dislodging werewolves from the tops of vehicles.

The fall had hurt her. She got back up, but was limping badly. Unless she made a sudden miraculous werewolf recovery, she wasn't going to be able to get out of the way of the car this time.

He floored the accelerator again.

And then, proving once and for all that he was better with spur-of-the-moment decision-making than things that required actual plans, he swerved at the last moment.

He threw open his door, bashing it into Ally, knocking her into the air and then onto her back.

He slammed the brakes again.

She lay in the middle of the road.

That impact would've killed a normal person, but Ally deserved *some* kind of benefit from being a werewolf.

George got out of the car. As he went to her, the fur disappeared. She lay there, bruised and battered. Even more so than she already had been.

But she was breathing.

George scooped her up in his arms and returned to the car.

She looked up at him. She didn't smile, and he could barely hear her, but she said, "Thank you." Then she lost consciousness.

———————

They drove through town, trying to figure out what to do.

"We can't just keep her," said Eugene.

"I know. But can we simply let her go? She can't control this. We stopped her from going on a killing spree, or maybe we only stopped her from running away from us, we'll have to ask her when she wakes up, but either way, she's a danger to others. She doesn't have any parents. Is it safe to just drop her off at a police station?"

Eugene shrugged. "I'm sticking with you for as long as you'll have me, but you did shoot Mr. Dewey in the head. I'm not sure it's all that safe to be around you."

"Fair enough."

George glanced up at the rear-view mirror. There was a van that he thought might be following them, and he'd made three unnecessary turns to try and shake it. It was still there. This wasn't good.

"Is that a bad van?" Eugene asked.

George made a right turn. Another van was in the middle of the road, blocking his way.

"I don't think you should ram it," said Eugene. "Not in this car."

"I wasn't going to."

"Should we surrender?"

George stopped the car. The van that had been behind them turned onto the road as well, stopping directly behind him.

A couple of men, dressed entirely in black and holding rifles, got out of the back of the van. They rushed up to the car.

"Out of the vehicle!" one of them shouted. "Now!"

"Yeah, I think we surrender," said George.

———————

"I fucking hate vans," George told Eugene, as they sat in the back, awaiting their fate.

About fifteen or twenty minutes later, the van stopped, and another man in black got into the back with them. He looked reasonably friendly, except for the rifle.

"Where's Ally?" George asked.

"She's fine. Getting medical attention."

"Eugene could use a turn with the doctor, too."

The man smiled. "As could you. Don't worry, George. You're with the good guys."

"Are we?"

"We've collected the bodies. Thank you for killing them all in the same area. Makes things easier for us."

"So is this some kind of cover-up?"

"You could say that. Do you disapprove?"

"No," said George. "I'm all for it. Where are we going?"

"Far away. But we'll stop for a burger before we get there."

"I love you."

CHAPTER THIRTY-THREE

Final Warning

Duncan Maven knew something was wrong as soon as he pulled into his driveway. His front door was wide open. Jennifer was practically a mental case over the issue of not letting bugs into the house, so she'd never let the door just hang open like that.

He walked into the living room and fell to his knees.

Jennifer's head rested on the floor, not so neatly severed. The heads of the twins were next to hers. Their bodies had been dismembered, the parts lined up in a row in front of the heads.

His cell phone vibrated. The display read *Private Number*. He accepted the call but couldn't speak.

"You get to be the messenger," said a low male voice that Duncan didn't recognize. "Your loss will prevent the losses of others. Have you found the bodies?"

"Yes."

"Do not seek retribution against George Orton for the death of Jonathan Dewey. Tell the others. He is off-limits. If you or your associates disregard this warning, more blood will flow than you can imagine. Do you understand?"

"Who is this?"

"I asked you if you understand."

"Yes."

"Good. Remember that you have parents. A sister. None of them are safe if any harm comes to Orton. Goodbye."

Duncan dropped the phone, weeping, then crawled over to caress the hair of his dead wife's head.

"I guess I'm just destined to hang out with one-handed people," said George, sipping a margarita as he and Eugene watched television. He didn't know exactly where they were, but they had satellite television, and he found it somewhat comforting that not much had happened on his favorite *telenovela* since he'd last watched.

"They said they'll revisit the issue." The people here had done some miracle work on Eugene—on both of them, actually—but they'd drawn the line at actually getting him a prosthetic hand. Too expensive.

The accommodations in the small compound weren't particularly comfortable, but they were better than he'd had for the past few months, so George wasn't going to complain.

Ally was doing amazingly well for a fourteen year-old girl who'd discovered that she was a werewolf, lost her mother, and watched her psycho father get his head run over by a car. George and Eugene didn't see much of her, but she told them that once she was sufficiently healed, her training would begin.

George and Eugene had been told that once they'd recovered, they'd either be given jobs in the compound, or the arrangements of their release would be worked out.

Right now, George was inclined to stay.

Lou would've wanted to stay.

Eugene definitely did.

And it was nice to not have to be constantly worried about Mr. Dewey's men coming after him. He'd mentioned his concerns about retaliation for Dewey's death to J.P., the guy from the van, and J.P. had assured him that he had absolutely nothing to worry about. George had taken him at his word.

George had a lot of questions and at some point he'd start demanding answers, but for now, he was content to sit back, relax, and enjoy life.

———

Desmond Reith hung upside down from the chains, blood running into his face.

"Are you sorry for what you've done?" asked the man in the cloak.

Desmond let out a crazed laugh. "Not at all!"

"We were living peacefully among them."

"And that's wrong!"

"How is it wrong? What are you trying to do, Desmond? Start a war?"

"That's exactly what I'm trying to do."

"It won't work. Maybe you could draw out a few of us. The least of us. Not enough to matter."

"If Shane Goldwyn didn't matter, we wouldn't be here right now, would we? You can't stay hidden. Look how little it took to your kind to expose themselves."

"Like I said, the least of us."

Desmond laughed again. "If you say so."

"You won't be doing this again."

"I don't need to. I'm happy to die for this. How many people do you know who'll die for their cause, in this day and age?"

"You're old and decrepit. Don't act like this is a huge sacrifice. You'd be dead soon anyway. The only difference is that your death here will be much messier."

"I don't mind getting dirty."

The man in the cloak shook his head with disgust and walked away. Before he left the room, he waved his hand. "He's yours."

The wolves looked at each other, as if unable to believe their good fortune, then at Desmond, and then they were upon him.

Jeff Strand is the four-time Bram Stoker Award-nominated author of such books as PRESSURE, DWELLER, A BAD DAY FOR VOODOO, DEAD CLOWN BARBECUE, and a bunch of others. He also conveniently wrote WOLF HUNT, which made it a lot easier to get permission to write the sequel. Future novels may or may not include WOLF HUNT 3, WOLF HUNT 4, WOLF HUNT 5, WOLF HUNT 6, or WOLF HUNT: ALL-VAMPIRE EDITION.

Foolish mortals can visit his website at www.jeffstrand.com.

About Dark Regions Press

Dark Regions Press is an independent specialty publisher of horror, dark fiction, fantasy and science fiction, specializing in horror and dark fiction in business since 1985. We have gained recognition around the world for our creative works in genre fiction and poetry. We were awarded the Horror Writers Association 2010 Specialty Press Award and the Italian 2012 Black Spot award for Excellence in a Foreign Publisher. We produce premium signed hardcover editions for collectors as well as quality trade paperbacks and ebook editions. Our books have received seven Bram Stoker Awards from the Horror Writers Association.

We have published hundreds of authors, artists and poets such as Clive Barker, Joe R. Lansdale, Ramsey Campbell, Kevin J. Anderson, Bentley Little, Michael D. Resnick, Rick Hautala, Bruce Boston, Robert Frazier, W.H. Pugmire, Simon Strantzas, Jeffrey Thomas, Charlee Jacob, Richard Gavin, Tim Waggoner and hundreds more. Dark Regions Press has been creating specialty books and creative projects for over twenty-seven years.

The press has staff throughout the United States working virtually but also has a localized office in Portland, Oregon from where we ship our orders and maintain the primary components of the business.

Dark Regions Press staff, authors, artists and products have appeared in FANGORIA Magazine, Rue Morgue Magazine, Cemetery Dance Magazine, Publishers Weekly, Kirkus Reviews, Booklist Online, LA Times, The Sunday Chicago Tribune, The Examiner, Playboy, Comic-Con, Wired, The Huffington Post, Horror World, Barnes & Noble, Amazon, iBooks, Sony Reader store and many other publications and vendors.

Support Dark Regions Press by ordering our titles directly at:
http://www.DarkRegions.com

Made in the USA
Middletown, DE
01 September 2018